They reached the car and got in. Liza fastened her seat belt and turned to him. "Just out of curiosity, let's see the picture Wright gave you."

Jim pulled it out and glanced at it. It had to be Grady's mug shot from thirty years ago. The man in the picture had a tough-looking, meaty face, topped off with an Angela Davis 'fro and a unibrow. "Very attractive."

He handed the picture to Liza and started the engine. He was about to pull into traffic when something about Liza's continuing silence got to him. He turned back to find her staring transfixed at the photo, with her hand trembling.

He cut the engine and turned to face her. "Baby, what is it?"

She looked at him, a horrified expression on her face. "Th-this man. I've seen him. I spoke to him. He was in the gas station when I went in there."

Jim swallowed. This man had been that close to her and neither of them had known how dangerous he was at the time. "What did he want?"

"Nothing. Or he didn't seem to want anything. At the time, I thought he was just being friendly. He showed me a picture of his son. I practically told him I was out here visiting my father. He told me to enjoy my time with him. When he said it, I thought it was his way of saying good-bye. But now . . ."

Now, Jim agreed, it sounded like a threat.

Books by Deirdre Savoy

Spellbound (Spellbound series)

Always (Thorne/Ward series)

Once and Again (Thorne/Ward series)

Midnight Magic (Thorne/Ward series)

Holding Out for a Hero (Spellbound series)

Could It Be Magic (Fitzgerald Brothers)

Not the One (Thorne/Ward series)

Lady In Red (Spellbound series)

Looking for Love in All the Wrong Places
(Fitzgerald Brothers)

"Fairy Godfather" (novella in the anthology
To Mom with Love)

Looking for Love in All the *Wrong* Places

Deirdre Savoy

BET Publications, LLC
http://www.bet.com
http://www.arabesquebooks.com

ARABESQUE BOOKS are pubished by

BET Publications, LLC
c/o BET BOOKS
One BET Plaza
1900 W Place NE
Washington, DC 20018-1211

All Kensington Titles, Imprints, and Distributed Lines
are available at special quantity discounts for bulk purchases for sales promotions, premiums, fund-raising,
and educational or institutional use. Special book ex-
cerpts or customized printings can also be created to fit
specific needs. For details, write or phone the office of
the Kensington special sales manager: Kensington Publishing Corp., 850 Third Avenue, New York, NY 10022,
attn: Special Sales Department, Phone: 1-800-221-2647.

First Printing: June 2005
10 9 8 7 6 5 4 3 2 1

Printed in the United States of America

For D.J. She knows who she is and she knows why.

ACKNOWLEDGMENTS

Right after my first book was published, a reader asked me if I would ever consider doing romantic suspense. My answer was an unqualified "no." I was much more interested in exploring relationships than wondering about who killed who.

Well, needless to say, I spoke too soon. *Looking for Love in All the Wrong Places* is my third romantic suspense, and it doesn't look to be my last (in fact, I've got two more scheduled).

I'd like to thank my readers for sticking with me for whatever I've chosen to write. You guys are the best!

Prologue

This morning

Liza Morrow woke, not to her alarm clock as she usually did, but to the sharp, insistent, buzzing of the smoke alarm in the hall. Groggy, but alert enough to detect the acrid smell of smoke, she got out of bed, donned her Elmo slippers and her trench coat as protection against the cool night air, and set about grabbing what few necessary possessions would fit down the fire escape outside her bedroom window.

She snatched up her purse, the case that housed her laptop, and for some unknown reason, a giant teddy bear some beau had won for her at a carnival she didn't remember. At this point, she didn't bother to question her own motives. She needed to get out of there.

She made it out of the window, shut it as best she could behind her, and started down. Below her, a plethora of flashing lights and sirens signaled the arrival of both the fire department and the police. Once she reached the street, she, like all the other building inhabitants, stood staring up at the rolls of black smoke that billowed up from one side of the building. Flames, bright orange against the black of the night sky, licked out of the second-story apartment windows and to a lesser degree the windows on the floor above.

As she stood looking up at the building, an odd sense of relief washed over her. For one thing, she heard her neighbor across the hall, Mrs. Chin—a diminutive Chinese lady who had earned the nickname Little Miss Nosy—say everyone had gotten out of the building. For another, it was the third bad thing that had happened to her lately. If bad luck traveled in threes, her streak should be over.

Two weeks ago, she'd lost her job at Women's Work, an employment agency devoted to helping women. Two days ago, the morning of her friend Jake's wedding, her fiancé had come to see her to break off their engagement. And now her apartment building was burning to the ground.

Suddenly, the gravity of her situation hit. To be honest, she wasn't too sorry to see her fiancé go, but her job she missed. She missed the camaraderie of other women and enjoyed knowing that the work she did mattered to other people. But her home? Everything she owned was in that apartment. Everything her mother left her. It was too much, especially since she overheard two of the firemen talking and one of them said something about the possibility that an accelerant was used. She could cope with everything she owned being lost accidentally. But on purpose—that she couldn't handle. All she could hope was that the firemen got the blaze out before it reached her side of the building.

A man wearing a uniform consisting of a white shirt and navy pants came up to her. "You live in the building, right?"

Her first temptation was to give a flip answer about walking the neighborhood in her nightgown and slippers, but decided to forgo that. "Yes."

The officer asked for her name and apartment number and wrote them down on a paper attached to a clipboard. "Do you have somewhere to go for the night? If not, we're housing everyone over at the Y on Third."

"That won't be necessary." She did have somewhere to go. With Jake and Eamon on their honeymoon, their apartment was empty. Neither of them would mind her camping out there for the night. She gave the officer the address and her cell phone number as a contact. They would let her know when it was safe to return.

"Are you all right, miss?" he asked after taking down all her information.

"I'm fine," she answered. But she wasn't fine. She hadn't been fine for a long time, and that had nothing to do with her fiancé or her job or even her apartment building. She'd been off, not herself, for the past year. Ever since her ill-fated trip to Florida where she'd met *him*—James Fitzgerald. Every time she even thought about seeing him something bad happened to her. He was a jinx, her own personal demon, may he rot in hell. Well, close to it. As far as she knew, he'd gone back to Florida for good. With any luck, she'd never have to see him again.

But as she turned to walk uptown in search of a cab, her thoughts turned to that time a year ago. . . .

One

The sun was just beginning to set when Jim pulled up in front of his friend Paul's house. Jim had promised to check on the house before returning to New York, which was why he'd come. But truthfully, he was anxious to get back to the Big Apple. Heaven only knew what Eamon might be doing in New York to mess things up with Jake. Again. He'd set his sights on Jake as a new sister-in-law, and didn't trust Eamon not to send the poor woman to the nearest sanatorium.

Okay, Eamon wasn't that bad, but in his mind, Eamon bore watching. Otherwise he'd saddle himself with another version of his first wife. What Eamon had ever seen in the selfish, scheming Claudia, Jim would never understand. Most people assumed Eamon had married her because she carried his child. But no force on earth or heaven above could convince Jim that the kid was Eamon's. Eamon had loved her as if she were his own, and it had nearly broken him when the two of them had died in a car accident.

Now that Eamon seemed ready to rejoin life, he needed a woman like Jake to shake him up, to keep him from sinking into his usual workaholic lifestyle. In the past few weeks, he'd done his best to get the two of them together. He'd started the rumor himself that something was going on between him and Jake, knowing that Margot Spenser, that British bloodhound who worked for Eamon, would sniff it out and report back to the boss. Although Eamon had obviously been eaten away with jealousy by that knowledge, he hadn't done a damn thing about it. Jim should have known such a plan would backfire. Eamon would never go after a woman he thought his brother wanted, even though he himself hadn't always been so gracious.

At least he'd convinced Jake, or he hoped he'd convinced her, to stay with Eamon until she got better. He hadn't called, partly because he'd been too busy packing up his own house and partly because if Eamon had really screwed up there was nothing he could do about it until he got there anyway. Luckily, his flight left in the morning, and he'd be back in the office in plenty of time to discover which way the land lay.

Jim let himself in the one-story Spanish-style house and tossed the keys onto the hall table. Paul decorated as he lived, in early beach bum. Consequently most of his furniture was made of wicker and almost all of that was on the verge of disrepair. He enjoyed comfort more than style. And as Paul often joked, any burglar would assume he was broke and move on to a more lucrative location.

Jim checked the two bedrooms, the bath, and the den. Paul must have had something there where burglars were concerned. Nothing seemed amiss, out of place, or stolen. He headed back to the front hallway that led to the kitchen, wondering if there was anything edible in the refrigerator. The hands on the wall clock read nearly seven o'clock. He hadn't eaten anything since breakfast.

As he drew nearer to the kitchen he noticed something dark lying on the ground just outside the glass door that led out to the pool. He bypassed the kitchen to inspect the mystery that waited outside. He pulled the door open and stopped short. Not only was the object on the ground a pair of black panty hose, its owner frolicked in the kidney-shaped pool in front of him. If he weren't mistaken, the girl had abandoned her skirt and every other item of clothing before getting into the water. Paul might have the burglars beat, but he had a little work to do where trespassers were concerned.

Silently, he slid open the glass doors and stepped out into the fading Florida sunshine. He made it to poolside without the girl noticing him. She lay on her back in the water, her eyes closed, her hands making little splashes on the surface. She looked young, maybe twenty, small breasts, a narrow waist, and long, coltish legs. For all he knew, he could be gawking at a teenager.

He crouched down and splashed a bit of water in her direction. "Whose little girl are you?"

Immediately, the girl shrieked, took in a mouthful of water, then coughed it up. Her hands crossed over her chest, but he'd already seen all she had to offer. She stared up at him, the expression in her eyes more indignant than frightened or abashed at being caught au naturel in someone else's pool.

Something in her gaze stirred a demon in him. He let a slow grin form on his face. "Paul promised me a present for my birthday, but I wasn't expecting it so soon. The big day isn't until next month. And look, you've saved me the trouble of having to unwrap you."

She extended her hand. "Give me my towel."

For some reason, the bluntness of her request surprised him. For one thing, her voice resonated with a deep smoky tone he didn't expect. For another, she acted as if she belonged there, not he. But if Paul had entertained another houseguest in the past five years beside him, that was the first Jim had heard of it. He made Howard Hughes look like Hugh Hefner. Besides, if Paul had given anyone permission to be here, he would have told Jim about it.

He glanced at the snowy white towel on the bench beside him, then back to the girl. "Or I could come in and join you. How's the water?"

Obviously this girl, whoever she was, lacked any sense of humor at all. Before he had time to blink, she vaulted out of the pool and snatched the towel from the bench. If he'd thought about it, he would have shut his eyes or turned his head, or maybe he would have forgone the jokes and handed her the towel in the first place. Instead, he gaped at her, his eyes riveted to her small, delicate hands as they fastened the towel around her just above her breasts. He watched those hands until one of them balled into a fist and punched him in his left eye.

He staggered backward, but it wouldn't have taken much more for him to have fallen from a combination of surprise and a mean right cross. She used this opportunity to run past him into the house and lock him out. She disappeared inside, where to, he had no idea. It didn't matter. The lock on the door had broken two years ago and Paul had never bothered to fix it. He followed her inside. He saw her immediately at the other end of the hall by the front door, fumbling with the lock on the front door. She assumed she'd locked him out one way and sought to bar his entrance the other way.

"That lock's broken, too."

She swung around, her eyes huge. Her stint in the pool had paled her skin and plastered her hair to her

head. Standing there, shivering in the frigid blast of the
air-conditioning, she appeared vulnerable and genuinely
frightened. "Touch me and I'll blacken your other eye."

Apparently not content to wait for that eventuality,
she turned and tried to yank the door open. Lucky for
him he hadn't wasted his time standing at the other
end of the hall. Now he was close enough to slam the
door shut the moment she got it open. Trespasser or
not, nothing good could come of a woman running out
into the street wrapped only in a towel.

Immediately, she turned on him, pummeling him
with her fists, screaming, but the knee to the groin was
what did him in. Under the haze of the pain and the
strength of her assault he went down. Heaven knew
where he got the presence of mind to grab on to her
and take her with him. And still she fought him, strug-
gling against his hold on her wrists, attempting to knee
him again.

Somehow he managed to flip her over so that she lay
beneath him with one leg thrown over her two and her
arms pinned over her head. He leaned down close
enough to shout "enough" in her face.

She blinked and glared up at him, obviously startled
by the sudden shift in position and power. That and the
fact that her towel had fallen away at the same time
they'd hit the floor.

Jim dragged air into his belabored lungs. At the moment, all he wanted to do was lie there cushioned by
her soft body and try to recuperate. No female had
given him such a workout since Veronica Simpson
pounded him into the playground asphalt in third
grade. Having had it drilled into his head at a young
age that real men didn't hit girls, not even if they were
bigger than you and could throw a better haymaker
than Mike Tyson, he'd been at her mercy. He'd keep
that bit of information to himself, as he supposed that

the first sign of weakness would send the virago beneath him into another rage.

Said virago, having recovered herself somewhat, struggled against him. "Get off of me."

"Not until you tell me who you are and what the hell you are doing in this house."

Her jaw clenched and her eyes narrowed, but she said nothing. He recognized in her gaze not surrender but the resolve to conserve her energy until she finessed a better fighting position.

"This may not have occurred to you, but I have you at a disadvantage." He hadn't intended them to, but his eyes strayed from her face down to her throat to the mounds of her breasts pushed upward by his weight on her. With some effort he refocused on her face. "Now I suggest you give me your name before I lose my patience."

"Scheherazade."

He knew a lie when he heard one. "Scheherazade what?"

"Jenkins."

Another lie, but this one almost made him laugh out loud. "Okay, Scheherazade Jenkins, what are you doing in Paul's house?"

"We have a mutual friend that s-suggested that I visit him."

If that wasn't an out-and-out lie, at best it was a half-truth. He admitted he didn't know what to make of her, but they couldn't lie here on the floor forever. "If I let you up, do you promise not to try to skewer my intestines with anything?"

A barely perceptible nod. He supposed that was the closest to acquiescence she would come. He pushed to his feet, and without looking at her he reached for the towel and extended it in her direction. She snatched it from his fingers. Since his brother had raised him to be somewhat of a gentleman, he gave her privacy this time, though his eyes were busy scanning their periphery in case she found something to bash him with.

After a few seconds, he called to her, "Are you decent yet?" Getting no answer, he turned to find himself alone in the hall. Where had she sneaked off to so quickly and so silently? He found her locked in the master bathroom. He pressed his ear to the door, but the only sound he heard was the water running.

"Damn!" Jim bit back a few more choice words on the off chance the girl in the bathroom might hear him and think him a worse pervert than she already did. Now that he'd thought about it, he'd been out of line way before their wrestling match on the carpet. Despite what Eamon thought, he knew how to treat women. Frankly, he didn't know what had gotten into him with this one. Usually when he had the fortune of having a woman lying beneath him, she might be screaming her head off but creasing his skull was not part of the equation.

"Scheherazade," he called in his most solicitous voice. The false name she'd given him tasted bitter on his tongue. "I assure you I am not a masher. But Paul did ask me to look after the place. So if you don't come out and tell me what you are doing here, I will have to break the door down."

To his mind that sounded like a potent threat, though he'd never in a million years try to bust through a solid oak door. He heard nothing from the girl, but he did hear another sound that alarmed him: police sirens. His gaze went to the cordless phone on Paul's nightstand. The receiver was missing. Undoubtedly she'd snatched it up on her way into the bathroom. From the sound of it, they'd be there any minute. Damn.

"Sweetheart," he called in his most solicitous tone.

"Would you mind coming out of the bathroom long enough to explain to the police that I am not a mad rapist?"

Only the spray of the shower answered him. He slumped against the wall and shut his eyes. He probably deserved that. His fingers probed the sensitive circle of flesh around his eye. In all likelihood, the girl in the bathroom would rather see him carted off to jail than explain that he hadn't really hurt her.

"Freeze!"

Jim opened his eyes to stare into the face of a young cop dressed in the navy blue uniform of the San Pedro police. He didn't look old enough to have grown his first whisker, but the kid had his weapon drawn and trained on him. Great! Now he had his chance to get gunned down by Macaulay Culkin.

"Turn around and put your hands on the wall."

Jim had been around enough to know the drill. He assumed the position, only to find his face pressed up against the wall by a forearm across the back of his neck.

"Where is the girl? What did you do to her?"

"I didn't do anything to her. She's in the bathroom."

"Fitzgerald, is that you?" a familiar voice said. Jim focused on the doorway in time to see his friend Bill Simpson enter the room. "When I got the call that some strange man was terrorizing a woman, I should have known."

"Hey, Bill. Would you mind?" He nodded as best he could toward the younger officer.

"Ease off, Harrison."

Harrison sputtered. "B-but this man—"

"Is a good friend of mine and one of those pesky taxpayers who pay your salary. Now ease off."

Harrison did as he was told. Jim straightened up and turned around to glare at Harrison, whose face bore an expression of profound disappointment that this was not a situation for which his gun was not required.

Bill rolled his eyes. "These young pups all want to be Dirty Harry. Now what's going on here?"

"I got here and found a girl swimming in Paul's pool. I thought she was a trespasser. She thought I was a masher. She hit me in the eye and ran in the bathroom. End of story." He left out the part about her nudity and the tussle in the hallway. That was none of Bill's business anyway.

In a droll voice, Bill said, "I'm glad to see you still know how to show a lady a good time. And as soon as we hear the same story from the young lady, we'll be on our way."

Jim leaned his back against the wall and crossed his arms. He knew that after hearing such a ridiculous story, even Bill would want to check it out before believing him. "Good luck."

Bill knocked on the door. "Miss, this is the San Pedro police. We need to speak to you to make sure you're all right."

When Bill's words were met by a yawning silence, Jim suggested, "Why don't you tell her you're going to break the door down? That should work."

"Don't make us come in there," Harrison shouted.

Bill shot his partner a chilling look. "Harrison, go outside and secure the car."

"But, but—"

Bill pointed. "Go."

Harrison stomped off like a little boy whose mother sent him to his room without supper. When he'd gone, Bill rolled his eyes again. "He's green, but he'll get there. If I don't kill him first."

Abruptly, the sound of the water stopped. Slowly, the bathroom door opened and she stood before them wearing a gray silk robe, obviously Paul's because it dwarfed her slender figure. Contrary to his first impression, she appeared older, possibly close to his own age of thirty-two. Her eyes weren't dark brown, as he'd first thought, but a rich whiskey color. And her lips, now that they weren't blue and trembling from the cold chlorinated water, were fuller and incredibly luscious.

For a moment, all he could do was stare at her, until he realized Bill was similarly afflicted. "Don't you have something you want to ask her?" Jim asked in an annoyed tone.

Bill recovered himself and cleared his throat. "You phoned in a report to 911 earlier. We just wanted to make sure you're all right."

"I'm fine, if a little embarrassed. I obviously jumped to the wrong conclusion."

"Are you sure you don't want to file a complaint? It wouldn't be too much trouble to cart this one off to jail."

Jim snorted, realizing Bill was flirting with her. He supposed even middle-aged white guys got the blues.

"That won't be necessary, but thanks for the offer."

"Can we take you anywhere?"

"No, thank you. I'll call a taxi. I'm going to get dressed and be on my way."

Bill pulled a card from his shirt pocket. "If this one gives you any more trouble, give me a call."

She took the card from him. And Jim noted that for the first time she glanced at him pointedly. "I will." She put the card in her pocket.

Bill turned to him. "See you around, buddy. Try to keep yourself out of trouble."

Jim shook the hand his friend extended. "Have fun raising Junior."

Bill gave a mock shudder. "Don't remind me."

After Bill left, Jim turned to the girl, glad she hadn't closeted herself in the bathroom again the minute she got the chance. "Do you want to tell me what you're really doing here now?"

"I told you the truth the first time. A mutual friend of Paul's and mine asked me to look him up. Do you know where he is or when he'll be back?"

"Last time I spoke to him, he was in San Francisco. As to when he's coming back, your guess is as good as mine."

"I see."

Her words were innocuous enough, but her face seemed to crumble in on itself. Her gaze lowered from his face to about his chest and her teeth worried the skin of her bottom lip. He didn't know what to say to her. Despite what she kept telling him, she'd obviously come here to do more than pop in on a friend of a friend, though he had no idea what that more could be.

He sincerely hoped Paul hadn't done something stupid like getting her pregnant and deserting her. Though if that had happened, Jim couldn't imagine when. This girl had obviously never been here before and Paul rarely left the island. It was only the funeral of a friend that had pulled him off the island now. Besides, Paul didn't have much use for women, not even ones as beautiful as the girl standing across from Jim.

When she looked at him again, unshed tears glistened in her eyes. "I'd better be going, then. I'll get dressed and get out of your way."

She started to retreat to the bathroom.

"Are you hungry?"

She stopped midstride and cocked her head toward him. "What did you say?"

"The least you can do is let me buy you dinner as an apology for the way I acted before. And considering there's probably nothing but mold in the refrigerator . . ."

He let his words hang there while he waited for a response from her. Her mouth opened, in all likelihood to decline his offer, but her stomach growled, giving the lie to any story she might concoct about not having an appetite. She pressed her lips together and frowned. "You've seen me naked."

She'd spoken those words as if they explained everything, and maybe they did. She worried that every time he looked at her, he'd be seeing her nude body. Since he couldn't deny that, he didn't bother. Jim let a wicked grin slide across his face. "I could always show you mine since you showed me yours. Then we'd be even."

She rolled her eyes, but her mouth turned up in a hint of a smile. "That won't be necessary. Honestly, I'm more hungry than I am embarrassed, so I'll take you up on your offer. Then I'll be on my way."

Forty-five minutes later, they were seated at a table at Fruta del Mar, an Italian seafood place he sometimes frequented. He glanced across the table at his dinner companion, wondering if it hadn't been a mistake to invite her out. For one thing, in dress at least, they were mismatched. He wore a Hawaiian shirt, Bermuda shorts, and topsiders; she wore a dove-gray Prada suit that, despite having been left in a heap by the pool, had fewer wrinkles than the maitre d's dress shirt. Luckily the management here didn't care what you looked like as long as you brought your American Express. For another, she barely looked at him, and when she did it was with a tight-lipped smile that announced her discomfort. *Uptight.* No one ever used that word in describing him, but it suited her. He wouldn't have expected it from a woman prone to skinny-dipping in a stranger's pool.

The waiter came to take their food orders and leave their drinks—a glass of white wine for her and two fingers of scotch for him. So unless she was completely reckless, there went his theory of Paul knocking her up. He lifted his glass. "What shall we drink to, Scheherazade? Your name is a mouthful in itself."

She swallowed and blinked. "Most people call me Sherry."

The name fit, with her whiskey-colored eyes and smoky voice. But she didn't quite look him in the eye when she said it and immediately averted her gaze afterward.

"Okay, Sherry, what will we drink to?"

A smile flickered across her face and disappeared to be replaced by a look of resolve. "To new beginnings."

He wondered about that look, but kept silent as he clinked his glass with hers. He watched her as he drank, noticing the grace of her movements. She'd barely taken a sip when she replaced her glass on the table. He set his down as well, though he'd already consumed two-thirds of its contents. "Mind if I ask you a question?"

Her wary gaze met his. "I guess not."

He'd intended to ask her what she'd been doing in Paul's pool in the first place, since what he'd seen of her since she got out of it suggested her behavior had been uncharacteristic. Instead he asked, "What do you want with Paul?"

"Why?"

He shrugged, trying to appear casual. "He doesn't get many visitors."

She sipped her wine. "It's personal."

Which meant she wasn't going to tell him. Smiling, Jim shook his head.

"Why are you looking at me like that?"

"You remind me of someone."

"Paul?"

"No, my brother. That's the same type of nonanswer he gives when he doesn't want to talk about something."

"Then I take it he's broken you out of the habit of prying?"

He grinned. "Not entirely."

The waiter arrived, cutting short their conversation. As they ate, he watched her. Something in her gaze intrigued him beyond the beauty of her eyes. Sadness or maybe loneliness, he wasn't sure which. Having endured both, he didn't want her to feel either. During the week a band played on the small stage at the center of the room. Tonight, canned music, a white-bread version of Chuck Mangione's "The Look of Love," wafted through the nearly empty room. "Do you want to dance?"

She glanced toward the small, empty dance floor at the center of the room. "Can we?"

"Nobody will come with the big hook if we do."

She stood and allowed him to lead her to the dance floor. He pulled her into his arms and she fit with him as if she belonged there. In heels, she was nearly as tall as he, which should have been disconcerting. He'd always favored more petite women, but he found he enjoyed being able to gaze at her levelly. And despite her reserved demeanor she moved to the music fluidly. His fingers flexed on her waist, inching her closer. "This is nice."

She nodded, as the first genuine smile she'd granted him crept across her face. "Can I ask you a question?"

He grinned. "Why do I have the feeling I'll regret it if I say yes?"

"You never told me your name."

No, he hadn't. She hadn't asked either. He'd been waiting for the moment she would. "James," he replied easily.

Her eyes narrowed, as if she was trying to fit the name to him and finding them ill suited. "James what?"

"James Brown, but you can call me the Godfather of Soul if you want to."

She tilted her head to one side. "Really?"

"That's my story and I'm sticking to it. Unless you have something you want to tell me." *Like your real name.*

She settled an assessing gaze on him, as if she was trying to gauge something in his character on his face.
Apparently, she found him wanting in some regard, because she shook her head and moved closer to him,
resting her cheek against his shoulder.

Jim let out a heavy breath. How was he supposed to
remain upset with her lack of candor when it rewarded
him with her soft body pressed flush with his own? His
hand wandered over her back. She was slender, maybe
too slender, but her body moved lithely against him.
Her sweet scent filled his nostrils and her warm breath
fanned his skin, firing his libido. He wanted her, and he
doubted that fact had escaped her, as his body didn't
have any qualms about demonstrating exactly how
much.

She lifted her head. At first he thought she intended
to call a halt to their stimulating dance. But her gaze
locked with his momentarily before straying over his
face to settle on his mouth. Then she shocked him by
leaning up and pressing her lips to his.

She pulled away from him almost immediately. The
wide-eyed expression on her face told him she'd surprised herself as well as him. She lowered her head. "I
don't know why I did that. I don't usually go around
kissing strange men."

He didn't doubt that. In fact, he suspected something that had nothing to do with him had prompted
that kiss. Paul's absence must have disappointed her in
some significant way he'd be damned if he could figure
out. But he doubted the relationship between them was
sexual, though that might only be because that's the
way he wanted it.

"Don't worry. I'm not that strange." He winked at
her. "Ready to go?"

She nodded.

He paid the check and the two of them drove the

three miles back to Paul's house in silence. Once there, he cut the engine and put his hands in his lap. "What now?"

"If you don't mind, I'll come inside and call a cab."

She got out of the car without waiting for him to open her door and preceded him toward the dark house. In other words, she didn't want him dropping her anywhere because she didn't want him to know where she was headed.

He followed her to the house, opened the door, and flicked on the hall light. She'd already warned him about prying, so he didn't. Once they were both inside the house with the door closed he turned to her. "I hate to tell you this but any taxi service that might have ventured out here a couple of hours ago has closed up shop for the day."

She sagged back against the wall. "I see."

"You can stay here if you like. I'll do the gentlemanly thing and sleep on the sofa."

She pressed her lips together a moment considering him. "Why are you being so sweet to me?"

He leaned against the opposite wall. "Why shouldn't I be?"

One shoulder lifted in a delicate shrug. "Does your eye hurt?"

It did, but since he figured he'd deserved that he shook his head. "No."

"Let me see."

He obliged her by stepping over to her side of the hall and bracing his hands on either side of her. "How does it look?"

He closed his eyes as she took his face in both her hands. She didn't answer him in words, but by placing a soft kiss on his eyelid, his cheek, and finally his mouth. She kissed him once, twice, three times, each kiss growing a bit longer, a bit more intense. She pulled back enough so that they could see each other's faces. For a moment their gazes, both full of longing, locked. He couldn't say which of them moved first, but their mouths found each other and their tongues met for a heated dance. Her arms wound around his neck, pulling him closer.

How they got from kissing in the hallway to undressing each other in the living room to falling onto the sofa in each other's arms blurred in the heat of the sensual haze that enveloped him. A fever gripped him, perspiration coated his skin, and his breath came in ragged spurts. All that mattered was the softness of her skin, the sweetness of her kiss, and the warmth of her body as it enveloped him.

Once inside her, he lifted himself on his elbows and gazed down at her. For a second, sanity returned. Who was this woman who lay beneath him? He knew virtually nothing about her, not even her real name. Never in his life had he done anything so reckless. And yet, from the moment she'd laid her lips on his, he'd felt powerless to do anything but the inevitable.

She stared back at him, her heavy-lidded gaze roving from his eyes to his mouth. Incapable of denying her what she wanted, he lowered his head to claim her mouth again. With a throaty moan, she wrapped her legs more tightly around him, pulling him deeper inside her. He was sinking, drowning in an abyss of erotic sensation. The scent of their passion filled his nostrils. Her fingers dug into his back as she tensed beneath him. She gasped and her back arched, as her orgasm overtook her. The strength of her reaction pulled him under. His body trembling, his head thrown back, his own release flooded through him.

Still shivering, he sank against her, his face burrowed against her throat. He'd never felt anything like that before, such intense pleasure combined with an utter lack of control. And for the first time in his recent memory, the urge to turn over and go to sleep or alternately to get the heck out of there as swiftly and silently as possible didn't assail him. He lay there, he didn't know how long; content to hold her warm, soft body against his until she fell asleep.

Later, once they made it to the bed, they made love again. Afterward, they lay together a long time, her cheek to his chest while he stroked her hair and told her nonsense stories to make her laugh. To hell with his flight in the morning. Jake and Eamon would be fine whether he showed up or he didn't. Another day might be the most time he'd have to spend with the beauty in his arms. He realized with some chagrin and a great deal of surprise that he wished the circumstances were otherwise.

He closed his eyes and settled into a deep dreamless sleep. But when he woke up in the morning she was gone.

Two

Three months later

Liza flopped into one of Jake's kitchen chairs, grateful that the six seven-year-olds who had been tearing Jake's apartment to shreds for the last few hours had finally gone home. If she could muster the energy, she'd help Jake clean up and head home herself. For one thing, as much as she'd like to consider herself a bigger person, the green-eyed monster was wreaking havoc with her psyche seeing Jake so happy with Eamon. They'd had a few bumps, but if Liza weren't mistaken, Eamon was *the guy.*

It didn't seem fair. Jake had always been the free-spirited type; Liza had always been the one who wanted a family as much as she wanted her career. Not that she wanted to deny Jake her newfound connubial bliss. Liza just wanted some of her own.

And then there was the fact that Eamon's baby brother, one James Fitzgerald, would probably make an overdue appearance tonight. He was supposed to show up hours ago, and Liza was glad he hadn't. Jake had told her a few stories of Jim's exploits. He sounded like an overgrown adolescent, the kind of man who changed women like other men changed their socks. In her present mood, she'd probably punch him in the nose the moment she saw him.

Or maybe it was just the name. As it often did, her mind drifted to the man she'd met in Florida. Not for a moment did she believe that his name was actually James Brown. The witty banter, the rakish grin. It was all part of the flirtation that led her to his bed that night. But rather than being swept away or seduced by him as she'd allowed Jake to believe, she'd practically instigated their lovemaking herself.

And Liza Morrow, the Liza Morrow she'd been for the past thirty years, didn't wake up in strange men's bed having bedded them the night before. She was too sensible, practical, reasonable, reliable for anything as tawdry as a one-night stand. The next morning, she'd been so mortified at her own behavior she'd run out before he had a chance to awaken.

That hadn't been the most brilliant move, either. That man, whoever he was, deserved better than that from her. She'd blackened his eye and almost had him arrested by the police, for heaven's sake. Yet he'd held her with such tenderness after both times they'd made love, stroking her hair and telling her funny stories. She'd fallen asleep in his arms. That didn't happen either. With most men, she was content to let them leave or let them fall asleep while she got up and balanced her checkbook or made a to-do list of what she needed to accomplish the next day. She didn't crave the sort of postcoital intimacy she'd shared with that stranger.

Then again, it wasn't every day that she arrived on the doorstep of the man she believed to be her father, either. It had taken her six months after she found his name among her mother's papers to decide to see him and another six months to track him down. She'd wasted four days in a Florida hotel room trying to get up the nerve to see him. When she finally got her courage together to make the trip to the little island he called home, he wasn't there.

She'd felt so tired, disappointed, and alone, she'd thrown herself in the pool as a means of cleansing herself of all of it. Then he'd shown up, a savior in her hour of need. And she'd run out on him. You'd think with all her complaints about the lack of decent men in New York, she would have latched on to the one decent one she found somewhere else.

To make matters worse, two days ago, she'd done the second stupidest thing in her life. She'd lopped off her long hair and now wore a short pixie cut. It wasn't that the cut didn't suit her. But in an odd way she missed her hair. Ever since she'd been a child she'd worn it long. She figured the only reason she'd chopped it off was wanting to get rid of the remembrance of some man running his fingers through it, not a very sensible reason for such a drastic makeover.

Liza sighed as Eamon joined her at the table, carrying a glass of merlot for each of them. A strikingly handsome man with ice-blue eyes and a sensible nature, he balanced Jake's more fiery disposition. Talk turned to the success of the party. Jake, who stood by the archway dividing the kitchen from the front hall, hugged her little niece Dani, praising her for the magic show she'd put on for her guests. Then Dani ran to Eamon for a hug.

Liza swallowed, feeling like the fourth wheel on a tricycle: unnecessary and in the way. She was about to make her excuses for a quick getaway when the doorbell rang. Jake went to answer it. A moment later, Liza heard her call, "Jim!"

An instant later, Liza was on her feet. Just what she needed. Maybe she could slip out the door as he was slipping in. But apparently she hadn't moved fast enough. A second later, Jake came through the archway with a man who had his arm around her shoulders, while Dani danced around trying to peek into the shopping bag the man carried, obviously looking for a present.

For a moment, she stood without moving, watching as this man advanced toward Eamon, his brother. But he stopped midstride and looked directly at her, a surprised expression on his face. She imagined her face bore a similar expression of shock. Her James Brown was the same Jim that Jake had been telling her about for months?

She backed a step away, her mouth uttering the one word her brain seemed capable of forming. "You."

His gaze narrowed as it raked over her. "What the hell have you done with your hair?"

Liza didn't remember picking up her glass or the fact that she was still holding it. Not until the contents of it splashed in his face and ran down the side of his neck. Horrified at her own behavior, she opened her mouth, but no sound came out. She whirled and fled the room, going to Jake's bedroom and slamming the door behind her. Good God! What had gotten into her? Well, maybe he shouldn't have made that comment about her hair, but that was no excuse for violence.

She paced the floor with her back to the door and her arms wrapped around herself. It was shock; that's what it was. The shock of learning that the man she regretted leaving so abruptly was himself a notorious womanizer. Here she'd been beating herself up for months about her treatment of him, while he probably thanked the luck of his stars that he hadn't had to throw her out.

"I'll say this, you do know how to get a man's attention."

Liza whirled around. She hadn't heard the door

open or close, but he stood on the inside, the same grin on his face, though this time it struck her as cocky rather than self-assured. "Who says I wanted your attention? I've heard people can drown in less than an inch of water."

He had the nerve to laugh. "Last time I checked, you were the one who skipped out on me, so what's with the death wish?"

Okay, so she'd overdone it a little with that comment. She didn't really want him dead, just gone, or herself gone from this room and this ridiculous conversation. "I don't know why you came back here. I don't think we have anything to say to each other, except good-bye."

She took a step toward the door. He stepped into her path, making her draw up short. "I think we do. Why did you leave the next morning without telling me who you were, where I could find you?"

He sounded so sincere that she almost believed he gave a damn. Her gaze wandered over him. Damn, the man was gorgeous. She'd thought so from the first moment she'd met him. Tall, maybe six-two or six-three, with soulful brown eyes and a complexion the color of rich maple syrup. But she wasn't about to be fooled by a pair of bedroom eyes and a few softly spoken words. "I would have thought you'd be grateful. Isn't that your usual m.o.?"

"Not this time."

Liza rolled her eyes. "Oh, please. Jake told me all about you. How you'll say almost anything to get a woman into bed." She swallowed. He'd said some of those things to her.

"Let me ask you a question then. What bothers you more? The fact that you slept with me or all the women you believe I've slept with?"

What bothered her most was that she should be immune to this sort of thing by now. She'd dated half the neurotic whiners and crybabies in New York, not to mention the macho creeps, the workaholics, and those unfortunate souls who had yet to discover they were gay. Usually she could spot a man's line of bullshit before he got ten words out of his mouth. But she hadn't with him. She'd actually believed he gave a damn one way or another. A stupid mistake, since in all likelihood she'd only deceived herself into seeing what wasn't there. And that wasn't like her, either.

In answer to his question, she said, "Both."

"Did it ever occur to you that what Jake told you might not be true?"

"No," she lied. Granted some of the stories Jake told her were too far-fetched to be believed and some possibly physically impossible besides. But even if she didn't consider those, her general impression of him as a man who treated women casually and discarded them remained. She'd been there, done that, and had the T-shirt printed up. She didn't need to go there again "It's really none of my business what you do. Now if you'll excuse me, I'm going home."

She stalked around him, toward the door. She had her hand on the knob before he moved. The next thing she knew, her back was pressed against the door with his hands at her shoulders. She gasped in shock. He hadn't hurt her in the least, merely surprised her with the speed of his actions. His face was close enough to hers for his breath to fan her cheeks.

She pushed against his chest with the heels of her hands. "Don't bother. I won't say our time together wasn't interesting, but I decline the invitation for a second performance."

"I don't remember asking for one."

"Good then you won't be disappointed." She pushed against his shoulders again. "Would you please get out of my way."

"Liza, would you please listen to me?"

She scowled at him. "Why?" Give me one good reason why I should listen to anything you say."

She looked up into his eyes—a mistake. They weren't brown, as she'd first believed, but a dark hazel. The softness of his expression nearly undid her, nearly had her believing he was sincere. His hand rose to cradle her cheek. It was all she could do not to melt into that caress.

"I've spent the last three months looking for you and you were right under my nose."

She opened her mouth to say something, what, she didn't know. But before she got anything out, his mouth was on hers, kissing her with an urgency she couldn't ignore. Heaven help her, she didn't want to ignore it. Her arms wound around his back, holding him closer as she welcomed his tongue into her mouth. His hips ground against hers, revealing the strength of his erection.

But while she felt herself drowning in the sensual haze he created, a thought, like a tiny germ, infected her brain. How many other women had he held like this? Kissed like this? Slept with? He said he'd been looking for her, but how could she believe that? If he'd been as busy as Jake said, how could she believe that she meant anything more to him than any of the others? Even if it were true, she'd been love's fool far too many times to chance it.

With her hands at his shoulders, she pushed him away. "Nice try, but I'm not interested." She yanked open the door and made it into the hall without him stopping her. So much for his claim of being unable to go on without her. On unsteady legs, she walked back to the kitchen where Jake, Eamon, and Dani still sat.

As she entered the room, she heard Jake say, "I'm going to kill him."

"Stand in line."

Eamon immediately stood. She recognized the look of a man fleeing from the presence of an irate woman. *Chicken.* He said, "Come on, Dani. Let's see if between you, me, and Uncle Jim, we can't figure out how to hook this thing up."

Once the two of them left, Liza sat in Eamon's newly vacated seat while Jake poured them each a glass of wine. Jake extended it toward her. "You're only allowed to have this if you promise not to throw it on anybody."

Liza sipped from her glass, then set it on the table. "I can't believe I did that. It was such a shock seeing him and when he made that comment about my hair, I freaked."

"To put it mildly." Jake slid into the seat next to her. "Now forgive me if I'm wrong, but the last time we discussed this mystery man of yours, you were feeling guilty for having run out on him the way you did. You finally see him again and you throw your wine in his face? I don't get it. What changed things for you?"

"You did. You told me all about Eamon's younger brother, Love-'Em-and-Leave-'Em Jim. Pardon-Me-If-I-Can't-Commit Jim, I-Have-the-Mentality-of-a-High-School-Senior Jim. Forgive me for being Not-Going-There-Again Liza."

Jake sighed. "Me and my big mouth. I only told you those things about Jim to cheer you up, as in at least you're not pining away over this guy. Sure, Jim is all the things I told you about him, but that's not all he is."

Liza sighed. She appreciated Jake's loyalty to Jim, who was not only her friend but by all accounts the man about to become her brother-in-law. But she also knew how Jake's mind worked. At one point Jake had tried to fix her up with Eamon until she wised up and decided to keep him for herself. If she didn't nip it in the proverbial bud, Jake's focus would shift to uniting her with Jim and that was not happening.

"Well, that's all he is to me," she said in a way that she hoped would end the conversation.

It didn't. Jake gave her an eagle-eyed once-over. "By the way, what happened to that lovely shade of lipstick you were wearing up until a few moments ago?"

Liza's hands flew up to cover her mouth. "He kissed me. Mostly to shut me up, I guess. And fool that I am, I let him. Good Lord, Jake, does that man know how to use a pair of lips!"

Jake grinned. "It must be a family secret."

Liza groaned. Why hadn't she kept her own big mouth shut? She could sense Jake's renewed interest in getting them together. Just because the man had the ability to kiss her senseless didn't mean she'd lost her wits enough to get involved with him.

"Don't try to humor me out of this, Jake. Here I was beating myself up for deserting a decent guy, when that's what he does, Jake. He probably would have sent me a thank-you note for disappearing and saving him the trouble of throwing me out."

Jake shook her head. "I know for a fact that's not true."

Liza stood. "Whatever. I'm going to fix my face, say good night to Dani, and go home. I can't deal with this right now."

She snatched up her purse and headed out of the kitchen in the direction of the bathroom. Once inside, she locked the door and surveyed her image in the mirror. Just from the brief contact with his, her lips were reddened and slightly swollen. That was easy to camouflage with a little lipstick.

What was more difficult to conceal was her feeling of

crushing disappointment. These last few months, she'd harbored the romantic notion that somewhere out there some decent man had been good to her when she needed it. She never expected to see him again unless she tried another time to contact her father. Since she wasn't ready to do that, she'd made up her mind to move on. But that proved harder than she'd hoped. Images of that night haunted her dreams and disturbed her waking hours. And she knew the real reason she'd cut her hair was an attempt to forget.

Now to find that this man and the man Jake told her about were the same person? It was too much. It was as if the cosmos had played a cruel trick on her. She couldn't even have a fantasy man worth a damn. And she couldn't even get away from him. She knew Jake imagined them all as this lovely little family she'd created. How was she supposed to handle something so mundane as handing him the mashed potatoes next Thanksgiving?

She couldn't think about it anymore. She'd go say good-bye to Dani and get out of there. She'd worry about the rest of it tomorrow.

After Liza left, Jim stood in the archway with his hands braced on either side of the narrow door. That had gone amazingly well. He'd spent months looking for the woman and here she was the whole time. Worse yet, he suspected Liza was the woman Jake had been trying to introduce to him. He'd turned her down, uninterested for the first time in his life in meeting another woman.

But the real kicker was that she didn't want to see him—and it was all his own fault. He'd told Jake those stories—half made up and half exaggerated to cheer her up—when she hit a rough spot with Eamon. He doubted

Jake believed much of what he told her, but obviously Liza did. Or at least she believed enough of it to hold it against him. Damn.

He pushed off the door frame and picked up pacing where Liza left off. He didn't understand himself. When had any one woman mattered so much to him that he actually hired someone to find her? The trail had run cold almost immediately. The only thing he'd found out was that she'd registered in a little hotel near the airport using the same fake name and paid cash. But an airline required a real name and real identification to back it up. Considering he hadn't even known which airline to check, that had been that.

"How's it going in here?"

Jim turned to see his brother leaning against the doorjamb, a broad grin on his face. "Come to say I told you so, or some other nonsense?"

"Actually, I wanted to make sure she hadn't pounded you into the carpet this time. Those bloodstains are murder to get out."

Irritated by Eamon's humor, he said, "Not that I don't enjoy being your source of amusement, but was there something you wanted?"

"All right." Eamon stepped farther into the room and closed the door. "I'll behave myself. What happened between you two?"

"Nothing."

"Oh? Then when did you start wearing lipstick?"

Damn. Jim pulled his handkerchief from his back pocket and swiped it across his mouth. It came back with a smattering of crimson.

"Want to try that again?"

Jim folded the handkerchief and shoved it in his pocket. "Okay, I kissed her."

"And you thought that would improve the situation, somehow?"

No. He'd seen an opportunity to do what he wanted and he'd taken it. For a moment she'd returned his passion, but he'd pushed her too far. He knew that, but having her in his arms again made him a little crazy. If given the chance he wouldn't make that mistake again.

"She's not one of your usual party girls."

"Don't you think I know that?"

Eamon shook his head. "Maybe I should explain something. Although they are nothing alike, Jake and Liza are more like sisters than best friends. The two of them and Jake's older brother, Dan, practically raised themselves, especially after Jake's parents died when she was sixteen. While Jake's mother was basically ineffectual but harmless, Liza's mother worked and wasn't around much. When she was, well, she wasn't a happy woman. Although Liza rejected her mother's bitterness, she's a serious woman. Frankly, both Jake and I were shocked to hear that she had been so reckless as to sleep with a man she didn't know. If I'd known that man was you, I could have told you you were wasting your time."

"Then, you'll be pleased to know you were right about something else."

"What's that?"

"You said my tendency to exaggerate would get me in trouble. I believe you called it my unfortunate over-reliance on hyperbole."

"What has that got to do with anything?"

"Everything. It seems some stories I told Jake made it to Liza's ears. Now she thinks I'm some sort of pervert and won't have anything to do with me."

"What do you intend to do about that?"

Jim sighed. Sure, he could pursue her, but to what end? He wasn't ready to promise the woman hearts and flowers, and from what Eamon told him, that's what she required. Even if she didn't, he had Jake and Eamon to consider. If things went the way that he thought they would, Liza would be his sister-in-law of a sort. If things ended badly with them, it might disrupt the perfect little family Jake and Eamon both wanted. Better to keep his pants zipped and his mouth shut.

For the first time in his life, he was going to do the wise thing. "Who, me? Not one thing."

Three

Two days ago

The morning of Jake's wedding, Liza woke up and stretched her back like a cat. Morning sunlight washed through her bedroom windows, though it was barely six o'clock. The weatherman had predicted a glorious summer day, and Liza was looking forward to helping her friend celebrate the big day.

She stretched again, got out of bed, and set about doing what she did every Saturday morning—tidying her apartment. She wasn't a neat freak, like Jake claimed. She simply liked to have a place for everything and everything in its place. Her mother had instilled in her a love of a sense of order, a lesson Jake's mother had never gotten around to.

After that, she showered, shaved, plucked, as the need called for it, washed her hair, and blow-dried it. When she got to Jake's, the hairstylist would have a go at it, so she didn't bother to do anything further with it aside from gathering it into a short ponytail.

As she left the bathroom, her gaze snagged on the one picture that sat on her nightstand, a picture of her and her fiancé, Ryan Gilchrest. They'd started dating five months ago and by mid-May he'd asked her to marry him. She knew she should be ecstatic, as she stood on the brink of having what she'd wanted all her life—a family like the one she'd lacked growing up. She'd wanted siblings, which was probably why she'd latched on to Jake and her older brother, Dan, for dear life. Dan's death two years ago had been nearly as devastating to her as it had been to Jake and Dani.

But she wasn't ecstatic. In the past couple of weeks she'd thought of any upcoming marriage between her and Ryan with a growing sense of disquiet. She was uncertain of his feelings for her or her feelings for him. Neither of them was shout-your-love-from-the-rooftop sort of people, though she wondered if there was much love to shout about in the first place. She had reached a point where her clock was ticking and he had reached a point where his father was looking for a grandchild. Sometimes she wondered if there wasn't any more to their relationship than that.

At any rate, she was glad he would be with her today when out of necessity she had to see *him*. In the past nine months she'd done her best to avoid seeing James Fitzgerald—not showing up places where she knew he'd be—even after she had Ryan as a buffer. Still, he haunted her dreams often enough to be truly annoying. Why couldn't he stay out of her subconscious where he didn't belong? Maybe it was because on some level she still worked at reconciling the sensitive man she'd met in Florida with the reprobate she'd heard about in New York. Being unable to do so unsettled her.

The doorbell rang and she went to answer it, surprised to find Ryan on the other side dressed in a pair of khaki pants and a pullover, not the suit she expected, not that she expected to see him at all.

"What are you doing here and why aren't you dressed?"

"I can't go to the wedding with you."

Liza glared at him. He arrived on her doorstep minutes before she was about to leave, and he wasn't going? "Why the hell not?"

"Don't shout at me, Liza. This is hard enough as it is."

Liza ground her teeth together. She'd never been late in her life and wasn't going to start now, the day of her best friend's wedding. She was supposed to help Jake get dressed and ride with her to the church. "What is hard enough?"

"I've come to a decision. I'm going to have to do what my father wants. You know he's been pressuring me to get married."

"And . . ." For a moment she imagined he wanted her to agree to a date considering she wore his ring on her finger. Although she'd put off setting a date in the past, she doubted he'd be this agitated over pressing her for one now. Besides, that wouldn't be something he'd skip Jake's wedding over.

"And I agreed. Debbie and I will be getting married in the fall."

What? She'd known his family had some debutante picked out and gift wrapped for him, but he'd always told her he wasn't interested.

"Don't you see, Liza? I have no choice."

"You're thirty-five years old, Ryan. Of course you have a choice."

"My father was going to cut me out of the business if I—"

He stopped there and she filled in the rest—if he married beneath the status his family thought they had. She didn't know why she didn't feel angry with him, or even disappointed at his defection.

"Fine." She started to take off her ring. "I suppose you want this back."

He shook his head. "Like I could give Debbie a ring like that."

That did it. She pushed him hard enough for him to stagger back across the threshold, threw the ring at him, and slammed the door in his face. She leaned her back against the door, her breathing harsh, waiting for some rush of emotion that never came. She didn't feel anything except annoyance at his lousy timing. She checked her watch. If she hurried, she could catch a cab and still make it to Jake's on time.

When Liza arrived at Jake's, Jake was still in her robe with her auburn hair piled high on her head. "Jacqueline Bouvier Troubat McKenna, I knew I should have spent last night over here with you. You are not anywhere near ready, and you're getting married in less than two hours."

"Good afternoon to you, too," Jake said as she moved aside for Liza to pass. "Who stole the prize out of your breakfast cereal this morning?"

Liza kept walking toward Jake's bedroom, where hopefully Jake had her things ready. "A little gremlin named Ryan. As of this morning, the engagement is off."

"It's about time you dumped that jerk. Frankly I don't know what you saw in him in the first place."

Having reached the bedroom, Liza turned toward Jake and forced a saccharine smile. "*He* dumped *me*, thank you very much, for some she-devil his father wants him to marry."

"The bastard. I hope the two of them rot in hell."

Liza shrugged. "Your vindictiveness on my behalf is touching, but wasted. I don't know what I saw in him either, except maybe he was a reasonably attractive, eligible man who didn't behave like an octopus on every given occasion." Or maybe like a million other women she'd succumbed to the myth that any man was better than no man at all. Liza sighed. One day she'd worry about it, but not today. "Tell me you at least showered already. And where's Dani?"

Jake grinned. "I did and the hairstylist will be here in ten minutes. Dani's in her room playing that infernal game Jim bought her." She sighed. "Are you sure you're feeling up to this today?"

What was Jake going to do? Cancel the wedding because some fool decided to act like a fool today? "I'm fine. Really." Maybe if she said that enough times to herself, she'd believe it.

Later, after the wedding guests had started to arrive at the restaurant where the reception was being held, Jim stood at one side of the room nursing a scotch. The new Mr. and Mrs. Fitzgerald had arrived a few minutes ago to the sound of resounding applause. He wondered which of the two of them had picked this place, or maybe they'd selected it together. The restaurant itself had an elegant feel with pristine white tablecloths and pricey artwork on the walls that suited Eamon's sense of elegance. However, he was certain that the band in one corner, which had already struck up a rocking version of "Celebration," had been Jake's idea. Left in Eamon's hands, some harpist would be causing the guests to snore into their champagne by now.

Either way, it didn't matter. They seemed to have married their two styles as easily as they'd wedded each other. Even to Jim's untrained eye, the wedding had gone perfectly. Lord knew only Jake could get away with getting married in a white lace minidress. Liza had worn a matching dress in a dark lavender. Her hair had grown back enough to be worn in a chin-length cut. Long enough for a man's finger to feel at home in. He scanned the crowd for her now, but didn't see her or the fiancé Eamon told him she'd acquired.

He'd behaved himself for the past nine months, so he supposed one more night shouldn't be a big deal. But in all those months he'd been careful not to see her anywhere except in his dreams. He had no choice about seeing her tonight, sheathed in that dress that clung to her curves in a way that made his mouth water. But she was taken and maybe it was best that way, since he'd never do something so foolish as hitting on another man's almost wife. Well, not with him there, anyway.

But Liza's mystery man hadn't made an appearance at the church, not as far as Jim could tell. After the ceremony, she'd allowed him to escort her from the church, his best man to her maid of honor. Then she'd disappeared before he had time to blink. He'd assumed the fiancé had whisked her off. But now that he spotted her across the room, standing by one of the tables talking with his uncle, he wasn't so sure.

If she had a man in tow, Jim couldn't find him. What was he? The Invisible Man or just plain stupid? Any sensible man would lay an early and obvious claim to the woman to keep hounds like him at bay.

"Don't even think about it."

Jim hadn't noticed Eamon come up beside him. Nor had he realized how obvious his perusal of Liza must have been. "All I'm doing is looking. A man can't get arrested for that."

"No, but he might get flattened for it."

"Then he shouldn't leave her alone. I'm not the only one looking."

"I wasn't talking about him, I was talking about me. Besides, they broke up this morning."

"Damn." Now he had to behave just because. He focused on Liza again. She looked none the worse for the loss of her intended. Still he'd like to find the guy and pummel him just on GP.

"She doesn't need any of your fun and games right now."

Jim cast his brother a disparaging look. "You know, sometimes, big brother, your faith in me is such a touching thing."

"I meant that instead of a lover she might need a friend right now."

Right. He could manage to merely be friends with the woman who haunted his dreams. Besides, no woman really wanted friendship from a man at a time like this. Not a man like him, anyway. He'd learned that lesson early on from Eamon himself, or rather his women. Any time Eamon started to care for a woman, he'd find some infinitesimal flaw in her and then she'd be dismissed, as if she didn't exist anymore. Those who knew him sought out a dose of feel-good and to have their egos stroked before flitting off to greener pastures. Since that's all he offered, he'd never minded too much. Eamon's marriage to Claudia had been one of convenience, not caring. Jim considered Eamon's ability to let Jake into his life and to let himself love her to be a testament to his evolution as a human being.

Jim cast his brother another sour look. "Don't you have anything better to do than pester me?"

"As a matter of fact, I do. I'd better find my wife and get this show on the road or no one's going to eat tonight." Eamon chucked him on the shoulder before moving off.

Jim smiled seeing the broad grin that came across Eamon's face after mentioning Jake. He was happy for his brother, for both of them, and for little Dani, who finally had the family she craved.

Sighing, he let his gaze wander back to Liza. For once, her head turned and she fastened her laughing gaze on him. Almost instantly she frowned and turned away. In between the two extremes he saw another expression. The same kind of distress he'd seen in Florida, though not as sharply pronounced. So, that fiancé of hers had wounded her, if only a little. Heaven help that man if Jim ever got his hands on him.

He knocked back the rest of his drink and left his glass on a nearby table as he advanced toward where Liza stood facing away from him. When he reached her, he placed his hand on her back to get her attention. "I missed you after the ceremony."

She turned around to face him slowly, as if she were reluctant to do so. In three-inch heels, she was nearly as tall as he. She looked at him levelly, one eyebrow arched. "What can I do for you, James?"

No one, not even his mother, had ever called him James, except when she wanted to wring his neck. He liked the way her name sounded in that sexy rasp of hers, as if she'd just pronounced the name of some exotic species of bird. *James.* He supposed he could get used to that, except that he suspected she used his given name as a means of distancing herself from him. That he couldn't allow.

"The name is Jim." He nodded toward the dance floor. "It seems the happy couple is about to take their first dance. If I remember correctly, we're supposed to join them."

She glanced in the direction he indicated and frowned. Sure she as about to decline him anyway, he added, "Couldn't we put aside what happened in Florida and call a truce for one night?"

He flashed her his most charming grin, waiting for her answer. Not that he could forget that night they shared. Not that he really wanted to know that she could cast aide the memory so easily, either. Truthfully, he didn't want her angry with him. And he wanted to hold her, even if only in the sterile environment of a restaurant dance floor.

She smiled in a way that gave him no clue to what thoughts ran through her mind. "I'm only doing this for Jake and Eamon's sake. I don't want to do anything to spoil their day."

"I appreciate that." Any pretext was better than none. He led her to the edge of the dance floor, where other couples had already joined in, and pulled her into his arms. The maneuver was familiar yet different. Before, she'd come to him willingly, molding her soft body to his. This time she established a discreet distance between them and did her best to pretend she wasn't dancing with him at all. Rather than looking at him, she looked over her shoulder, at whom or what he couldn't know without turning to look himself.

He searched his repertoire of witty comments and surprising came up blank. Liza wasn't the type of woman to be impressed by his usual line of banter. What on earth could you say to a woman who had already decided to hate your guts, that would make her appreciate you anyway? "I'm having coronary bypass surgery in the morning and I'm not expected to live?" He doubted even that would win him any sympathy from her if it were true. She'd probably figure any calamity falling his way was just deserts for whatever sins she imagined he'd committed.

He focused on her face again. Her eyes had taken on a faraway quality and she was frowning. He recognized the look, one of a woman thinking about a man who'd wronged her. Her damn fiancé. He wanted to wipe that look off her face and that man from her mind. He gave her waist a squeeze. "I can't be that bad a dancer."

She blinked and focused on him in a way that said she'd forgotten his existence. "My mind was somewhere else."

No doubt. "Not on me?"

"Excuse me, but your ego is showing. I have better things to think about."

He grinned. "Or worse?"

"World hunger, AIDS, and typhoid come to mind."

"Hey, I made the top ten."

She shook her head as one does when dealing with a crazy person. "Why don't you go back to your thoughts and leave me to mine?"

"That wouldn't help me any. I was thinking about the first time we danced like this. Do you remember what happened then?"

She shot him a warning look that would have caused a lesser mortal to clam up.

She tilted her head to one side and glared at him. "Since there's zero chance of a repeat performance, maybe we should let the subject drop."

"If that's the way you want it, but promise me something?"

"What?"

"If you ever run into that fiancé of yours again, tell him he's a fool."

She sighed. "Jake told you about that?"

"No, Eamon. I'm sorry."

For a long moment she scrutinized him through narrowed eyes. "That makes one of us," she said finally. "It was a mistake, but he was the only one smart enough to do anything about it."

He stared at her a moment, nonplussed by the idea that any man was stupid enough to walk away from her. He'd assumed it was the other way around. "Then he's twice a fool."

"Though I'm inclined to agree with you, I'd rather not discuss him either."

She was back to staring over his shoulder, but this time when he pulled her closer, she didn't resist. She laid her cheek against his shoulder, facing away from him. He buried his nose against her hair and concentrated on enjoying holding her in his arms. He suspected the minute the music stopped the moment between them would be over.

In that regard, she didn't disappoint him. When the song drew to a close, she lifted her head and pulled away by slow degrees. For a moment, their gazes met. In the instant before she blinked them away, he saw two things flash in her eyes that he hadn't expected: interest, or maybe he'd even go as far as desire, and disappointment.

That surprised him. Up until that moment, he would have sworn what Jake told her had rendered her as immune to him as she claimed. He smiled to himself, unaccountably pleased by that revelation. He brought her hand to his lips and kissed the back of it. "Thank you."

She pulled her hand out of his grasp and stepped back from him. "I have to go."

She sounded so earnest he couldn't resist teasing her. "As long as you save me another dance later."

She cast him a scoffing look before heading off and leaving him at the edge of the dance floor. He watched her departure, noticing the swing of her hips, the shapeliness of her legs in those high, high heels.

"Jake says it's not polite to stare."

Jim had been so taken up with his own thoughts and the view in front of him that he hadn't noticed Dani coming up beside him. Jim ruffled her hair. "Maybe not, but who feels like being polite every day?"

"Not me."

Jim laughed. He could believe that.

Later, after the cake had been cut and eaten, the bride and groom and most of the guests departed, Liza stood in the small courtyard at the rear of the restaurant leaning her back against the railing. Inside she could see Jim and Dani dancing. Dani stood on his feet while Jim took comically large steps around the dance floor and Dani giggled. Liza wondered if he knew how deep a crush the little girl had developed on her new uncle.

Liza sighed. In some ways, so much had changed in the past two years. Two years ago, they'd all been reeling from Jake's brother's unexpected death. Dani had gone to Jake, as Dani's mother, Sylvia, was nowhere to be found and had given up her parental rights a week after Dani's birth anyway. Then Jake had gone to work for Eamon at his family-owned magazine. Just as life seemed to finally be on track again, Sylvia had come back into their lives, not to claim Dani, but in an attempt to share in her life. In a few minutes, Liza would collect Dani to take her to her apartment for the night. Dani would be staying with Sylvia and her new stepfather while Jake and Eamon enjoyed a monthlong honeymoon in France.

Okay, so a lot had happened for Jake in the past year, while her own life had remained basically in place. Despite her temporary claim to a fiancé, she was actually worse off than she had been two years ago. At least she'd been employed then. And she'd had hair. The hair, at least, would grow back.

Hearing Dani giggle, she shifted her attention again to the couple on the dance floor, Jim in particular. Seeing him today, she could almost see him as the same man she'd met in Florida. Almost, though she still didn't know what to make of him. She'd expected him to spend his time hitting on every unattached woman in sight. She'd even noticed a couple of women approach him, but he hadn't seemed interested. Instead, he'd spent most of his time letting Dani tag along behind him. What kind of Casanova could the man be if he didn't press his advantage when he had one?

Liza sighed. He hadn't even pressed her for the other

dance he claimed she owed him. She had to admit, part of her wouldn't have minded if he did. Part of her had been looking forward to it, since in truth she couldn't seem to get that night out of her mind, despite what she knew about him.

Being in his arms hadn't exactly helped in that regard. Annoyed at her body's immediate reaction to him, she'd at first tried to maintain some distance from him. But once she'd laid her cheek on his shoulder, memories flooded through her, swamping her. She'd barely noticed when the music ended, and then it had taken her a moment to work up the will to pull away. The only saving grace was that Jim hadn't noticed her predicament, or at least hadn't made a big deal out of it.

She was really going to hate it if she had to revise her opinion of him. Believing him to be a cad offered her a little bit of a safety net, as she knew she could never really be attracted to that sort of man. She was having enough trouble maintaining her equilibrium around him as it was.

As soon as the song ended, Dani bounded off the dance floor toward her, Jim following close behind. "Did you see us dancing?"

Liza ruffled Dani's hair. "I sure did."

"Are you ready to go?" Jim asked.

Liza nodded. "Dani and I will get our things and catch a cab."

"There's no need. I'll drop you."

She shook her head. What she needed was less Jim Fitzgerald, not more. She needed some distance from him to get her head together where he was concerned. In her present mood, she didn't trust herself not to do something unwise. "That won't be necessary. Jake gave me money for the cab."

"I'll let you in on a little secret. Dani's bag is already in the car."

Huffing out a breath, she looked from Jim to Dani, who gazed back with an expectant expression on her face. She returned her attention to Jim, who appeared to be the picture of innocence. Yeah, right. She didn't know when the two of them had cooked this up, or more importantly why, but she knew when she was licked. Liza threw up her hands in defeat. "Fine."

Jim grinned. "I'll meet you ladies downstairs after I bring the car around."

Watching his departure, Liza sighed. So she was saddled with him for a few more minutes. He'd drop her off at her apartment and that would be that. She understood from Jake that he'd be heading back to Florida in a day or two. He'd be out of her life and if that out-of-sight, out-of-mind thing could manage to kick in, she'd be a happy woman.

Just as she and Dani made it outside, Jim pulled up in Eamon's big black Town Car. Although there was no need, he came around and opened both her and Dani's doors and helped each of them inside. Dani giggled at her uncle's uncharacteristically formal behavior. Liza wondered what he was up to.

He slid in beside her and started the engine. "Everyone comfy?"

"Yup," Dani said with a yawn.

"Buckle your seat belt, munchkin," Jim warned before pulling from the curb.

Once she was sure Dani had complied, Liza settled back in her seat. She hadn't exactly expected Jim to drive like a speed demon, but neither did she expect him to start out and maintain a sedate speed, either. Most Manhattan drivers drove as fast as they could as far as they could before a traffic light or another car or some pesky pedestrian got in their way. New Yorkers elevated riding someone's tail to an art form. Maybe he was just being cautious because Dani was in the car.

She glanced at his profile. His attention focused on the road in front of him. "Do you have any idea where you're going?"

"Sort of. You live near Jake."

Or where, as of today, Jake used to live. Tomorrow, after Sylvia collected Dani, Liza would oversee the removal of the few furnishings left in the apartment. "Around the corner."

"When we get close, tell me where to go."

Liza widened her eyes and covered her mouth in pretend shock. "Do my ears deceive me? Did I just hear a man asking for directions? Where are the people from Ripley's when you need them?"

He stole a glance at her. "Make fun if you want, but contrary to popular belief, men have no problem asking for directions."

She folded her arms. "Is that so?"

"Actually, it's you women's fault."

Her eyebrows lifted. "How do you figure that?"

He shot her another look, this one laced with a suggestiveness the first one lacked. "If you'd be more precise about where you wanted us to go . . ."

Heat stole into her cheeks with her understanding that the sort of directions he had in mind had nothing to do with four wheels and turn signals. "Turn right at the corner."

As he made the turn she looked back at Dani. She knew that bit of conversation would have gone over her head had she been awake.

"How is she?" Jim asked.

"Out." Which unfortunately meant that Liza would have to wake her to get her in the house. They were only two blocks away. Damn.

When Jim double-parked in front of Liza's building a few moments later she tried to get the little girl to stir.

"Leave her. I'll carry her up."

"That isn't necessary." She shook Dani's leg. "Sweetheart, we're here."

"You'll have as much luck rousing her as you would waking the dead. Once that girl is asleep, she's asleep. Come on."

He popped the trunk and got out of the car. Liza gritted her teeth. Couldn't anything with this man ever be simple? She got out of the car and claimed the suitcase he'd lifted to the sidewalk by its handle. He opened the car door, lifted Dani to his shoulder effortlessly, and kicked the door shut.

"Can you handle that?" he asked, nodding toward the suit case.

She shot him a droll look. The only items Dani had packed were some toys and special items she didn't want to do without, and a change of clothes in case they were needed on the trip. She had more than enough clothing at her mother's house in Atlanta to make packing the ones she had here redundant. Not to mention the thing rode on wheels. "I've got it."

"Then let's go."

He smiled at her, a gesture she found completely disarming for its lack of guile or suggestiveness. "Fine," she said. She turned and led the way into the building.

Four

When they reached her apartment, Liza unlocked the door and stood aside to let Jim carry Dani in.

"Where do you want her?" he asked.

"In the bedroom." She pointed to the left. "The second door down the hall."

He started off in the appropriate direction. She kicked off her shoes and left them under the coffee table before joining them. By the time she got to the bedroom, Jim had laid Dani down on the bed.

Straightening up, Jim said, "Seeing her asleep like that you'd never guess what a hellion she is."

She had to agree with him. Dani slumbered with an angelic expression on her face. "I'd better get Sleeping Beauty tucked in properly."

"I guess that's my cue to leave."

She nodded. "Thank you."

He winked at her. "All in a day's work."

As he moved off, she sat on the bed facing Dani and took one of the little girl's feet into her lap to remove her shoe. When she reached for the other foot, Liza noticed Dani's eyes snapped shut.

Liza's mouth dropped open. "Dani McKenna, you weren't asleep at all, were you?"

"I was. Kinda."

"What kind is that?"

"The kind where you close your eyes and pretend."

Liza groaned, replaying the conversation in the car in her mind, trying to remember if they'd said anything damaging to little ears. Finding nothing, she shrugged. "Since you're awake, help me get you into your pajamas."

"Okay."

Once she'd settled Dani under the covers, pajamas in place, Liza leaned down to kiss Dani's forehead. "Sweet dreams, sweetheart."

"Auntie Liza, can I ask you a question? You don't have to answer if you don't want to."

Liza sat back and scanned the little girl's face. By the serious expression on Dani's face, Liza knew whatever Dani wanted to ask meant a lot to her. "Sure, sweetheart."

"You like Uncle Jim, right?"

Liza's eyebrows lifted. She hadn't expected that and wondered exactly where this conversation was heading. But she answered honestly. "He's okay, I guess." She was big enough to admit she no longer wanted to string him up for the sake of all womankind everywhere, though she was reserving any other judgment for the time being.

"I mean like him, like him. Like kissing and stuff."

How on earth was she supposed to answer that? And what had prompted Dani to ask that? What the hell had they talked about in that car? She settled on the time-tested parental prerogative of answering a difficult question with another one. "Why do you want to know?"

"If you two got married, that would make you my aunt for real."

That would make her Dani's stepaunt, but she wasn't about to quibble semantics with a child. "That's not going to happen, Dani."

"Why not? Uncle Jim is so nice. He takes me to the park to ride my bike and he taught me how to fish and he buys me things Jake says no to."

"And that's a recommendation? That he goes against Jake's wishes?"

"Jake only says no to things she can't afford. Or she used to."

Liza could imagine that. Jake's financial situation had improved dramatically once Eamon came into the picture.

"Don't you want to be my aunt for real?"

Hearing the plaintive note in Dani's voice, Liza thought she finally understood what had led to this discussion. With Jake and Eamon about to leave on their honeymoon, she needed reassurance that she was still cared for. "You listen to me, Dani McKenna. I am your aunt in every way that counts. I'm always going to love you and help take care of you, and if you don't cut this nonsense out right now, I'll be forced to give you a spanking to prove it."

That last part was an idle threat. Dani'd never received a spanking in her life, though she'd deserved quite a few of them.

Dani's eyes widened. "Would you really?"

"Yes, I would, so don't tempt me."

In response, Dani reached up and hugged her. "I love you, Auntie Liza."

Liza hugged her back. "You better. Now go to sleep. And real sleep this time. We have to get up early in the morning."

Dani nodded and settled down. Liza lingered at Dani's bedside, watching as her breathing deepened. When she was reasonably sure that Dani had fallen asleep, she turned on the lamp beside her bed to serve as a night-light.

Liza went to the door, but lingered in the room resting her side against the door jamb. So he was gone. No muss. No fanfare. The two of them hadn't even said a proper good-bye. Not that that mattered. She should simply consider herself lucky that she hadn't done anything foolish that she could now regret at her leisure.

A peculiar sort of melancholia claimed her, which she was certain had nothing to do with the presence or absence of Jim Fitzgerald. It was probably the letdown of the wedding finally being over after months of planning. All the excitement, the buildup, and unlike the happy couple, she wouldn't be going on any honeymoon to keep the thrill going. About all she had on her agenda was looking for a new job, which was an anti-thrill, if anything.

She pushed off the wall. She couldn't stand here forever deliberating her moods. She had to get up early to see Dani off. She switched off the overhead light and walked to the linen closet farther down the hall to retrieve her spare sheets and pillowcases. With Dani in her bed, she faced a night on the living room sofa—another treat to look forward to.

The first thing she noticed as she made her way back to the living room was that the radio she hadn't turned on was playing. So she wasn't entirely surprised to find Jim still in her living room, though she wasn't sure why. He stood near one of her speakers making a mess of the neat stack of CDs she kept on a shelf. In the time she'd been gone he'd taken off his jacket, rolled up his sleeves, and loosened his collar and tie. He looked nicely mussed and so damn sexy her mouth watered.

As she approached he looked up at her and winked. "How's the princess doing?"

She drew to a halt a foot away from him. "You mean *not* so Sleeping Beauty? It turns out we've both been duped. She was wide awake the whole time in the car."

"So I risked my sacroiliac for nothing. Is she asleep now?"

"Seems that way on both counts." She crossed her arms. "Don't take this the wrong way, but what are you still doing here?"

"I didn't want to leave until you could lock up after me. This is, after all, still New York."

So it was, but she doubted the location of her apartment had anything to do with anything. He'd been busy making himself comfortable while she put Dani to bed and didn't look as if he planned to bolt for the door any time soon. That left her with the task of kicking him out—a tough job, but she was just the woman to handle it.

"Well, it's been a long day," she said pointedly.

He put down the CDs in his hand and turned to face her. "Yes, it has. How are you doing?"

Liza sighed. He had that sympathetic look on his face again. He supposed he was asking how she was handling her breakup this morning. No way did she intend to discuss Ryan with him. "I'm fine. You know if you leave your car where it is, you'll probably get a ticket."

"Then I'll pay it." He shoved his hands in his pants pockets. "Why do I get the feeling you're trying to get rid of me?"

"You're observant?"

He had the nerve to laugh. "Is there anything wrong with wanting to make sure you and my niece are all right before I leave?"

"No." But that was the problem. It was sweet in an overprotective sort of way. At the moment, she didn't need to be thinking any nice thoughts about him, not when his presence alone wreaked havoc with her emotions. "But we're both fine."

She left it to him to get her implication—that there was no longer any reason to stay.

Abruptly the song on the radio changed. She didn't know its name then or now, but she recognized the sultry Latin melody as the one they'd danced to in Florida. For her, that song carried with it sense memories that caused her body to both heat and moisten.

Obviously, the song had a similar impact on him, too. His eyes narrowed and a suggestive smile tilted his lips. "Looks like they're playing our song."

"Looks like it."

"Come dance with me."

She shook her head. "It's late and I have to get Dani up early in the morning."

"You still owe me a dance."

"No, I don't."

"Dance with me anyway. One dance and I'll go."

Now that he put it that way. How much could one dance hurt, especially if it guaranteed he'd leave without a fuss? Oh, who was she kidding? She should just admit she wanted to be held by him. Something about him called to her on a primitive level that defied logic and reason.

She took the hand he extended to her and gasped when he pulled her toward him roughly, bringing their bodies to instant intimate contact. His arms closed around her, sealing their positions. Of their own accord, her arms wound around his neck and she buried her nose against his neck.

A demon must have seized her. That was the only explanation for it. After a while, she lifted her head and said, "I kissed you."

He brushed a strand of hair from her face. "Excuse me?"

"You asked me before if I remembered what happened the last time we danced like this. I never answered you. I kissed you."

"And is there still zero chance of a repeat performance?" His voice was low, husky, very sexy, and his eyes were intense.

"You tell me."

She watched avidly as his mouth slowly lowered toward her, waiting until the last moment to close her eyes. When they finally met, she inhaled sharply from the heat of the contact. His tongue invaded her mouth to mate with her own. One of his hands roved lower to caress her bottom, while the other rose to tangle in the hair at her nape. She moaned and clung to him, lost to the fire raging in her veins.

When he finally pulled away, they were both out of breath. Her fingers went to his tie, swiftly undid it the rest of the way. She tossed it aside, then started on his shirt buttons. She parted the material, revealing the broad expanse of his chest. Her fingers wandered over his skin, until she found what she sought. She strummed her thumbs over his nipples.

His hands grasped her wrists to still her hands. "What are you doing, Liza?"

She smiled a wicked smile. "Kissing you." She pressed her lips against his chest and circled his nipple with her tongue. He jerked and his breath hissed out through his teeth. Inspired by his reaction, she drew his nipple into her mouth. A groan rumbled up through his chest and reverberated through her, too.

He lifted her in his arms and carried her to the sofa. He settled them at one end so that she lay across him with her back braced against his arm and the arm of the sofa. His fingers traced the path of her neckline. His gaze traveled over her, from her face to her throat to her décolletage. "Have I told you how beautiful you looked in this dress tonight?"

"No, but you can if you want to."

His hand dipped deeper into her gown so that the backs of his fingers grazed her nipples. Her breath drew in on a gasp. "Wh-what are you doing, Jim?"

He pushed her neckline low enough to expose her breasts. "Returning the favor." His head lowered and he took her nipple into his mouth. His tongue flicked against her sensitive flesh, making her back arch and her hands close around his neck, holding him where she wanted him. His hand strummed down her body from waist to hip and finally to grasp her buttocks in his palm. Her legs pressed together restlessly. God, she wanted him, all of him, reason and logic be damned.

The sound of someone pounding on her door reached her, followed by another sound that froze them both in place. Ryan's voice saying, "Liza, open this door, I know you're in there."

"Oh God." What was Ryan doing here and what could he possibly want at this hour of the night? Whatever he wanted, she didn't want to see him. "Ryan, go home," she shouted toward the door.

The banging intensified. "I'm not leaving until I speak with you."

"I could get rid of him for you."

She glanced up at Jim to see the feral expression in his eyes. Good Lord, that's just what she needed, two men duking it out in her living room. Well, one man anyway. Ryan would probably faint at the first sign of a punch. Then she'd have to revive him just to get him out the door.

But she had to do something before Ryan's racket woke both her neighbors and Dani. "I'll be right back." She extricated herself from Jim and stood. For good measure she told him, "Stay where you are." If he stayed put, she could open the door to Ryan without him being able to see Jim.

She padded toward the door, fixing her clothing and hair as best she could as she went. She opened the door partway. "What do you want, Ryan?"

"Do I have to say it standing out in the hall?"

That would be her first choice, but she could see that was not to be. She opened the door a little wider. Ryan stepped over the threshold, but rather than shut the door behind him, she stepped backward, blocking him from entering her apartment any farther. "What do you want, Ryan?"

He took a step toward her. He frowned when she stood her ground and didn't allow him to pass. "I've spent all day thinking about you," he said in a voice that was almost a whine. "I couldn't get you off my mind."

She crossed her arms. "That's what you came here to tell me?"

"I never should have broken things off with you the way I did this morning. I know that now. No one has ever been as good to me as you have."

She didn't doubt that. Who else would put up with a grown man's whiny rants and ramblings about his father? Just call her Liza the Enabler. "And . . ." she prompted, hoping to get to whatever he wanted to say so she could get him out of there.

"I stood up to my father, Liza. I told him I didn't care what he wanted. I had no intention of marrying Debbie since I was in love with you."

Liza stared at him a moment, not knowing what to say. While she was glad he'd finally grown a backbone, there was no way she could take him back. He'd given her enough time and distance to really see him as he was. She shook her head. "It's too late."

"What do you mean it's too late? We only broke up this morning."

Thankfully, that was long enough. "Go home, Ryan. There's nothing for you here."

"I should have known."

She had no idea what he was talking about. Worse, he wasn't even looking at her but at something over her head and in back of her. She turned to see what caught Ryan's attention. A shiver ran through her seeing Jim standing behind her. Illuminated only by the sliver of light coming into the apartment from the hallway, he looked dark and dangerous with his feet braced apart and his hands fisted. His shirt was still open the way she'd left it. His gaze was set on Ryan, not her. "The lady asked you to leave."

Hearing his voice, low and mean, another shiver passed through her. She didn't doubt he'd carry through on his threat to get rid of Ryan for her. Since she didn't want to see Ryan beaten to a pulp, at least not enough to witness the actual beating, she turned back to him.

"How could you do this to me, Liza? My God, you couldn't even wait a day before picking up some man?"

Anger flashed in her. In his own roundabout way, Ryan had called her a whore. Obviously Jim didn't miss his meaning either. She felt him come up behind her. She made sure to block his path, not because she cared any more what happened to Ryan. Jim could have him as soon as she was through with him.

She glared at Ryan. "Who are you to question anything I do? The whole time we were together you had Debbie the Debutante on the side and I never once questioned you."

"True," he said in a quiet, defeated voice. "But I never touched her. I never even thought about her unless my father brought her up. I'm going." He directed that comment at Jim. "Good-bye, Liza. I hope you find what you're looking for." He turned and walked out the door.

As soon as he'd gone, she shut her eyes and gritted

her teeth. It was bad enough that Ryan had been here at all, but Jim had heard every word they'd spoken. Not only that, he'd actually come to her defense. If that thing about floors opening up and swallowing people could work right now, she'd be eternally grateful.

Instead, she felt his arms close around her from behind, pulling her against him. For a moment, she relaxed against him, craving his strength and his protection and mostly his warmth.

He kissed her shoulder. "Sweetheart, are you all right?"

"Other than profoundly embarrassed, I'm fine. I'm sorry you had to hear all that."

"*You* have nothing to be embarrassed about."

Maybe not, but she did have something to fear. She'd just gotten out of one mistake; she wasn't about to leap into another one. She shrugged out of his embrace and headed to the living room. She retrieved his jacket from the sofa and his tie from the floor and extended both to him. "You have to leave now."

"Right this minute?"

She heard the amusement in his voice but refused to be deterred. "Yes."

"Why?"

"If you want to know the truth, I don't trust myself around you. Every time I get near you, it's like my brain falls out of my head and I do something stupid."

He grinned. "What's your point?"

She tilted her head to one side. "Let's face it, where do you think we'd be right now if Ryan hadn't come here?"

He shoved his hands in his pockets. "Precisely nowhere, considering Dani is sleeping in your bed and I doubt you'd risk making love out in the open where she could walk in on us."

"Oh," she said in a small voice. He'd planned on

stopping while that thought had never crossed her mind. Someone please remind her which of them was supposed to have a lack of sexual self-control.

She sighed. How could she say this without really offending him. "Look, I'm willing to admit I judged you a bit harshly at first. You're probably a decent guy. But we both know you are exactly the kind of man I think you are—around for the good times but nothing else. That's fine. We all have our roles to play in the world, but that's not what I want. I need more than that. I need a life. Can you understand that?"

While she spoke, an emotion flashed in his eyes, but came and went before she had a chance to decipher it. "Sure, baby." He took his jacket from her and shrugged into it. He shoved his tie into one of his pockets. "Take care of yourself." He placed one soft brief kiss on her cheek. "Remember to lock up after I'm gone." He turned and strode out the door in the direction of the stairs.

Liza closed the door and locked it, then leaned her back against it. She let her breath out through her teeth. He was gone. He'd done what she asked with a minimum of fuss and left. She'd gotten exactly what she wanted, so why did she feel so disappointed?

When Jim got down to the car, it was to find a bright orange traffic ticket tucked under the windshield wiper on the driver's side. He snatched the ticket up as he rounded the car. In truth, he'd been lucky the car hadn't been towed as well. He opened the door, tossed the ticket onto the passenger side, and got in, slamming the door behind him.

Gripping the steering wheel with both hands, he banged his forehead on the top of it. "Stupid, stupid, stupid," he muttered. She'd thrown him out, and he'd gotten exactly what he deserved. It wasn't like he hadn't known what he was doing. He'd already told himself he should leave her alone. Despite her outwardly cool demeanor, he'd known that losing her fiancé must have cost her something, even if the guy turned out to be a complete s.o.b. Just like in Florida, she'd been vulnerable, and he'd taken advantage of that vulnerability.

He wasn't proud of that. The only thing he could cite in his favor was that he hadn't intended to take things so far with her. Honestly, he'd only wanted to hold her. But once she'd put her sweet mouth on him, he'd been a goner.

He turned off the hazard lights and started the car. Well, at least he wouldn't have to worry about it too much. In a few days he'd be back in Florida, she'd be here in New York. He'd have no opportunity and no excuse to see her, except maybe over one of Jake's inedible family meals. He supposed they could manage to be civil to one another for the sake of their loved ones.

That's not how he wanted it to be, though, in truth, he wasn't sure what he wanted. He only knew he regretted leaving her this way, since all he'd managed to do was reinforce every negative thing she believed about him. He pulled into traffic, headed for his brother's house on the west side of Central Park.

Five

Four o'clock this morning

Liza let herself into Jake and Eamon's apartment, kicked the door shut with her foot, and let her belongings slip silently to the floor. She was physically exhausted, mentally drained, and soaked to the skin besides. Catching a cab uptown hadn't proved to be as easy as she'd thought. Apparently no one wanted to pick up a half-clothed woman clutching an enormous bear and a briefcase. She'd resigned herself to walking at least part of the way here, when the heavens opened up and spat out raindrops the size of cats. If it weren't for some cabbie that'd given her a ride without charging her a penny she'd still be wandering up Sixth Avenue muttering to herself like a madwoman.

Now, too tired to do anything as practical as shower, all she wanted was a warm bed. Rather than turn on any lights she'd have to backtrack to turn off, she clomped through the dark apartment in her sodden slippers without managing to bang into anything. Standing by Jake and Eamon's bed, she shrugged out of her trench coat and let it slide to the floor. She toed off her slippers and slid into one side of the nice, warm, king-sized bed. Maybe it was a bit too warm, she mused as she settled under the lightweight covers. Or maybe in her wet, chilled state, it only seemed so. .

Then something beside her moved. She recognized it immediately as the form of a nude man, because it draped itself half over her before she had time to move out of the way. She shrieked and scrambled from the bed. An instant later, one of the bedside lamps flickered on, momentarily blinding her. From the bed, a familiar voice said, "Liza? What are you doing here?"

Oh God, she should have known it was him. Just what she needed on top of everything else. She shoved her feet into her slippers. "I didn't know you were here." She snatched up her trench coat. "I'll go now."

She pivoted and hurried from the room, putting on her coat as she went. She heard him calling to her but she ignored him. She simply couldn't deal with him right now. But the hall light flicked on and a moment later he pulled her back with a hand on her arm.

"Liza, will you please tell me what's going on? What happened?"

Liza blinked, trying to find somewhere for her eyes to focus. How he'd managed to slip on a pair of jeans that fast, she didn't know, but he'd only managed to zip them halfway and his chest was bare. She settled on his hand wrapped around her wrist. "Nothing a good night's sleep and a new apartment won't cure. Now if you don't mind, I'll be on my way." She tried to pull away from him, but his grip didn't budge.

"Where exactly are you planning to go at this hour dressed like that?"

"I'll get a hotel room." Or she would if he ever let go of her arm.

"Why?"

"I cannot share this apartment with you."

"Why not?"

She shot him a droll look. Maybe he'd forgotten what happened the last two times they'd been alone together, but she hadn't. And those times they both at least started out clothed.

"Oh, for heaven's sake. Even I'm not up for any fun and games at the moment. It's four o'clock in the freaking morning."

When he put it like that, her reluctance did seem ridiculous. The whole situation was ridiculous. Since she had to agree with him that not much good could come from her wandering the streets as she was, she had to give in. "I'll be in Dani's room." She broke free of his grasp, hurried to Dani's room, and shut the door.

Too drained for anything else, she fell on Dani's bed, pulled a corner of the covers over her, and was instantly asleep.

The next morning Jim sat on the living room sofa nursing his second cup of coffee. Although it was nearly eleven o'clock, Liza slumbered on. He decided to let her sleep, though the temptation to wake her was strong. He didn't know what had caused her to flee her apartment in her nightgown and slippers in the dead of night, but possibilities circled in his brain, none of them good. And the items she'd brought with her—he could understand her purse, laptop, and portfolio, but for what earthly reason had she dragged that bear along? Its presence here suggested she hadn't been thinking clearly when she left.

Or when she got here for that matter. He'd been as surprised as she to find themselves sharing the same bed. He'd been dreaming about her and then there she was. At first he thought he was imagining things. Part of his reason for latching on to her was to prove to himself that she was real.

But she wanted nothing to do with him. Despite her denial, he suspected she did believe he'd taken advantage of her and wanted to protect herself from more of the same. Granted, he hadn't given her much reason to trust him, but it still stung that she would rather risk God only knew what on the street than stay in the same apartment with him.

He sighed, starting to worry about her now. Letting her sleep didn't mean he couldn't check on her. He went to the smaller bedroom and slid the door open. She lay on her side with one arm flung over her head and the other hanging off the side of the narrow bed. One corner of the blanket was curled toward her as if she had used it to cover herself. If so, it wasn't doing its job. During the night, her gown had ridden up, exposing the length of her slender legs. Jim swallowed as his body hardened just from the sight of her. No wonder she didn't trust him; he couldn't even trust himself.

Leaving the door open he went to Jake and Eamon's room. If nothing else, she'd need something to wear. Jake's clothes had to be at least two sizes too big for her, but they would have to do for the moment. He found the necessary articles along with a hairbrush and left them at the foot of the bed. He left the room again, this time shutting the door behind him. After pouring himself a fresh cup of coffee, he went back to the sofa to wait.

He was on the verge of falling asleep again when the sound of the bedroom door opening brought him back to consciousness. A couple of seconds later, Liza walked into the room. She'd pulled her hair into a short ponytail. That combined with the too-large clothes lent her a fragile look. The first words she said to him were not hello or good morning, but, "Where are my slippers?"

"You mean those two rags that looked ready for the garbage heap?"

He'd meant to tease her. He hadn't thrown out her slippers, he only meant they needed to be. But her face crumbled and her eyes glistened with unshed tears. Her shoulders drooping, she pivoted in the direction she'd come.

He was off the sofa before she'd taken two good steps. He took her hand and led her toward the sofa. "Come here, sweetheart." He sat on the sofa and pulled her down next to him. He pulled her to him and pressed her cheek against his chest. "I didn't really throw out your slippers."

She surprised him by going to him without protest, but she pulled away from him long before any tears she might have needed to shed had been spent. She sat back and surveyed him with dry eyes. "I'm sorry. I don't do that very often."

She'd barely done it now. "I didn't mind." He remained silent, waiting for her to elaborate and tell him what had happened last night. Since no such elaboration was forthcoming, he asked, "Is there any hope you're going to tell me why you showed up here last night?"

"None whatsoever."

That was blunt. "Why not?"

"Because in my experience, if you tell a man you have a problem, he can't just listen and mouth sympathetic nonsense like a woman would. A man wants to fix things for you. Ergo, since there's nothing for you to fix, there's no need for you to know."

How did anyone, man or woman, argue with logic like that? "How about if I promise to just say, 'There, there' and nod in appropriate places?"

She turned her head and glared at him. "Let's not and say we did."

He chuckled. "You do realize you are leaving me to think whatever I want."

"That's your prerogative. As soon as you tell me what you did with my slippers, I'm going."

She stood to leave, but he grasped her arm and pulled her back down. "Oh, no, you don't. You're not leaving here until you tell me what happened. Does this have anything to do with your former fiancé?"

"Ryan? What makes you think that?"

"Did he hurt you?"

"Of course not. The last time I saw him was the same time you last saw him. What has he got to do with anything?"

Jim gritted his teeth. He supposed he should be thankful that Gilchrest wasn't responsible for whatever brought her here. But that didn't get him any closer to learning what did happen. "Look, Liza, I realize we didn't leave it on the best of terms, but I hope we can at least be friends."

"Why would you want that?"

"I figure we don't have much choice. For Jake and Eamon's sakes, at any rate. Do you think either of them will tolerate us not being on speaking terms? I don't know about you, but I don't want to do anything to ruin their happiness. They've both waited long enough for it."

"You fight dirty, do you know that?"

He offered her a tight, fake smile.

"Fine, if you must know, my apartment building just burned to the ground."

A fire? In all his imaginings he'd never considered that.

"Were you hurt?"

"No, but everything I own was in that apartment."

And now she feared she'd lost it all. He patted her thigh. "I'm sorry, sweetheart."

She sighed and all the bluster seemed to have gone out of her. She looked away from him. "Thanks. And thank you for letting me stay here last night."

"What did you expect me to do? Toss you out on the street? And let Eamon find out you'd come here in trouble and I let you leave here alone? No, thank you. My brother already thinks the day they handed out common sense I overslept."

She chuckled. "I know how you feel. Jake is under the impression that I'd fall into complete dysfunction without her."

Considering Jake could barely get to work on time on her own, that notion surprised him. "How'd she get that idea?"

She shrugged. "What do you do when someone you love needs to be needed?"

"Consider yourself lucky. Try living with a brother who's a control freak and most of what he wants control of is you. I don't think I'm what he expected when the folks told him he was getting a baby brother."

She laughed as he expected her to. "What do you know, we have something in common: other people's expectations to live up to."

"Or not, as the case may be. We probably have something else in common. Are you hungry?"

"Starved."

"There's a place around the corner that probably won't poison us. Feel up to it?"

She nodded. "If the police department gets around to letting us in today, I gave them my cell phone number to call."

As it was a reasonably warm day with a light breeze blowing, they decided to sit at one of the restaurant's outdoor tables decorated in a red and white check pattern. Liza opened the menu the waiter presented to her and scanned the list of Italian specialties.

"Anything look good?"

"Several things." She lifted her gaze to meet his. "But I think I'll settle for the penne."

He folded his menu. "Sounds good. I'll have the same."

When the waiter returned, Liza watched Jim as he gave him their order. Despite having made love to Jim, she knew very little about him, not even what he did for a living that allowed him all this time to spend with her on a Monday afternoon. She knew it had to be something artsy considering he'd once served as art director for his family-owned magazine that Eamon now ran, but what, she had no idea.

After the waiter left, he turned back to her. "Why are you looking at me like that?"

She blinked, unaware until then that she'd been staring at him. "I was wondering, what do you do?"

His eyebrows lifted in surprise. "You mean for a living? I'm a photographer."

"A photographer as in your work is hanging in a gallery?"

"Some of it is, but mostly I do commercial work. Does that surprise you?"

She tilted her head, considering him. Her answer, if she gave one, would be yes and no. She didn't know him well enough to make that determination. And despite his in-your-face persona, she suspected that he, like the camera, was capable of hiding more than he showed. "How did you get into that?"

"By accident, really. My mother believed that all young boys should have a hobby, something to keep them occupied, probably to divert us from abusing ourselves as adolescents. While Eamon tinkered with his magic sets and trick handcuffs, I took pictures."

"Of what?"

"Mostly Mrs. Obermeyer, who lived across the street and liked to sunbathe in the nude on her back porch. Needless to say, this defeated the purpose of the camera in the first place."

"How old were you?"

"Eight, I think. Or maybe nine. Young enough that no one suspected what I was shooting until the photo lab called to say they didn't develop *those* sorts of pictures."

She shook her head. Whatever tendencies toward women he possessed, he'd formed at an early age. "Shame on you."

"Yeah, well, you would have felt sorry for me if you saw me after my mother got a hold of me. All I can say is ouch!" Without missing a beat, he added, "I hope you don't mind that I ordered us some wine."

"Not at all." For a moment she wondered about his abrupt change of subjects, until she noticed the waiter approaching their table. No, she didn't mind him ordering them *some* wine. With all that had happened to her in the last few days—and the natural effect the man seated across from her inspired—she wouldn't mind something to take the edge off. But *some* wine was a couple of glasses of the house Chardonnay, not a bottle the waiter opened with such flamboyance as to telegraph its expense. Was Jim trying to impress her? More likely, the man just liked a good bottle of wine.

As the waiter withdrew, she sipped from her glass. The wine was delicious, not too dry or too sweet, the way she liked it. She set her glass on the table, unwilling to turn him loose as the subject of conversation yet. "I take it you switched to a more appropriate subject matter."

He shrugged. "For a while and then I sort of forgot about it. I stumbled back into it when I was at NYU, majoring mostly in taking up space. Some ambitious friends of mine had entered a regional advertising competition and needed someone to take some shots for their slide presentation. I was the only person they knew who owned a decent camera. I was persuaded to help out."

She wondered if he was aware of the wicked grin that spread across his face. She could imagine what brand of persuasion had been used. "And that started you back on your career path?"

"That and the fact that one of the judges of the competition, an ad agency art director, liked my work. He hooked me up with a studio that did commercial photography. I found my niche and Eamon got to save the money he was wasting on my tuition."

He sat back in his chair and sipped his wine. "Turnabout is fair play. What do you do for a living?"

"At the moment, nothing. I got fired from my job two weeks ago."

"I'm sorry. What did you do?"

"Believe it or not, I was an employment counselor."

"Seems like you should have been looking for your own job."

"Maybe. Actually, I volunteered to get fired."

His eyebrows lifted. "I wouldn't have figured you for a martyr complex."

"I don't. I knew Daphne, my boss, had to fire someone. With most of the world looking for employment online, there simply weren't enough clients to sustain us. Although I'd been there the longest, I knew I'd probably be the one to go. Unlike the others, I didn't have a family to support or a sick mother to care for. I saw the handwriting on the wall, but this way I got to be noble about it." She shrugged.

"Do you regret your decision?"

She sighed, surprised at how adeptly he'd seen into her soul. "I regret it had to come to that. But God, I miss that job, the people I worked with." And she realized something else. "Do you know this is the first time I've been unemployed since I was fourteen years old? I lied and said I was sixteen in order to get a weekend job in a shoe store."

"Why so young?"

Liza gulped a mouthful from her glass. Now she'd gone and done it. She rarely spoke about her mother to anyone, not because she hadn't loved her. She had, but the two of them hadn't exactly gotten along. Liza had never told anyone, not even Jake, that her real reason for wanting that job was that the hours required were on Saturday and Sunday, the days her mother was off from work. Since her mother could appreciate an industrious daughter, it had been an easy ruse for Liza to pull off. But how did you put a nice face on that?

Luckily, her cell phone rang, making an immediate response unnecessary. After a brief conversation with a representative from the fire department, she hung up the phone. She looked at Jim, whom she'd felt watching her during her time on the phone. "The fire turned out not to be as bad as they thought. They're letting us in for two hours today to get our belongings."

"If the fire wasn't that bad, why can't you stay?"

"They're not sure yet, but they think the building might nave sustained structural damage. That will need to be fixed before we can move back in." She scrutinized the disappointed look on his face. "Why? Ready to get rid of me?"

"Not at all. But I had been planning on going back to Florida in a couple of days."

"So go. I told you that you don't have to babysit me. As far as Jake and Eamon go, we just won't tell them. I'll be back home by the time they get back, so what they don't know won't hurt them."

"If you say so." The waiter chose that moment to appear with their food. "Do we still have time?" Jim asked.

She nodded. "They wouldn't be letting anyone in for another hour."

"But something tells me you're anxious to go."

"It'll be nice to get into some of my own clothes, at least." She plucked at the shoulders of the T-shirt she wore. "I can't even fill out one of Jake's tops."

He winked at her. "Baby, didn't anyone ever tell you more than a mouthful is wasted?"

Despite herself, heat stole into her cheeks and it was difficult to hold his intense gaze. "Other than by one of my equally poorly endowed sisters? No. Besides, I thought all you men were obsessed with the breast."

"Not all of us. I'm a leg man myself. Nothing beats a good drumstick."

Smiling, she shook her head, grateful he'd diffused the heat of their conversation with humor. But her appetite had dried up. A feeling of foreboding gripped her, making it impossible to muster the urge to do more than push her food around on her plate.

After a few moments, Jim tossed his napkin on the table. "Are you ready to go?"

She nodded. Ready to go, but not sure she was ready for whatever awaited her at home.

When their cab pulled to a stop on Mercer Street, Jim looked up at the wide, squat structure that was Liza's apartment building. The east side of the building showed boarded-up windows and char marks on the outside of the brick, while the west side seemed untouched. He'd only been there once and couldn't remember where in the building Liza's apartment sat. He only hoped it was somewhere on the burn-free side.

While he paid the driver, Liza got out of the cab. A police barricade had been set up in front of the building. Three uniformed officers, one of whom held a clipboard, stood on the other side. Jim joined her as she showed her driver's license as proof of identity and address so that they would be allowed inside. The odor of burnt furnishings as well as another unfamiliar chemical smell assaulted them the minute they entered the building.

When they got to Liza's apartment—which was thankfully on the west side as he'd hoped—Jim took her key from her. The lock didn't turn as easily for him as he remembered it turning for her the other night, but once he got the door open, he stood aside to let her precede him.

She took a step forward as if in a haze. "Oh my God," she whispered.

He turned to see what caused that reaction and did a double take. The last time he'd been in her apartment it had been neat as the proverbial pin. Now books and papers were scattered around the floor. The contents of her sofa cushions had been emptied and her coffee table lay broken on its side. The stereo was missing from its perch. Someone had ransacked her apartment.

His gaze settled on Liza, who stood rooted to the same spot looking around. As if to no one in particular she said, "Who could have done this?"

That was his first question, too, followed closely by why. Anyone simply looking for something to steal wouldn't have bothered making all this mess. They'd have grabbed the VCR and the stereo and been done with it. At first glance, it seemed that someone had been looking for something in particular—or someone had trashed the place out of anger. Immediately one possibility sprang to mind.

She took another step forward, but he stopped her

with a hand on her arm. On the off chance that whoever did this hadn't finished yet, he didn't want her inside. "Why don't you go downstairs and get one of the
policemen up here?"

She looked at him questioningly. "What are you
going to do?"

"Don't worry about me," he said in a voice that he
hoped proved both gentle and persuasive. He nodded
in the direction of the stairs they'd just come up. "Go."

Reluctantly, she turned and did as he asked.

Six

Jim waited until she hit the stairwell to go into the apartment himself. He stopped in the living room first to retrieve one of the wooden legs that had broken off the coffee table.

The kitchen was to the left. All of the cabinets had been opened and emptied. Broken dishes littered the floor and counter spaces. The contents of every box and bag in her pantry had been emptied onto the floor: cereal, rice, flour, pasta. Even the ingredients in her spice rack had been dumped out and apparently sifted through.

The bedroom was just as bad. Her mattress had been slashed and all of her dresser drawers stood open. Various articles of clothing had either been dumped on the floor. Her jewelry box had been emptied and its contents scattered.

As he looked around at the decimation, Jim's anger boiled over. He felt like smashing something himself, or rather someone. Even someone searching her apartment wouldn't have wreaked this much destruction. To Jim's mind that left one possibility—that someone seeking vengeance had trashed her apartment. As far as he knew, that left only one possibility—her former fiancé, Ryan whoever. Jim ground his teeth together. He knew he should have beaten the crap out of that sniveling jackass while he had the chance.

He was turning to leave, when one article caught his attention. Lying on the floor next to what used to be her bed was her address book. He picked it up and thumbed through the pages until he found the name he wanted under G. He tore the sheet out and tucked it into his pocket.

He dropped the address book to the floor and went back into the living room in time to see Liza entering the room with a young, blond officer in tow.

The officer stopped on the threshold. "Whoa, what happened here?"

Jim ground his teeth together. For some reason, this kid reminded him of the young cop in Florida and immediately Jim itched to brain him with the table leg. To prevent himself from being charged with assaulting an officer, he tossed the leg onto the sofa. "That's what we were hoping you could tell us. I thought no one was let in or out of the building since the fire."

The officer nodded. "No one but fire marshals and police, until a half hour ago. Then tenants started coming in to get their stuff."

"Then how do you explain this?"

"I'd better go get the sarge."

As soon as the officer was out the door, Jim felt Liza's gaze on him. She glared at him with her arms crossed. "What exactly did you do in here while I was gone?"

She was angry with him, but he preferred that to the wounded look he'd seen in her eyes when they'd first walked in. "Just looked around."

"And what would you have done if someone was still here?"

"I was perfectly prepared to run and scream like a girl."

She shook her head. "Is it all as bad as this?"

"Pretty much."

She bit her lip and her eyes brimmed, but she didn't say anything. He closed the small gap between them and pulled her into his arms. For once she came to him willingly and rested her cheek on his shoulder. "I'm sorry, baby," he whispered against her ear.

She lifted her head to look at him. "What are you sorry for?" She hit him on the shoulder with the side of her fist. "You didn't do this, did you?"

"You know I didn't." He also knew she wasn't really angry with him, just blowing off steam.

"I'll tell you one thing. I am not cleaning this mess up."

"I tell you what. As soon as they catch who did it, we'll lock them in here with a broom and dustpan."

She hit his shoulder again. "This is not funny."

He caught her hand and kissed her palm. "I know, sweetheart."

"Damn, what happened here?"

He and Liza broke apart at the sound of the unfamiliar baritone voice. It belonged to the officer with the clipboard they'd met downstairs.

Liza said, "Obviously, someone broke into my apartment and did . . . *this*." She spread her arms in a way that encompassed the whole apartment.

The older policeman ignored her and focused on Jim. "And you are?"

"James Fitzgerald. A friend."

The officer's skeptical look told Jim what he thought of his self-definition. Considering the scene he'd walked in on, Jim couldn't blame the guy for thinking more existed to his relationship with Liza. Luckily Jim didn't give a damn what the man thought.

"Is it all as bad as this?"

Without thinking, he answered him the same way he'd answered Liza. "Pretty much."

The officer cast him a disparaging look. "It didn't occur to you that this was a crime scene?"

Jim shrugged.

The older officer nodded to the younger one, who disappeared in the direction of the kitchen and the bedroom beyond. "We'd like to check it out for ourselves if you don't mind. In the meantime, could you two wait outside? We'd like to get a CSU team in here and then we'll need a list of anything taken."

Jim took Liza's hand and led her out into the hall. He leaned against the wall while she paced in front of him. He sensed the anger in her, the frustration, and the sorrow for the decimation of everything she owned. He wanted to comfort her, but unable to come up with anything remotely soothing to say, he decided to let her be.

After a while, she turned to face him and threw up her hands. "Could someone please tell me, why me? Why would someone want to break into my apartment to steal things? Aside from the TV and the stereo, I don't keep anything valuable here. I don't even own anything valuable."

"I don't know, sweetheart." Obviously she believed robbery had prompted the break-in. He debated the wisdom of sharing his suspicions with her, but in the end decided to tell her. If Gilchrest could do this to her apartment, who knew what he might try to do to her in person? Jim wanted to make sure she didn't allow him anywhere near her.

"Maybe whoever broke in wasn't really looking to steal anything?"

"Then why is the stereo gone?"

"To make it look like a robbery, maybe. Think about

it, Liza. Would someone trying to rob you need to make all that mess? I think whoever was in here just wanted to trash your apartment."

"Who would want to hurt me like that? And why?"

"When he left here the other night, Ryan seemed angry enough to want to take some sort of retribution against you."

She shook her head. "Do you honestly think Ryan did this? Can you imagine Ryan of all people sullying his pristine hands that way?"

That was a difficult picture to imagine, he'd admit. "That doesn't mean he couldn't have hired someone to do it."

She shrugged, considering that. "But how would he even know when to do this? And on such short notice? The fire didn't happen until this morning. You're reaching, Fitzgerald. Face it, you just don't like the guy."

He conceded all her points, including the fact that he wouldn't mind making a little trouble for her former fiancé if he could. Hell, he'd like a few minutes in a locked room with the guy just for the hell of it. So, maybe he had it in for the guy, but that didn't make him wrong.

He decided to let the subject drop, as it wasn't getting him anywhere with her. There were others who might be more interested in what he had to say. He hoped so, anyway.

She turned away from him, resting her hands on the railing that ran the length of the stairwell, her shoulders slumped, her head down. "I hate this."

Jim sighed. He'd only considered her safety in telling her about Gilchrest. He hadn't considered how she might take knowing someone she'd once loved and trusted might want to hurt her.

He closed the gap between them and circled his

arms around her waist. He rested his chin on her shoulder. "It'll be okay, Liza. I promise you that."

She shook her head. "Thanks for trying to put a brave face on it for me, but you can't possibly know that."

No, he couldn't. He only knew how he wanted it to be.

The crime scene people came a few moments later, followed by a craggy-faced man who introduced himself as Detective Mike Sloan from the NYPD.

"Ms. Morrow, I'm very sorry this happened to you, and I assure you that we'll do everything possible to find out who did this."

"Thank you, Detective."

"I want to take a look at the apartment first, then we'll talk."

Liza nodded. "Okay."

As soon as the man was out of earshot, she turned to Jim. "I swear, everyone and has mother has been in my apartment but me."

To Jim's mind, that was a good thing. "I don't think it will be much longer."

"I hope not."

Sloan returned a few minutes later, his face grim. "Sorry to keep you waiting, Ms. Morrow. There's quite a bit of damage in there. More than I expected."

Jim ground his teeth together. He'd spent the last he didn't know how many minutes trying to convince Liza that things were better than they were. Sloan shot that to hell in one sentence.

"I see."

"Can you think of any reason someone might choose your apartment to break into?"

"That's the question I keep asking myself. I don't keep anything valuable in the apartment."

"Do you know offhand if anything is missing?"

"Aside from the stereo, who could tell?"

"Is there anyone you can think of who might hold a grudge against you?"

Liza glanced at him before answering. "Why do you ask?"

"You don't usually see this sort of destruction with a simple robbery. You're sure you don't keep anything here someone might be looking for?"

She shook her head. "Nothing I can think of. Why?"

"If the person who broke in was looking for something specific, something small, it might explain some of the damage."

"I can't think of anything like that."

"I'd appreciate it if you could put together a list of missing items. We'd also like to fingerprint both of you to rule your prints out when we run them. We can do that here. If I think of anything else, I'll contact you." Sloan went back into the apartment.

Jim rubbed his hand on Liza's back. "Ready to go in?"

She sighed. "I guess."

He watched her face as they walked through the apartment. He didn't know what reaction he expected from her, but the calm detachment she displayed wasn't it. Once they reached her bedroom door, she peered in and shuddered. "I am *really* not cleaning up this mess."

"Why don't you see what's missing in here? I think I'll take care of the kitchen."

She eyed him skeptically, but said, "All right."

He walked down the hall, but rather than going to the kitchen he detoured to the living room where Sloan and the two other officers stood talking. He caught Sloan's attention and nodded toward the area next to the sofa. "Can I talk to you for a moment?"

Sloan sauntered over to him with the kind of swagger

and suspicious expression only a cop who thinks he's in control can muster. "What can I do for you, Mr. Fitzgerald?"

"What do you really think happened?"

Sloan shrugged. "Opportunistic crimes when a building is vacant aren't unheard of. On the other hand, you might want to tell the lady to be careful until we can determine that's what this was."

In other words—nothing. Sloan didn't tell him anything he didn't already know.

"What do you think happened?"

"My money's on her former fiancé. Ryan Gilchrest."

"Ms. Morrow didn't mention him. What makes you think he did this?"

"When he left here two nights ago, he was not a happy camper."

Sloan folded his arms. "Really? What role did you play in this breakup?"

Jim knew what the man was asking—how much of a stake did he have in wanting Ryan picked up. "Me? None whatsoever. I just got to catch the fallout."

"I see. If you have some information on this Gilchrest, we'll check him out."

Jim handed him the slip of paper from Liza's address book, which Sloan copied down on a notepad. Flipping it closed, Sloan said, "Anything else?"

"That's it."

He took the paper from Sloan and put it back where he'd had it and headed for the kitchen. It didn't take him long to sweep up the mess on the floor and clean the remaining debris from the sink and countertops. Afterward, he went back to the bedroom to check on Liza. He found her sitting on the floor next to her closet. Her knees were pulled up and her head was down.

He crossed over the debris and knelt beside her. "Baby, what's the matter?"

She twisted around to face him. "They took my box."

"I beg your pardon?"

She sighed, exasperated. "I had a lockbox, you know, one of those security-type things, at the back of my closet. He, they, whoever took it. As far as I can tell, that's all they took."

He cleared a spot and sat down beside her. "What was in it?"

"Nothing anyone but me would want. Some mementos, everything my mother left me. They're all gone. Why would anyone take those things?"

Sherry-colored fire flashed in her eyes, and he realized that she was angry, not upset as he'd first believed. That surprised him. Any other woman he knew, most men for that matter, would have fallen apart by now. He admired her for the fact that she didn't. "I don't know, baby. Maybe they didn't know what was in there."

"There was a big label on it that said 'Mementos.'"

Maybe her thief hadn't taken her label at face value, but he doubted it. The longer he spent in the apartment the more convinced he became that this attack had been personal, not the work of vandals or petty thieves. His gut had told him from the beginning that Gilchrest was responsible.

She pushed to her feet. "I really hate this." She kicked at a shoe lying on the floor beside her, sending it flying.

He rose to his feet and pulled her against him. "Do you really want to make *more* of a mess in here?"

She rested her forehead on his shoulder. "Is that possible?"

He tugged on her ponytail. "Liza, look at me." When she complied, he almost lost every thought in his head. Even with her face clean of makeup and her hair in that dreadful style, she was the most beautiful woman he'd ever laid eyes on.

"You were saying . . ." she prompted in a way that let him know she knew exactly what he'd been thinking.

He inhaled, willing his emotions to settle. "It's really not that bad. "We'll hire someone to clean up. There's got to be a company that does that. They've got one for every damn thing else. Anything else can be replaced."

"My box can't."

Her prized mementos. Funny, he'd never pegged her as a sentimental woman. Besides, if Eamon was right, she didn't even get along with her mother. Well, it wouldn't be the first time a person's memory proved more precious than the person himself. "We'll go to Hallmark later. I'll buy you a card."

She laughed. "You're crazy, do you know that?"

"That's what they tell me."

She sobered. "Seriously, though, thank you. You've been very sweet to me today, when I treated you terribly this morning. I have no excuse for that."

"None needed." He brushed an errant strand of hair from her face, then let his fingers trail down her cheek. She inhaled, and her lips parted slightly. His thumb traced the rim of her lush lower lip.

"Jim," she protested.

She barely got the word out before his mouth was on hers. But she didn't push him away as he expected her to. She kissed him back and her arms wound around his back. Her tongue rubbed against his in a way that made his pulse quicken and his breathing stall.

"Um, Ms. Morrow?"

Liza sprang away from him, at the sound of the young officer's voice. "What can I do for you?"

"If you're ready, we can do the fingerprinting now."

"Sure." She walked over to her dresser where the officer cleared a place for a stamp pad and fingerprint card. Liza was finished in no time. When she was through, she walked over to the corner of the room without looking at Jim. In another minute, he was done. The young officer offered him a wet-nap to get the ink off his hands, then hurriedly left the room.

Liza rested her forehead against the wall. "Well, that was embarrassing."

"I'm sorry. I shouldn't have done that."

"I shouldn't have let you. But I get around you, and I lose my head."

She did the same to him. "Where does that leave us?"

"Maybe we could try to stop tormenting each other. Keep our distance."

He'd give it a try, but touching her was as natural to him as breathing air. "Let's start by getting out of here. I'll help you pack whatever you want to take with you."

She lifted her hands in the universal sign for a disgusted woman. "I'm not taking a single thing out of here unless it's to the laundry. Whoever was here was in my underwear drawer."

He chuckled. "I thought you wanted to get out of wearing Jake's clothes."

"I do. I'm going to do what any woman in my position would do. Go to Bloomies."

"Want some company?"

She tilted her head to one side. "I told you that you don't need to babysit me. Besides, I think it's better if I visit the lingerie section alone."

"I see your point. Are you sure you'll be okay?"

"I'll be fine. I'll meet you at the apartment later."

"I may be a little late getting back. I have something I need to take care of myself."

"I'll see you later then." With a little wave of her hand, she left.

Once she was gone, he pulled out his cell phone and called his friend Jackson. Jackson had once been a cop, but had opened up his own investigation firm a few years back.

Jackson answered on the second ring. "Hey, Jim, what's up?"

"Meet me for dinner and I'll tell you."

Jim spotted his friend Jackson the moment he entered the East Side restaurant where they'd agreed to meet. He'd met Jackson a few years ago when he'd first opened his own detective agency, right after leaving the NYPD. The first thing Jackson said once Jim seated himself at the table across from him was, "What's so important you had to drag me away from dinner with my in-laws?"

Jackson had defected from the Confirmed Bachelors' Club a year ago when he met and married the owner of a cosmetics company. Since then he'd developed a wry sense of humor that suited him. From the tone of his voice, Jim knew that whatever Jackson had been pulled away from, he hadn't minded.

After the waitress took his drink order, Jim said, "Remember that girl I had you looking for?"

"The one from Florida where the trail dried up? What about her?"

Last year when Dani's mother had turned up and no one yet knew her intentions, Jim had asked Jackson to look after Dani. "Turns out she's Jake's best friend."

Jackson laughed. "Only you, Jim. Only you. When did you find this out?"

"A few months ago when I showed up at Dani's birthday party."

"So, what's the problem? She skip out on you again?"

"Early this morning there was a fire in her apartment building. They let the tenants back in a couple of hours ago. Her apartment had been trashed. My place looked better after the hurricane blew part of my roof off. But apparently hers was the only one touched."

"I'm sorry to hear that. Is she all right?"

"She's fine."

"Then what do you want me to do about it? You know I'm back on the job."

"I'd heard something about that." He pulled out the slip of paper he'd taken from Liza's apartment. "You might want to make sure your brother officers take a look at this guy." He tossed the paper onto the table.

The waitress came then to deposit Jim's drink and take their dinner order. After she left, Jackson asked, "Who is he?"

"Her former fiancé. They broke up two days ago. He's not taking it very well."

"Why didn't you give his name to the boys on the scene?"

"I did, but I don't know if they are taking my suspicions very seriously. They suspect I have ulterior motives for wanting to have the guy questioned."

"Do you?"

"Sure. He's an ass."

Jackson swirled the contents of his glass. "That's it?"

"That's all I'm telling."

Jackson shook his head. "Why do you think he's the one?"

"For one thing, the only items missing from her apartment were the stereo—probably to make it look like a robbery—and a box of mementos she kept in the closet. Personal things. I think he took them to punish her for tossing him out."

Jackson tucked the paper in his pocket. "You may have something there, but you could have told me all of this on the phone."

"Here's the problem. I'm heading back to Florida in a couple of days. I don't feel good about leaving her unprotected."

"You distrust this guy that much?"

"Maybe I'm biased, but yeah."

"What does she say to this?"

Jim sipped from his glass. "I haven't told her."

"I see. You want me to get someone to tail her without her knowing. Let me tell you, that's the kind of thing that can backfire on you but good. That's how I met my wife, Carly, and she was not amused."

Jim sighed. "Does that mean you don't think it's a good idea or that you won't do it?"

Jackson lifted one shoulder in a noncommittal way. "If you're that worried about her, why don't you take her with you?"

"For one thing, she doesn't want to have anything to do with me."

Jackson chuckled. "That is a problem. Do you mind if I ask why not?"

"Seems she's the type who wants a ring and whatever the modern-day equivalent of a white picket fence is."

"And you're not ready to fight for her?"

Jim shook his head. Not unless he was willing to change everything he believed about himself and what he thought he wanted. "Not yet."

Jackson gave another of his noncommittal shrugs, his eyes on his glass. "Here's something else to think about. You say the fire took place this morning? That's a very narrow opportunity for mischief." Jackson shot him a pointed look. "If your guy is the one responsible, how do you think he knew when it was safe to go in?"

Jim muttered a curse. He must have been watching her. Maybe it was best if he tried to get her out of New York after all.

Seven

Liza barely made it through the door to Jake and Eamon's apartment when the phone that connected to the front desk downstairs buzzed. She set down her numerous packages by the front door and picked up the phone. She knew the doorman well enough to be on a first-name basis, though he never used hers. "What can I do for you, Freddy?"

"Miss Morrow, there's a guy down here that wants to see you."

Liza groaned. Who could that be? Unless it was Ed McMahon with the Prize Patrol, she wasn't interested. Exhausted from a night without enough sleep and an afternoon of shopping, all she wanted was to sit down. "Who is it?"

"He *says* he's your fiancé."

But Freddy didn't believe him. Smart man. She neither wanted to see Ryan, nor could she imagine why he'd bothered to contact her again. "Please tell Mr. Gilchrest that I'm not receiving visitors right now."

"Will do," Freddy came back, then a muffled "She says she don't want to see you."

Liza groaned at Freddy's translation, but a second later she heard him exclaim, "Hey!"

"Liza, would you please tell this person to let me pass? I need to speak with you."

"Haven't we done this scene before? What could you possibly say that you haven't said before?"

"Because of you, I've been arrested."

"Arrested?" If nothing else, that was novel. "When? What for?"

"Let me up and I'll tell you."

Liza ground her teeth together. She had a sinking feeling she already knew. She supposed she did owe him a hearing if nothing else. "Put Freddy back on the phone."

"Yes, Ms. Morrow?"

"You can let him up."

"You sure, 'cause it wouldn't be no trouble to toss him out of here?"

For Freddy, a former Golden Gloves contender, it would probably be like old times. "That won't be necessary, but I'll call you if I need you."

Before Freddy hung up, Liza heard a muffled "You can go up, but don't start no trouble."

She hung up the phone and waited by the open doorway for Ryan's arrival. A few minutes later, he stormed off the elevator and into the apartment, kicking one of her bags in the process. Unfortunately it happened to be the bag from the lingerie department. Bras and panties spilled out onto the floor, but Ryan seemed not to notice.

He halted at the center of the living room and pivoted to face her. "This is beyond the pale, Liza."

Inwardly, Liza groaned. Just what she needed—more of Ryan's histrionics.

"Why don't you calm down and tell me what hap-

pened? The police arrested you? For what? When did
they let you out?"

"They dragged me out of a board meeting of all
things to pepper me with questions about what happened in your apartment building."

"I thought you said you were arrested."

"Arrested, picked up for questioning. What's the difference, when you're dragged off by the police? They
think I had something to do with ransacking your apartment."

She shook her head. "Why would anyone think you
had anything to do with that?"

"It appears someone suggested my name to the police. That wouldn't have been you, would it?"

"Of course not." But if someone was singing to the
police, she thought she knew the songbird in question,
damn him. Jim had voiced his suspicions to her and
hadn't listened when she'd tried to shoot them down.
How could she suspect a man of trashing her apartment
who'd never emptied a trash can in his life? It was pre-
posterous.

"I'm sorry that happened."

She meant that sincerely, but Ryan was apparently
not through with his rant. "They don't let suspected
criminals become heads of publicly traded companies,
Liza. I didn't tell you this before, but the reason my father wants to see me settled is that he's planning to retire soon."

Liza almost laughed. Did he have to do everything
the way his father said it should go? If Daddy said to
take a leap off the Empire State Building, would he
jump? She knew part of Ryan's problem was that his
mother had deserted him and his father almost a year
ago. She understood devotion to the one parent who
remained, but come on.

Whatever his problem, she'd had enough of dealing

with him. Looking at this man, she couldn't remember what she ever saw in him or if there really had been anything at all.

To placate him and hopefully get him out of the apartment she said, "If you want, I'll tell the police you had nothing to do with it."

"You would do that for me?"

A suggestive note crept into his voice that immediately put her on alert. He took a step toward her. She tried to take an equal step away to maintain their distance, but backed into the wall. Damn.

He didn't miss the opportunity to use this to his advantage. He crowded her against the wall with his hands braced on either side of her.

She pushed against his shoulders with her palms. Not hard, but strongly enough to let him know she didn't appreciate his closeness. "Cut it out, Ryan. I'm not interested."

"I want you back, Liza. I know I said some things I regret. I was angry with you for being with another man the same day we called off our engagement. You can understand that, can't you?"

"No, I can't, Ryan. And we didn't call off our engagement. You told me you were marrying another woman. Don't you think dear Debbie might object to you seeing me?"

"She wouldn't have to know."

That did it. She'd half expected him to say that he'd changed his mind. Her answer would have been the same, but it would have salved her ego a little. And she'd really had enough this time.

She pushed him away, harder this time. "Go home, Ryan. Go back and be the dutiful little boy your daddy wants you to be and leave me alone."

"Don't you see what I'm offering you? I could put you up in a nice apartment, not like the fleabag you were living in. You could have clothes, furniture, money, whatever you wanted."

The man had to be out of his mind. For a moment, she simply stared at him. He acted as if he were offering her the world, but it only showed how little he knew her if he thought she could ever agree to such an arrangement. God, the sex wasn't even good enough that she'd want to subject herself to more of it without gaining anything she needed.

"That's not good enough."

He shook his head, incredulous. "You have nothing, no job, no family, no real home."

And therefore she was nothing in his eyes. Had he always seen her that way? Someone beneath him whom he could feel superior to? She remembered his comment about not being able to present Debbie with the quality of ring he'd given her and knew it was true.

She walked to the door and pointed toward the hall. "You have three seconds to get out before I call Freddy. He'll be more than happy to remove you."

Ryan's expression grew harsh. He stalked toward her. "You're making a mistake," he said as a parting shot as he walked through the door.

"If I am, it's obviously not the first time."

She slammed the door shut, then braced her back against it. That had been fun, learning that a man she thought at least cared for her actually believed she was one step up from a common whore. Not that his opinion mattered to her, not anymore, but it was one more straw on the back of a very weary camel. She hurt and she wanted to stop hurting.

But there was a cure for what ailed her. At least a temporary one. Finding what she wanted in the cupboard above the refrigerator in the kitchen, Liza smiled.

* * *

Jim arrived at his brother's apartment a little after ten to find it dark save for a flickering light he assumed to be coming from the living room TV. Judging by the number of shopping bags strewn in the foyer, Liza'd beat him home. "Liza," he called as he walked farther into the apartment, switching on the light as he went.

"In here."

Her voice sounded funny, not different, really, but a little bit off. Maybe she'd fallen asleep watching television and he'd awakened her. He drew up short at the entrance to the living room. He took one look at her and knew he was in trouble. She definitely had not been asleep, at least not recently. She was sitting on the living room floor with her back to the sofa and her legs folded under her. An open pizza box sat on the table, as well as a bottle of wine and two glasses, one of which was partially filled. Most troublesome of all, she wore nothing but a black lace peignoir set that bared her long legs.

Jim swallowed. "What are you doing?"

She offered him a lopsided grin. "Getting a little tipsy. Every now and then a girl just needs to get a little drunk. It's like having a good cry without the tissues. Want to join me?" She patted a spot on the sofa behind and to the right of her.

"Some other time." She seemed to have done a good enough job of getting tipsy for both of them, considering the pizza was barely eaten while the wine was almost gone. The question was why? He didn't believe her good drunk theory, but decided not to challenge it. He'd bet something had happened in his absence, or maybe the destruction of her apartment bothered her more than she'd let on. Either way, he regretted leaving her alone, even if out of necessity.

For his own peace of mind, if nothing else, the best thing he could do was get her into bed—alone—as soon as possible. Maybe then he could prevent himself from doing something stupid, though he doubted it. But first he needed to know what had happened. He crossed the room and sat on the edge of the sofa next to her with his hands clasped between his knees. When he did, she shifted to face him. She drew her knees up and wrapped her arms around them, drawing his attention to her bare, shapely legs. He tried to focus somewhere north of them, but didn't benefit himself any. Her robe had parted, revealing the gown beneath that dipped low between her breasts. He locked his gaze on her face. She smiled back in a way that left him no doubt that his distress hadn't gone unnoticed.

He couldn't do anything about that, so he pressed on. "What all have you been up to since I left you?"

"Nothing much. I told you I was going shopping. As you may have guessed, Bloomies had a sale." She shrugged. "Oh, and Ryan was here."

"Ryan?" She'd tossed that last part out as if it meant nothing to her, which immediately made him suspect whatever happened meant more to her than she wanted him to know. What had that bastard done to her? He doubted it was anything physical, but considering he believed the man was responsible for trashing her apartment, he wished he hadn't left her alone at his mercy.

In a voice much more calm than he felt, he said, "What did he want?"

"First to complain that he'd been questioned by the police."

A wicked smile crossed his face. Too bad they hadn't kept him. "Then what?"

Shaking her head, she turned away from him, but not before he saw the pained expression that came into her eyes.

"Tell me," he urged.

She rested her chin on her upturned kness. "Then he offered to take me back, sort of."

"What does that mean?"

She did look at him then. The pain in her eyes was nearly a palpable thing. "As long as I didn't mind being his squeeze on the side, so to speak."

"That bastard." That was the least of what he wanted to say, but he bit back the words, doubting she'd appreciate the sentiment at the moment. He knew how much such an offer would hurt a woman like her and didn't want to add his own grief to the mixture.

He stroked her hair. "I'm sorry, baby."

She tilted her head from one side or the other as if considering options. "Actually, it's been a learning experience for me. I wasn't aware men actually kept women anymore in this day and age. With all the tramps and hoochie mamas practically giving it away, you'd think a man would settle on what he could get on the cheap."

He had absolutely no idea what to say to that. Mr. Glib, as his brother used to call him, rendered speechless. At any rate, it was time to get her into bed. "Come on, sweetheart." He grasped her elbow, trying to help her stand.

She rose up on to her knees, but that's as far as she went. "Where are we going?" She rested her forearms on his thighs in a way that brought the tips of her breasts flush with his leg.

"I'm putting you to bed." The sooner the better, as he saw it.

"Why, James Fitzgerald," she said, affecting a southern accent. "You didn't even buy me dinner."

"I meant alone."

"Oh. Who'd expect you not to be any fun? Are you going to tell me, 'sweet dreams'? Did your mother ever tell you that?"

"No, my mother used to say, 'James Fitzgerald, you stop talking in there or I'm going to sew up your mouth.'"

Laughing, she slapped his leg. "You must have been some pain in the butt to raise."

"So I'm told."

"Do you miss her? Your mother, I mean."

"Yes, a great deal sometimes."

"I don't. Miss my mother, I mean. She died a couple of years ago. Don't get me wrong, I loved her. But she was never satisfied with anyone or anything. She'd been disappointed by life and I don't think she intended to let anything disappoint her again. Not even me. I loved her, but now that she's gone it's like a heaviness has been lifted off of me. Do you think that makes me a bad daughter?"

If she was looking for someone to condemn her for a lack of parental devotion, she'd have to look elsewhere. He'd been there, done that, and had the pictures to show for it. Although he considered Peggy Fitzgerald his mother, what he hadn't told her, what he rarely told anyone, was that the Fitzgeralds had adopted him as an infant. Way back when Jackson first opened his P.I. business, Jim had been one of his first customers, seeking the identity of the woman who'd given birth to him. It had taken him three years just to unseal the envelope Jackson's report had come in. Although he knew who she was, he'd never made contact with her. He doubted he ever would.

"Let's try this again, shall we?" Grasping both her elbows, he stood, pulling her with him. He finally got her to an upright if wobbly position. Now to make it to the bedroom.

"You know, I was thinking, before, about all these bad things that keep happening to me. You know what I decided?"

"I haven't the faintest clue."

"Well, then, I'll tell you. It's you. Every time I get near you something bad happens to me. That's what I think. You, sir, are a jinx." She poked him in the chest.

"And you, madam, are drunk, so I'm not paying any attention to anything you say."

"Spoilsport."

"Walk." He turned her so that she faced the bedroom.

His hands were at her waist, steadying her. She brushed them away and turned to face him. "I can do it myself. Just kiss me good night and I'll go to bed. Scout's honor." She held up the wrong number of fingers.

"You'll fall flat on your face in two seconds."

She wrapped her arms around his neck and pressed her body against his. "Kiss me good night and we'll see."

"Liza," he said in warning, but he knew she wasn't listening. She rubbed herself against him in a way that made him wish he really were the sort of man she thought he was. Maybe then he could take what she offered without worrying about the consequences in the morning.

She took the decision away from him by going on tiptoe and pressing her mouth to his. Of their own, his arms closed around her, which turned out to be a good thing, as she went slack in his arms a moment later. He scooped her up and carried her to the bed in Dani's room and arranged her under the covers. With any luck, she wouldn't remember any of this in the morning.

He went to the doorway to turn off the light, but he stood there a long time watching her sleep in the darkened room. Did she really think of him as her own personal demon, the source of all the recent havoc in her life? He hoped it was only the alcohol talking, but in the end it didn't matter. He would get her to come to Florida with him, if he could. That would probably be the easy part. Spending any length of time with her without touching her—that would probably kill him.

But he, as he was now, couldn't give her what she wanted. She was right about not settling for less than she deserved. But for the first time in his life, he thought about the moment when a woman would walk out of his life. When she was ready to leave, would he be ready to let her go?

Eight

Liza woke up the next morning feeling as if she'd slept with a big wad of foul-tasting cotton in her mouth. She brushed her hair from her face and sat up. Her temples throbbed both from the wine she'd consumed and the memories of the previous night that washed over her.

One minute she was waxing maudlin about her mother, the next she was coming on to him like a sailor out at sea too long. She'd called him a jinx and passed out in his arms. And to top it off, she had to remember it all in stark, gory detail. Where was a good alcoholic blackout when you needed one?

Annoyed at herself, Liza huffed out a breath. She'd known adversity before. The trouble was, this time she'd let herself fall apart. Well, usually her tragedies didn't pile up one on top of the other. They had the decency to come at her one at a time so she could deal with them.

So, okay, her life was one big screaming nightmare. Ryan was right about that. But now it was time she did something about it. She had to get herself together and start acting like the responsible, mature woman she was. She couldn't let a few catastrophies turn her into a ball of mush.

Granted, that was better than going her mother's route and becoming a sharp-tongued, bitter harpie, but not much. She'd do what she always did: tackle one problem at a time, restore order. She'd start with the thing that mattered most to her, whatever that was.

But what did she want most of all? At the moment, she couldn't care less if she ever set foot in her apartment again. Considering the state her assailant had left it, the greatest temptation was to find a really big garbage bag and sweep everything she owned into it. Most of it would have to be replaced anyway.

With no job, not even any friends tying her to New York for the present, she knew she wanted to finish what she'd started in Florida. She wanted to find out if Paul Mitchell really was her father while she had nothing as prosaic as a job or an apartment tying her to New York. Maybe then she'd have the closure she had sought since childhood, the certainty of knowing whether or not her mother had told her the truth in her letter.

The best way to accomplish that was to ask Jim to take her with him when he went. He'd probably laugh his head off at the suggestion. She suspected half his urgency in heading south was to get away from her. She didn't want much from him, though, just an introduction. She could take it from there and he could be on his way to do whatever he wanted. That wasn't too much to ask, was it?

Maybe it wouldn't have been before last night. They'd made a truce and she'd broken it. And not for any valid reason, but because she'd overindulged and couldn't hold her liquor. She didn't imagine the pained look she'd seen in his eyes when she'd accused him of tormenting her. If nothing else, she owed him a whopping apology. She only hoped he accepted it with the sincerity with which it was offered.

She rose and showered. After toweling dry, she put on one of her new outfits, a lavender sundress with spaghetti straps that crisscrossed in the back. It didn't occur to her until she was almost dressed that Jim must have brought her bags into the room while she slept. Another example of his consideration for her. Damn!

She followed her nose to the kitchen where Jim stood at the stove, one hand wrapped around the handle of a frying pan while he stirred the eggs in the pan with a spatula. She leaned her shoulder against the wall, considering his profile. Her mind was thinking there ought to be a law against any man looking so good first thing in the morning, but in her ears she heard her mother's voice. *Never marry a man who can't take care of himself. He'll expect you to do all those things his mama should have taught him how to do.*

She shook her head to clear Eloise Morrow and her caveats on selecting the proper man out of it. It was one thing to admit that the man wasn't the womanizing monster she'd once believed him to be, quite another to start picking out the dining room furniture. All they shared was an incredible case of lust.

Without looking at her, he said, "Hungry?"

That was the right word for what she was feeling, but not the way he meant. "That depends. What have you got?"

"Eggs in the pan, bacon staying warm in the oven, toast, if it ever pops up."

Her stomach rumbled, though she doubted she'd get away with eating much before it rebelled. It still hadn't forgiven her for the previous night. "Sounds good. I'll take care of the toast."

Wordlessly they worked until both their plates were

filled and they sat across the kitchen table from one another. Liza scooped some eggs onto her fork and brought it to her mouth. Not bad. The eggs were fluffy and seasoned nicely, but she put her fork down, not really interested in food. "About last night—" she began.

At the same time, he said, "Look, Liza—" He shook his head, smiling. "You go first."

She dabbed her napkin at the corner of her mouth, then sat back. "First, let me apologize for my behavior last night. I don't usually overindulge and I don't usually let my mouth run away with me."

"Then you didn't mean it when you said I was the bane of your existence?"

"I didn't exactly say that, but no. I was upset and I took it out on you. I promise that won't happen again."

"Don't sweat it. It's not like I spent all night torturing myself with all the ways I've wronged you."

Despite the humor in his words, she saw none of it in his eyes. "I never said you'd wronged me at all. Can't we just forget whatever it was I did say? I know I'm trying to."

"We do a lot of that, don't we?"

There was a quiet intensity to his words and a seriousness in his expression that caused heat to rise in her body. "Do a lot of what?"

"Forgetting what happens between us."

He watched her in an expectant way, as if he was waiting for her to say something in particular. If he was, she had no idea what it could be. Part of her wanted to tell him the unequivocal truth, that it was near impossible to forget anything that had happened between them. Part of her wished she were reckless enough to throw caution out the window and see where a relationship with him would take them. But could her heart survive a fling with him when he was destined to move on? That much of what Jake told her she believed. When the time came, he wouldn't look back, but she wasn't built that way. Since she couldn't tell him that, she said nothing.

With a sigh, Jim leaned back in his chair. "Okay, Liza. We'll play it your way." He smiled at her, but his gaze remained as intense as before. "Was that all you wanted to say?"

So, her silence had disappointed him. She wondered how he'd take what she said next. "I want to go to Florida with you."

His eyebrows lifted, and for a moment he scrutinized her. "Why would that be?"

"I need to meet Paul Mitchell. You obviously know him better than I do."

"And you want me to make the introductions?"

"Something like that. But that's all I'm asking. I'll get my own hotel room, so I will be out of your way."

He remained silent so long that at first she thought he wasn't going to answer. "What do you want with Paul?"

"That's personal."

"Then it's none of my business."

Liza sighed. In other words, she either told Jim what she was up to or he wouldn't help her. She supposed she couldn't fault him for that. Not only must he be generally curious as to why she would want to meet the other man, Paul Mitchell was his friend. He'd want to make sure she didn't intend to cause trouble. Oh well. "I have reason to believe Paul Mitchell is my father."

A look of amused surprise crossed his face. "Paul? What would make you think that?"

"A note my mother left me. Why would Paul's being my father be so shocking?"

He shrugged, not a particularly helpful gesture. "What did this note your mother left you say?"

"It says, 'Paul Mitchell is your father.'" Or at least

that's what she'd always believed it to say. It was obvious her mother had been crying when she'd written the letter, as tearstains mottled the apricot-colored stationery on which the letter was written. One large tear had landed in the middle of this particular sentence, obscuring the letters, but what else could "Paul Mitchell . . . our father" mean?

"Do you still have the letter?"

"Yes." As it was the one thing from her mother that she kept in her wallet, it hadn't been stolen or destroyed.

"Get it."

He actually expected her to offer him proof? She started to protest, but that look of steel came into his eyes again. For a man with the reputation for being happy-go-lucky he was nowhere near as easy going as one would expect. "Fine."

She retrieved the note from her purse and handed it to him. As he unfolded it, she slid into her seat. She couldn't imagine what possible difference actually seeing her mother's note could make. Especially since he refolded it almost immediately.

"Here's what I'm offering. If you can live with that, that's fine."

"Go ahead."

"I will get us two tickets on the same flight, which I will pay for."

"You don't have to do that. I can afford the airfare."

"While you're in Florida, you'll stay with me. I have a spare bedroom, so the sleeping arrangements shouldn't be a problem."

"That really isn't necessary."

He sat back in his chair. "That's my deal. Take it or leave it."

Given the high-handed way he'd spoken those last few words, she was tempted to leave it and give him a few other choice pieces of her mind. But it made more sense to go with him than to go on her own. As usual, sensibility won out. Then again, once she'd met Paul Mitchell, she could do as she damn pleased. She wouldn't need Jim Fitzgerald anymore.

"Fine." She pushed her chair back. "Since you were kind enough to cook breakfast, I'll do the dishes. Then I'm going to go pack."

He didn't say anything to that, but as she washed and rinsed their dishes, she felt his gaze on her. She had the feeling he was debating whether to tell her something, which seemed fitting. As sure as she knew her own name, she knew he withheld something from her. Why else would he insist that she stay with him where he could keep an eye on her? They both agreed that sharing the same living space was torture.

Or maybe she was just becoming paranoid under his persistent scrutiny. The man had a way of making her nerves stand on end, even when he didn't have anything cryptic to impart to her. Not nervous, exactly, but very aware of her own body and its reactions to him. Hyperalert, if that was a word. Not an unpleasant feeling, but certainly unusual for her.

Unable to stand him watching her anymore, she turned off the tap. "Would you just say it, already?" The last of her words trailed off to a whisper as she turned to face him and realized he'd already gone.

Jim fastened his seat belt in the first-class cabin of the plane that would take them to Miami International Airport. The flight wasn't a long one, just over three hours, but for the exorbitant price he'd had to pay for last-minute accommodations, the seats ought to have been lined with gold. He looked over at Liza, who'd taken the window seat, and offered her the best smile he

could muster. He didn't feel good about this trip. He'd
spent the better part of the previous day trying in subtle
ways to convince Liza to abandon her plans, to no avail.
All he'd succeeded in doing was making her suspect his
motives. But he knew, without a doubt, that this foray to
the Florida coast would end in disappointment of some
kind for her.

For one thing, as far as Jim knew, Paul didn't have
any children, abandoned or otherwise. Then again,
Paul wasn't the most forthcoming individual on the
planet, either. Who knew what secrets the man held?
Jim had known him for five years before learning he'd
originally hailed from New York.

But if by some strange confluence of events, Paul
proved to be her father, what then? How would she feel
knowing that her father was a reformed con man and a
thief? As conventional a woman as she was, that wouldn't
sit well with her. Jim didn't understand his own friendship with the man. They'd "met" when Jim awakened
one night to the sound of a strange noise. He'd turned
on the light beside his bed to find a man standing at his
dresser. For a moment they'd stared at each other, each
equally surprised by the other's presence. Then the
other man's gaze darted to the open window, presumably the way he'd gotten in. Silently, Jim thought, *Go for
it.* He'd be happy to see him go. He'd survive the loss of
a few items as long as both he and the woman beside
him were left unharmed. Vaguely he was aware of her
stirring beside him. The last thing he needed was for
her to wake during the middle of this.

The man bolted toward the window, but before he
made it out, a large pop sounded and an odd odor, like
burned sulfur, filled the room. The man grunted and
fell to the floor. Slowly, as if still in a dream, Jim turned
to his companion of that evening, Linda or maybe
Laura—something with an L. She held a tiny revolver in

both hands, still pointed in the man's direction, as if waiting for the chance to shoot him again. A tiny wisp of smoke curled up from the barrel. He'd heard the expression "smoking gun" before, but never realized that it was a literal, not figurative, reference.

"Are you totally insane?" He snatched the gun from her, burning his palm on the hot metal. "You just shot a complete stranger."

Indignation flashed in her eyes. "Who should I shoot then? My friends?"

Jim shook his head. His only excuse for such a ridiculous exchange was the fact that he was still half asleep. Or maybe he was still dreaming. He'd had dreams like this before, ones that seemed so genuine at the time that when he awoke he had difficulty reconciling that they weren't real. But if he was dreaming and he realized he was dreaming, shouldn't he wake up?

He blinked, and since the room was still the same, he had to assume the worst. "Call 911," he said to Laura or Linda, whatever. When she moved to pick up the phone on the bedside table, he added, "From the other room." She scootched across the bed and got to her feet. As she left, she picked up his shirt and tugged it over her head.

Jim sighed. He was definitely going to have to be more selective about whom he allowed into his home—both those who came in the door and those who got in by other means. He found his jeans and tugged them on. He stuck the gun in the front of his pants just in case either Annie Oakley decided to come back for another round or the guy on the floor got frisky. Right now, he was groaning and complaining, but as yet hadn't managed to get up. Jim supposed he should be glad she hadn't killed him. As it was he'd have enough to explain to the police.

But what the hell was he supposed to do now—aside from watching the man's blood seep into his carpet? If he'd been wounded anywhere else, Jim would have considered offering assistance. But Laura or Linda, whatever that woman's name was, had hit him square at the center of his left butt cheek. As far as Jim was concerned, the guy was on his own.

Since he didn't appear to be going anywhere, Jim sat at the foot of his bed, confident that the man was unarmed. Otherwise, he would have found a way to shoot back by now, if only to assuage his wounded dignity. No man wanted to be shot in the ass by a woman he hadn't been cheating on. And in that instance, the relief came from knowing one's assailant had missed another, more vital part of the body.

He nudged the man's leg with his foot. "How are you doing, buddy?"

The man lifted his head and glared at him. "How the hell do you think I'm doing? She shot me."

Jim scrutinized the man's face. Lines etched his forehead and around his eyes. Jim hadn't noticed that before, but he'd put the guy in his late forties or early fifties. "Aren't you a bit old for this line of work?"

Whatever rejoinder the man might have given was cut off by the appearance of two policemen in the doorway. The younger of the two uniformed officers looked from Jim to the man on the floor, still clutching his buttocks. "What's going on in here?"

That's how Jim met Bill Simpson, his savior when Liza'd locked herself in Paul's bathroom. Honestly, Jim couldn't say why he'd maintained a friendship with either Bill or Paul. Well, having a friend on the force had come in handy a few times in the last few years. As for Paul, Jim supposed he was like the rest of the population—equally curious and repulsed by the workings of the criminal mind. Many a night he'd sat on Paul's patio facing the pool and the sunset beyond, listening to some tale of the older man's exploits, which always began with,

"Did I tell you about the time when . . ." and whatever came after.

In some ways, Jim was glad Liza hadn't asked him anything about Paul. If she had to find out her "father" was an ex-con, he didn't want to be the one to tell her. In other ways, her lack of curiosity surprised him. Wouldn't any woman in her position—about to meet the man who fathered her—want to know as much about him as she could? Why didn't she? Maybe he should simply count his blessings instead of wondering why he'd been blessed.

After they touched down on Floridian soil after an uneventful flight, they took a taxi to the dock. It was late afternoon, hot, humid—normal weather for that part of Florida. A year-round version of August in New York. He glanced at Liza. While the short, non-air-conditioned wait for a taxi had caused him to perspire, she looked cool as a cucumber. Her only concession to the heat and brilliance of the Floridian sun was to put on a pair of sunglasses.

One of her hands rested on the seat. He wrapped his fingers around hers. "How are you doing over there?"

She focused on him and lifted one shoulder in a shrug. "Fine, I guess. A little hungry, maybe."

Not surprising since the airlines seemed to have forgotten how to serve anything vaguely resembling food. "We can fix that."

She said nothing to that, but a slight smile turned up the corners of her mouth. Mentally, he shook his head. He didn't understand her. There was no harm in admitting that, was there? She was no Chatty Cathy like her friend Jake, who'd blab all her secrets given enough time and enough stamina on the part of the listener. She possessed enough self-containment to keep most of what she thought to herself. A trait most people could stand a little more of, only now it annoyed him. It kept him from knowing what, if anything, she was feeling at the moment.

Now, there was a laugh. Most times, when he asked a woman how she was feeling, it was a thinly disguised after-sex prompt for her to praise his masculine prowess. But with Liza, he really wanted to know. He sensed something different in her today, a distance from her and resoluteness, about what he couldn't begin to fathom. He needed to know that he was doing the right thing in bringing her here. Not only would he have to answer to Eamon and Jake if he let anything bad happen to Liza, but his own underused conscience had to get into the middle of it, too. Where was that devil-may-care attitude that his brother always complained about now that he really needed it?

Jim sighed. She was a grown woman. She knew what she wanted and why she wanted it. But if anyone asked him, which no one had, she was on a fool's mission that was likely to end in disaster. But in that moment, he made himself a promise. If he couldn't keep her from getting hurt, he'd at least stick around to pick up the pieces afterward.

Jim's home was a ranch-style house with an Italian tile roof painted an exotic shade of blue. Tall palm trees and other foliage framed the house and azaleas and other colorful flowers flanked each side. The shrubbery was a bit neater than she'd expected, but otherwise, the house suited him. What she knew of him, anyway, which wasn't much. She still had no idea why he'd insisted on this arrangement and no idea what secrets he withheld from her. She'd tried, in a way she'd hoped was subtle, to probe him for information on the plane. The only thing she'd succeeded in acquiring was a mutual agreement not to try to see Paul today. They'd head over to his house the first thing in the morning.

He opened the door and stood aside to let her pass. "Welcome to my humble abode."

From what she could see, there wasn't much humble about it. The interior was painted a bright white from the bottom molding to the high, arched ceilings. Heavy Spanish-style furniture decorated the foyer and the living room to her left. Sunlight streamed in through the large windows and the panes of the pair of French doors in front of her. She smiled, running her fingers along the bottom edge of the wooden frame that housed an oversize black-and-white photograph of a kid in a rowboat, presumably asleep while a fish nibbled on his line.

She glanced at him over her shoulder. "One of yours?"

He set down their suitcases by the door. "Guilty as charged. One of my neighbor's grandsons right before the fish took off with the rod—reel, leaders, and all. "Want the two-cent tour of the house?"

"Sure." When he'd made his stipulations about bringing her here, he'd promised her a bedroom of her own. Now was as good a time as any to find out if he'd reneged on that promise.

With a hand on her back he led her forward. "This is the living room," he said, gesturing to the left. "To the right is the kitchen."

Unlike the living room that boasted aqua accents, the kitchen was accented with a soothing shade somewhere between peach and salmon. They continued on until they reached two doors, each painted in a similar but not matching shade of tangerine.

"This is the guest bedroom," Jim continued. "It's a bit small, but I hope you'll be comfortable here. The bath is next door."

He moved away from her to flick on the light,
though the afternoon sun was doing a pretty good job
of illuminating the room. The space was at least as large
as any bedroom she'd ever laid claim to. The furniture
here, a four-poster bed, dresser, and nightstand, was
made of ash or maybe a pale pine that contrasted starkly
with the heavier orange accents on the bedspread and
draperies. Still, it struck her as a very feminine room,
leading her to wonder whom the room had been decorated for.

"It's fine," she said, but she didn't look at him, aware
that her gaze might be a little green at the moment.

"I'm glad you said that. I redid the room with Dani in
mind. I promised her she could spend the last week of
the summer down here if Jake and Eamon agree."

"In that case, you're going to need a few Jeff Gordon
posters and a trampoline in the backyard."

"Speaking of which, do you want to see it?"

She shrugged, surprised his room didn't figure anywhere on the tour. Or maybe he planned on saving the
best for last. They'd end up on his doorstep and with
nowhere else to see, maybe he planned to linger awhile.
Part of her still believed he had some sort of seduction
scenario in mind, or why else would he insist that she
stay with him?

He led her back to the French doors and opened
both of them wide. "*Et voila.* The pool."

The oblong pool was lined with the same exotic blue
of the house, while the tiles beneath her feet were white
flecked with blue in a way that reminded her of sand. A
large blue and white umbrella shaded the white patio
furniture to her left. A high, latticed fence draped with
bougainvillea surrounded the property, adding to the
tropical feel of the house, and she suspected, shielding
swimmers from the prying eyes of neighbors.

"What do you think?"

"Tell me you didn't decorate this place yourself."

"Not a chance. I actually paid someone to have my house look like someone hit it with a bag of tropical-flavor Skittles."

She laughed, thinking how apt that analogy was. Still, she hadn't changed her mind about the house suiting him. "Is that the end of the tour?"

He smiled. "For now. What do you want to do first— go for a swim or eat?"

Her stomach rumbled, settling the question. "Dinner it is. Give me a few moments to freshen up, okay?"

He nodded. "Meet you by the front door."

Liza went to the bathroom adjoining the bedroom he'd shown her and flicked on the light. She surveyed herself in the mirror. Heat and perspiration had smudged what little makeup she'd put on that morning. After splashing some water on her face from the tangerine-colored sink, she quickly reapplied mascara and a rose-colored lip gloss. Rubbing her lips together, she put away her cosmetics and zipped her handbag.

Giving herself one more once-over in the mirror, she sighed. The feeling of foreboding that claimed her before came back threefold now. Maybe she simply had the jitters knowing the hour of reckoning was at hand. In a few short hours she'd know whether or not Paul Mitchell was her father, which could be either a good thing or a bad one depending on the man himself.

Or maybe she was simply nervous about being alone with Jim. They'd played this scene before—out for dinner, then in for a little dessert. She didn't intend to re-play that little drama, though she was more susceptible to him now than before. Though she had to admit, part of her salivated at the notion of sharing a bed with him.

She sighed again, contenting herself with the knowledge that by this time the next day, she'd either have her answers or be on a plane back to New York. It would all be over tomorrow.

If only she could get through tonight.

Nine

He didn't know why he brought her back to the same restaurant to approximately the same table they'd shared before, but he was tired of questioning his own motives where Liza was concerned. He leaned back in his chair, while studying the menu, though he already knew what he'd order. "See anything you like?"

She closed her menu. "I'm thinking of the scampi."

"Shrimp or lobster?"

"Who's paying?"

She had to be kidding. He hadn't allowed her to pay for a meal yet. "I am."

"The lobster, then."

He smiled, closed his menu, and laid it on the table. The waiter came by and Jim gave him both of their orders, hers for scampi and his for broiled scallops, as well as an order for a bottle of Chardonnay. When the wine came, he watched her take a delicate sip. For all her straightforwardness, she was a very feminine woman, with long graceful limbs and a slender beauty that knocked him on his ear.

She set her glass on the table. "Not bad."

"Not bad at all," he echoed, though his mind was far

from the wine. But he knew he ought to behave himself. If his mind veered too far down the path it was heading, he'd end up in bed that night frustrated, miserable, and alone. He'd probably end up that way anyway, as he'd done every night since he'd met her, but there was no point rubbing his own nose in it.

Jim cleared his throat and straightened up, determined to turn the train of his thoughts to something more pertinent. "Do you mind if I ask you a question?"

"That depends. What about?"

"Your father. Paul. Why haven't you asked me anything about him?"

She laughed, not with mirth, but with a different emotion he didn't understand. "You've got me pegged wrong if you think I'm expecting some teary-eyed reunion of father and child. I've lived thirty years without one; I don't need one now."

"Then why?"

She shrugged, looking down at the tablecloth where one of her fingernails traced a pattern on the fabric. "That's what I want to know. Why did he leave us? Why did my mother change into such a bitter woman? I've seen pictures of her as a young girl, always laughing, always smiling. What was she like before he abandoned us? Did she tell me the truth when she said Paul was my father? On my birth certificate, my father is listed as unknown."

Jim frowned, picturing in his mind the note she'd shown him. To his thinking, the missing space was large enough to have housed any number of words. *Paul Mitchell knew your father. Hated your father.* Or the one he found most likely: *is not your father.* But then why bring up the man's name if he had nothing to do with her parentage? He wished now he'd read the letter more closely, because he feared Liza was simply reading into it what she wanted to see.

"I didn't ask you those questions," she continued, "because even if you knew the answers, I'd want to hear them from him." She sipped from her glass. "You don't know those answers, do you?"

"No."

"He's never mentioned me to you, has he?"

"No."

"Well, then," she said as if that said it all. To his mind, it didn't, but the waiter appeared with their food, silencing conversation for the moment.

After he left, Liza sampled a morsel of lobster and chewed it with an expression of joy on her face. "Delicious."

Jim watched her, remembering a time when something other than food had brought a similar expression to her face. He shook his head and forked a bit of his own food into his mouth. Hadn't he already decided not to torture himself this way?

She saved him with her next comment. "I like your pictures, what I saw of them in the house. Do you always work in black and white?"

"Not always. It depends on what the job calls for. For my own personal use, I do."

"Why?"

"I like the contrast, dark and light, the starkness of the images. Color is an overrated commodity."

"Who's J.T.?"

She must have noticed his signature at the bottom of every picture. "Unfortunately, that's me."

Her brow furrowed. "Why unfortunately?"

He grinned. "Most people think I was named James after my father. Little do they suspect my mother was a sci-fi junkie who named me after a certain starship captain."

"Your middle name is Tiberius?" She laughed, a throaty sound that pleased him.

"That's me. James Tiberius Fitzgerald. And I'd appreciate it if you kept that to yourself. As far as the rest of the world knows, my middle name is Thomas."

She sobered just a little. "Well, I'm honored that you confided in me, Jim. Or should I start calling you Captain?"

"Jim is fine."

"If you say so, Captain."

"Watch it, you." Since they'd finished most of their meal, and as long as a humor-filled smile still turned up her lips and her eyes sparkled with sherry-colored amusement, he figured he'd risk it. "Come dance with me."

She shook her head. "Isn't that where we got in trouble last time?"

He lifted his hands as if in surrender. "I promise to be a perfect gentleman. Besides, if I remember correctly, last time it was you who made the first move. Now if you're trying to tell me you find me irresistible . . ."

She shot him a droll look, but he could sense the anticipation in her nonetheless.

"Tell me you don't want to, and I'll let it drop."

She shook her head, not in denial, but in exasperation. She wanted to be with him, he knew, but didn't want to want him. That was fine by him. He didn't want to convince her he was any Sir Galahad. He just wanted to hold her.

She gazed up at him. "I should have my brain examined for defects."

But she did put her hand in his and walk with him to the dance floor. She offered no resistance whatsoever when he pulled her close, close enough that she rested her cheek on his shoulder. He buried his nose in her soft, fragrant hair and inhaled. For a long moment, he was content to move with her to the slow beat of the ballad played by the small group of musicians in the center of the room. Her soft body molded to his in a way that made him wish for things he couldn't have. There went the question of whether he'd be indulging in a cold shower before bedtime. He would, and he doubted that Liza had missed knowing he'd need one.

Then she lifted her head, and for a moment he feared she'd pull away from him. Instead, she regarded him with a bemused expression. "Do you mind if I ask you another question?"

"Of course not."

"Why don't you look more like your brother?"

His eyebrows lifted in surprise. "Why?"

"Don't get me wrong, I'm not complaining." She lifted one shoulder. "But I was just thinking that if you'd looked anything like your brother I probably never would have gotten involved with you in the first place."

"He's not your type."

She shook her head. "Too pretty. But that's not what I meant. If the two of you shared some resemblance, and definitely if you shared the same eye color, I might have suspected you were related. But you guys look nothing like each other."

He cleared his throat. "There's a simple explanation for that. Eamon and I aren't related by blood. The Fitzgeralds adopted me when I was a baby."

She bit her lip and her brow furrowed. "Oh, Jake didn't tell me."

"Wonder of wonders, Jake managed to keep her mouth shut about something."

"I didn't mean to pry."

"You didn't. Honestly, it's not like it's a state secret, I just don't talk about it much."

"Have you ever tried to find them? Your birth parents, I mean."

"Not really," he lied. "Maybe if I knew exactly who and where to look I would. You didn't start looking for your father until you thought you knew his name, did you?"

"No."

"Well, then," he said with the same finality she had before, hoping that would put an end to the discussion of his least favorite topic. It did. She laid her cheek on his shoulder again, but the gesture didn't move him the way it had the first time she'd done it tonight. Feeling unaccountably testy, he pulled away from her when the song ended. "Let's get out of here."

She nodded, but he saw the expression of concern in her eyes. He didn't want to see it there. He'd never wanted anyone's pity, which was why he'd never discussed the circumstances of his adoption with anyone save for his brother. It was his own fault. He could have sidestepped the issue or changed the subject. But for the second time that night he'd shared with her information he usually kept to himself. He didn't understand why he'd felt compelled to tell her the truth.

They stopped at the table briefly enough for him to deposit enough cash to cover their meal. They drove the short distance back to his place in silence. He left her at her bedroom door with a platonic kiss to her forehead and an exhortation to get a good night's sleep. He went to his own room, stripped, and got into bed. Looked like he wouldn't need that cold shower after all, but that didn't mean he'd be able to sleep either.

Hours later, Liza checked the clock at her bedside for the umpteenth time that night. Two-fifteen, and still she couldn't sleep. She'd expected that. The prospect of meeting her father in the morning was enough to keep her tossing, without having watched Jim's transformation after she asked him about the lack of family resemblance. She'd been teasing him, expecting him to say that he looked like one parent while Eamon resembled the other. She'd been surprised by his admission and floored by his reaction to the subject. A coldness, the like of which she never expected to see in him, had come into his eyes and his body had gone rigid. It was as if someone had taken the man she knew and replaced him with someone else.

Liza shifted onto her stomach and hugged her pillows. Until that moment, she'd been certain that she wouldn't be spending this night alone with only a thin blanket for warmth against the strength of the air-conditioning. Or maybe she might have summoned some great store of willpower and sent him packing. Dancing so closely with him, she knew she excited him. That knowledge served as a powerful aphrodisiac by itself. Add to that the strength and heat of his embrace, and she'd been a goner. Or she had been until the conversation turned the way it did.

Even now, she felt the urge to go to him, not as a lover but as a friend. That was what they agreed to aspire to, wasn't it? They would become friends so peace could reign in the kingdom of Jake and Eamon. What a laugh! Not only couldn't they keep their hands off each other, she'd made him hurt without even trying. Though she'd give anything to take back those thoughtlessly chosen words, she couldn't deny the pain she'd seen in his eyes. And as much as she hated to admit it, tonight's episode proved to her once again that James Fitzgerald possessed more depth than she'd first imagined. Deciding whether that was a good thing or a bad thing was the problem.

She punched her pillow for want of anything better to strike. "Way to go, Morrow. Just what you need, to fall for a commitment-phobe with birth mother issues."

That idea stopped her cold. Was she falling for him? That was the most disturbing thought of all.

* * *

Jim woke early the next morning as he did every day, but his whole body felt listless from the lack of sleep. It hadn't taken long for his animus to wear off, but he'd lain awake a long time thinking of Liza in the small bedroom at the other end of his house. Part of him wanted to go to her and offer some sort of explanation for his behavior, but what would that be? He didn't understand himself the virulence of his reaction, so how could he explain it? Most of the time he didn't even think about it and when he did it was with little more than indifference. Or that's what he told himself, anyway.

But once his thoughts turned to Liza, his discomfort began in earnest. He imagined her warm and pliant in sleep, dressed only in the thin nightgown she'd worn to bed at Jake and Eamon's apartment. He'd wondered what she would have said if he'd simply slid in next to her and drawn her beside him. After the way he'd behaved, she probably would have kicked him out posthaste. But the thought of her body anywhere in proximity to his drove him from his bed into the icy blast of the shower in pure sexual frustration. Especially since he suspected that, before his display of temper, she would have come to his bed last night with very little prompting.

In a way, he should be glad she hadn't. She might have come to his bed willingly, but would she have regretted it later. And didn't she have enough on her plate coping with meeting her father or whatever Paul turned out to be to her? Jim might be forced to turn in his lifetime membership at Players R Us, but he knew the next time she came to his bed, he wanted it to be because she truly wanted to be there, not because someone or something had disappointed her or because any warm body would do.

He sat up and stretched, trying to muster some impetus toward starting the day. Yet, for the umpteenth time, he wondered what it was about this one woman that intrigued him so. Hell, he'd even hired Jackson to find her, though he hadn't come up with anything. Why couldn't he leave her alone? If he were honest with himself, his motives for having her stay here were not entirely altruistic. Or mostly altruistic.

He knew Paul would never hurt her physically, even if he broke her heart by not being the man she hoped him to be. Jim sighed. She didn't really need him. Even the one time she'd deigned to cry on his shoulder, it had lasted such a brief moment her tears could have been figments of his imagination. Yet he'd tried to bind her to him by means of an agreement he never should have made in the first place. That was so unlike him that it was scary. He'd never in his life tried to hold on to a woman who wanted to be free.

True, there was the possibility that someone wanted to harm her. In his gut, he believed that someone was her former fiancé. The bastard had probably been watching her and saw the fire as his chance to take vengeance on her. Who else would stoop to stealing the few items her mother had left her except someone out for personal revenge? Liza would be as safe from that jackass with Paul as she would be with Jim. Even at the advanced age of sixty-two, Paul wasn't a man to mess with.

After showering and dressing, Jim wrote a note for the still slumbering Liza and drove to the market since his refrigerator lacked even the requisite spoiled milk. She was still sleeping when he returned, so he started some bacon in the pan and gathered the ingredients he would need for French toast. Hopefully, her nose would wake her and lead her to the kitchen.

Fifteen minutes later, she made her appearance, dressed in a beige linen shirt and matching slacks. She looked calm, but faint circles under her eyes attested to a night without much sleep.

"Have a seat," he said. "Breakfast will be ready in a moment."

She slid into one of the kitchen seats and unfolded her napkin in her lap. "What are we having?"

"French toast with bacon."

"You are definitely spoiling me. If you keep this up, I'll be as big as a house."

Yeah, if he had a good twelve years to fatten her up. "Not to worry. Breakfast is the only thing I know how to cook. All other meals, you're on your own." He fished two pieces of French toast from one pan and arranged them on her plate beside the bacon. He set it in front of her. "Cinnamon and syrup are on the table."

"Thank you."

He retrieved his toast from the other pan, made sure both burners were off, and then joined her at the table. They ate silently for a moment, until he said, "About last night—"

At the same time, she said, "Look, Jim—"

The last time they were at a similar impasse, he'd allowed her to go first. This time he claimed that option for himself. "I want to apologize for the abrupt way I dragged you back home last night. There was no excuse for that, and I'm sorry."

"There's nothing to apologize for—"

"Let me finish. I also should not have insisted that you stay here. You're a grown woman. You can do what you like."

She put down her fork and stared at him for a long moment. "Does that mean you're kicking me out?"

He detected just a bit of humor in her voice, which surprised him. "No, I just realized that making outrageous demands is more my brother's style. The very idea of following in his footsteps put the fear of God in me."

"I guess that saves me the trouble of ditching you later."

Jim forked a square of toast into his mouth. Never, if he lived two lifetimes, would he ever understand the workings of the female mind. "You planned on ditching me?"

She brought her coffee cup to her mouth and sipped. "I'd considered it."

"Why?"

She tilted her head to one side. "You have to ask? Where would we have been headed if I hadn't opened my big mouth last night?"

While they were on the subject of opening big mouths, he opened his. "Would it have been so bad if we had ended up there last night?"

She bit her lip and stared at him a moment. "You want an honest answer?"

He nodded. "That's what I was shooting for."

"Well, my honest answer is, how the hell should I know? We're both adults here. And okay, I don't really care how what we do affects anyone else anymore. I don't believe I've made any headway at convincing you I don't want to be with you."

No, she hadn't. "But—"

"But, fool that I am, I've started to care for you in ways that have nothing to do with ravishing your body. And considering all you're offering is a fling, that's an invitation to have my heart stomped. Considering everything else that's going on, I don't think I could take that right now." She tossed her napkin onto the table and rose with her plate in her hand. "Now that we've finished with the 'truth' segment of our show, I'd better finish getting ready to go."

She stepped away from him, toward the trash, ostensibly to clean her plate. He caught up with her before she'd taken another step and reached around her to relieve her of her dish, which he set on the counter. He pulled her back against him. Though she didn't fight him, she didn't come that willingly either. "You had your say, let me have mine."

She nodded, but now that he had her ear, he didn't know what to say. "I don't want to hurt you, Liza. The truth is, I don't know what I want. You have me tied up in so many knots, I don't know which way is up."

"What a pair we make: confused and confuseder."

He snorted. "That's us. But make no mistake, I don't want to pressure you into doing anything you aren't ready for."

She turned to face him, arms crossed. "You have to know I'd never allow you to do that."

"I do." He brushed an errant strand of her hair from her face. "I called Paul this morning to let him know I was coming over just so he wouldn't be out. I didn't tell him I was bringing you. I told him I'd be there around noon, but something tells me we ought to leave now."

She offered him a little half smile. "I'll be ready in ten minutes."

He winked at her. "I'll be waiting."

She pivoted to leave the room. He couldn't resist swatting her cute backside for emphasis. When she turned to glare at him over her shoulder, he speared her with a look that dared her to challenge his right to do so. Making an exasperated sound in her throat, she continued on to her bedroom.

After she'd gone, he cleared the remainder of the dishes and rinsed them before loading them in the dishwasher. He poured himself another cup of coffee and leaned his elbows on the counter to drink it. Their exchange that morning had gone better than he'd thought. She'd surprised him by admitting that she felt more for him than simple lust. He surprised himself by admitting the same. He still didn't know where that left them. But as long as she didn't know what she wanted, he knew he wouldn't push. He'd take his cue from her and wait to see how things would turn out.

Although Paul lived less than five blocks away, Jim insisted on driving. In the event Liza wanted to make a quick exit, hoofing it home wouldn't cut it. She sat beside him now, as silent as a plank of wood and just as rigid. He reached across the seat and took her hand. "Relax, sweetheart."

In the periphery of his vision he saw her turn to face him. "I am relaxed."

Perhaps she was no more jittery than she'd ever been. Maybe he'd only learned how to read her better. Not for the first time, he wondered if he shouldn't tell her what he knew about Paul and hope that changed her mind about her desire to see him. He doubted it would, the same way he hadn't told Paul about Liza for fear he'd bolt. She needed to settle this now, and he'd do everything in his power to see that what she wanted happened.

He pulled the car to a stop at the curb in front of Paul's house and cut the engine. He turned to her. "Ready?"

She nodded. "As I'll ever be, I guess."

She opened her door and got out. He followed her up the white stone path to Paul's house, but before they'd made it halfway, the door opened. Still tall and muscular from daily workouts in his pool, Paul strode out of the house. For a moment, he and Liza simply stared at each other. In the quietest, most somber voice Jim had ever heard from the man, Paul said, "I didn't think this day would ever come, child."

She tilted her head to one side, considering him. "You know who I am?"

"Of course I do. Come give your old dad a hug."

Liza, who swore she had nothing emotional vested in this meeting, burst into tears.

"Don't cry, sweetheart," Paul said in a solicitous tone as he closed the gap between them and wrapped his arms around her.

Looking at the two of them together, Jim knew Paul couldn't be her father. His nut-brown complexion owed very little to the heat of the Florida sun, while Liza's fair skin had begun to freckle the moment she got off the plane. But aside from that, they shared not one feature, not eyes, not nose, not mouth. And besides, Paul's face held a quality utterly lacking in Liza's: deceit.

Liza stepped away from him, swiping at her eyes. "I'm sorry. I don't do that very often."

"It's understandable. Why don't you go inside and get a glass of water? I have another surprise for you in the house."

"All right."

When she turned to look back at him, Jim offered her the best smile he could muster.

After she left, Paul turned to him with fury in his eyes. "Are you out of your mind bringing that girl here?"

Jim's eyebrows lifted. "You mean this isn't a good time for a family reunion? That girl, as you put it, is no more your daughter than I am. Why did you tell her otherwise?"

"Because she is. The closest thing I'll ever have to one, anyway."

Confused, Jim shook his head. "So why are you all bent out of shape about her being here?"

"Because you made a big mistake in bringing her here. You've put her in danger. The real reason I misled her is that I figured if she thought I was her real father she'd listen to me enough so that I can protect her. What I can't figure out is why she thinks I'm her father to begin with."

Questions swirled in Jim's brain, namely how he had put Liza in danger and from whom, not to mention how Paul knew about Liza being here to begin with. He'd get to that right after he told Paul what he wanted to know. He explained about the missing words from the letter Liza's mother had written.

"If I know Eloise, the only thing she would have said was 'Paul Mitchell killed your father.'"

Ten

"You killed Liza's father? According to her he ran off."

Paul sighed. "That's what Eloise told her. Better that than what really happened." Paul shifted his weight, looking uncharacteristically anxious. "Can't this wait until later? I don't want to leave her alone too long."

Without waiting for an answer, Paul started toward the house. Jim followed at a much more leisurely pace. He didn't know what Paul was up to, what he had to do with either Liza or her father. He was tempted to drag Liza out of there and hie her back to New York, before either of them got too enmeshed in whatever it was. But then they would never know what danger Paul referred to. Better to bide his time and see what developed.

Liza was just coming back into the living room from the bathroom as he came in from the other route. Paul had already ensconced himself on the sofa. He stood and gestured toward the cushion next to him. "Come sit next to me. We have a lot of years to catch up on."

"All right." She settled next to Paul. "If you promise to tell me why you and my mother split up."

"The same reason most people do, I suspect. We just

weren't getting along. But in those days there were no weekend fathers or joint custody arrangements. Your mother asked me to stay away and I did."

"All the way out here?"

Paul chuckled. "My job brought me out to Florida. I liked it so much I stayed. You can ask Jim, the summers here are so hot and humid it's the next best thing to living inside a tropical fish tank, but the rest of the year is quite pleasant."

Liza glanced at Jim, but he found it difficult to hold her gaze. He didn't like either the possessive way Paul's arm draped across her shoulders—considering the man wasn't really her father—or that he couldn't tell how much, if any, of what Paul said she believed. So much for learning to read her better. Luckily, she turned her attention back to Paul.

"What did you do?"

"Medical supply sales."

Jim wondered how Paul managed to utter such nonsense with a straight face. No legitimate job had brought Paul to the Sunshine State. He'd come along with some widow he'd been trying to con out of her life savings and whatever else he could get out of her. The widow had wised up before Paul had managed to do too much damage to her, but years later, she'd left him this house and the rest of her possessions in her will. It turned out the woman had really loved him and would have given him anything he asked for if he'd only returned her affections. Or so she'd said in the videotaped will she'd made for her lawyer. That bequest changed Paul's life. Realizing what he'd missed out on had finally given him the impetus to go straight.

Jim shifted in his seat and tuned back into the conversation in time to hear Liza ask, "Do you have any pictures of me?"

Paul reached behind him to retrieve his wallet from

his back pocket. From it, he extracted a photo that even Jim could tell from his vantage point across the coffee table had seen too many years in one place.

Paul handed the picture to Liza. "You were six months old then."

Liza studied the picture for a moment before handing it back. "Is that the only one?"

Paul replaced the photo in his black leather billfold and tossed it onto the table in front of them. "Your mother wasn't big on taking pictures in those days."

"Really? What was she like then?"

Paul tilted his head to one side, then the other, pensively. But rather than saying anything about Eloise Morrow, he launched into a monologue about his memories of Liza's earliest days: her favorite toy, her first word, the fact that she preferred to suck on her index and middle fingers rather than her thumb.

After a while, he sat back and sighed. "Unfortunately I have a meeting this afternoon that I can't get out of. But promise me you'll come back and see me tomorrow?"

Liza smiled. "Of course. I'll just freshen up a little, then Jim and I will get out of your hair."

If Liza had ever been that pliable in her life, he'd yet to have seen it. Yet she rose demurely from the sofa, crossed in front of Paul to stand beside Jim. "I won't be long," she said, before leaning down and pressing her lips to his. The contact was brief, but nonetheless surprising. She allowed her hand to skim along his chest as she walked away. Without thinking about it, he turned to watch her stride away, his concentration centered on the gentle sway of her backside.

"I suppose it was too much to hope that you'd kept your hands off her."

Slowly, Jim turned to focus on Paul. "You've got five seconds to explain exactly what is going on here."

Paul leaned forward in his chair. "My past coming back to haunt me. In spades." He put his face in his hands and sighed. "Did I ever tell you about the last job I pulled in New York?"

"I think I missed that one."

"Four of us youngbloods break into this candy store—that's what we used to call them before everything became a bodega. The shop did a good business, but the guy who owned it didn't trust banks. He kept every cent he owned in a safe hidden under the floorboards in the back room. Grady's girl worked in the store for a while and the poor guy trusted her with his secret. According to her, the old man had something like forty grand stashed in there. In those days that was a fortune."

"Why didn't he keep that kind of money at home?"

"Apparently, he didn't trust his wife, either. With good reason, too, I guess, since he was cheating on her. Every Thursday night he went to see this woman he had on the side. That's the night we broke in. Grady and I were supposed to work on the safe and Slim was waiting around the side in the car. Since this was in a residential neighborhood, we wanted to be in and out quick.

"What we didn't know was that the old guy must have been into something he wasn't supposed to. Along with the money we found a bag full of diamonds. Most of the stones were small, of low quality and little value, but there was one stone, much larger than the rest. In today's market, it would probably be worth millions."

"What went wrong?"

"For one thing, the old guy came back. To this day I don't know why. Maybe he forgot something or maybe he had a fight with his old lady and with the excuse he cooked up at home he couldn't go back yet. Who knows? But in he walks and all hell breaks loose. I was the only one to make it out there—with the money. Two of my buddies ended up in jail."

"Why didn't they rat you out?"

"And take the chance that I'd have to turn the take in? Neither of them was that stupid. Besides, when Slim got out, I gave him his share and Grady's. Grady would have been out years ago if he hadn't stabbed some guy to death in the shower."

"So what's the problem?"

"Grady got out less than a month ago, and he's convinced I held out on him for the diamonds."

"Did you?"

"Of course not. I don't know what happened. In the confusion I must have dropped them. I don't know. But there's no convincing him that I didn't cheat him out of what he thinks he's supposed to have."

"What has any of this got to do with Liza?"

"Nothing, really. Except Grady knows about her. But it didn't occur to me that she would be in any danger until you showed up on my doorstep this morning. As far as the world knows, I haven't seen her since she was a baby."

"And you're afraid your friends will come after her now?"

Paul shook his head. "Not Slim. He drove for us that one time, but his big thing was setting fires. He'd torch a house and after the family ran out and before the firemen would show up he'd ransack the place. He made a mint that way. Grady is the real problem."

Jim had stopped listening at the word *fire*. Anger blazed in him at the prospect of Liza being put in real danger by Paul's past misdeeds. "Would it surprise you if I told you that a week ago Liza's apartment building was set on fire and her apartment trashed?"

Paul said a word that exactly described Jim's own sentiment on the matter. "Was anything taken?"

"Only the stereo and a locked box Liza kept in her

closet. What do you suppose they were really looking for?"

"Damn. How would they have even known to look for her?"

"She was out here. Last year. Remember the girl I told you about looking for you?" At the time Paul had dismissed it as unimportant. "That was her."

Paul shook his head. "I suspected it might have been her, but I figured since we never hooked up nothing would come of it. But if someone had been watching the house . . ."

"I had someone looking for her, but she gave me a fake name when we met. She used the same name when she signed into the hotel. She paid extra cash so the desk clerk wouldn't ask for a credit card for incidentals."

For the first time since Liza had left the room, Paul smiled. "She takes after her old man."

Jim craned his neck to see if Liza was about to return. He had no idea what was taking her so long, but he was glad for whatever reason. "Before you break your arm patting yourself on the back, realize this: whatever problem you have with your old con buddies, you better resolve it, because if anything else happens to Liza because of what you've done, you won't have to worry what they'll do to you."

Paul nodded. "I hear you. I'm seeing Grady tonight. I'm figuring all he really wants is a few dollars now that he's out. With any luck, this will all be over tonight."

Jim huffed out a breath. As sure as he knew his own name, he knew there was more to this story, much more. All he needed to know, though, was that the danger to Liza was real. He didn't know what to do about it, lacking any training in anything that might tell him what to do. She was no safer here than she was in New

York. Maybe they should get lost somewhere until the trouble passed. Maybe they should just lie low until after Paul's meeting. Maybe things would turn out all right, but he doubted it. He only knew he was glad to be able to get her out of Paul's house for the moment.

"What's the matter with you two? You look like someone stole the last Malomar off the plate."

Hearing Liza's voice, Jim started. He'd been so lost in thought he hadn't noticed her approach. She stood at the edge of the room watching them both. He rose from his chair. "Ready to go?"

Paul stood. "I almost forgot. I have something for you." He disappeared into the bedroom before Jim had a chance to protest. He came back a few seconds later carrying an oblong jeweler's box wrapped in silver paper. "This belonged to your mother. You can open it later if you want."

Liza took the box from him. "Thank you."

Jim got her out to the car for the short drive home. He watched her as he started the engine. She seemed much more subdued than she had been at the house, clutching the box Paul had given her as if it were a live thing that might manage to get free. "How are you doing?" he asked.

She offered him a tight smile. "I'm fine."

He recognized that voice, the tone of a woman biding her time until she got her man home before lighting into him. He'd expected as much. He suspected she'd taken so long in the bathroom because either she'd been listening all along or she was giving him enough time to find out what Paul was up to. Her "father" would be so proud.

He pulled away from the curb, noticing that almost as soon as he did, a big, black Buick a couple of spaces down did, too. But the driver stayed far enough back that Jim couldn't get a good look at him in the rearview mirror. Damn! He might be new to this game, but he knew better than to go straight home. Instead, he headed for the island's one gas station and pulled up in front of one of the full-service pumps. As he did so, he watched for the guy who'd been tailing them. A little old man wearing a hat. Jim let his breath out on a sigh. "Get a grip, Fitzgerald," he muttered under his breath.

"What was that?" Liza asked, looking at him questioningly.

"Can you believe the price of gas has gone up again?"

As Jim filled the car, Liza got out and stretched. She hated the smell of gasoline, one of the many reasons she'd never attempted to maintain a car in the city. There was a minimart attached to the station. Liza nodded in its direction and said to Jim, "Do we need anything?"

"Actually, some milk, if you don't mind."

"I'll be right back." Later on she'd have to discuss with him the wisdom of buying milk at a gas station. For now, she was grateful to get away from the smell. It wouldn't do her any harm to get out of the midday sun as well.

A frigid blast of air-conditioning hit her as she opened the door, altogether not a bad thing at all. Liza glanced around the store. The mart had looked more mini from the outside than it proved to be on the inside. The milk was housed in a refrigerated case at the opposite end of the store.

She picked up a half gallon and headed toward the cashier. On the way there she spotted a familiar red box with a little string attached. Animal crackers—she used to love those things. The store had three boxes. She claimed them all by the strings and got at the end of the line to pay.

She'd only been in the line a moment when the man in front of her turned toward her. He glanced at her purchases. "Stocking up for the kids?"

Liza slid a glance at the man. He was older, maybe in his early sixties, with salt-and-pepper hair that could probably use a good trimming. His broad features and the sheer size of him would make him the kind of man you wouldn't want to meet in a dark alley, if it weren't for the engaging smile on his face that brought twin dimples out in his cheeks. She guessed everyone couldn't age as gracefully as Sidney Poitier.

She also guessed she was being rude. As a New Yorker, she sometimes needed a moment to remember that outside the city, complete strangers who spoke to you were not necessarily wacko perverts trying to molest you, thieves trying to pick your purse, or even tourists who asked for directions to places you didn't know in languages you didn't understand. Most places, especially small communities, people just liked to be friendly.

"No. My only kid is the big one out there pumping gas." She glanced at the three bottles of motor oil in the man's hands. She'd seen a display of them by the front door when she came in. "I see you're stocking up for a baby of another kind."

The man's smile deepened. "Just a beat-up Ford in need of a loving hand." The line moved down and it was the man's turn to pay. He pulled out his wallet and handed a twenty to the cashier. "I do have a kid though," he said to her. "Would you like to see a picture?"

Inwardly, Liza groaned. Now she'd gone and overdone the friendly routine. What was she supposed to say to that? No? She could only hope the man was true to his word and only had one. "Sure."

He handed her a worn photograph, which for some

reason reminded her of the one Paul showed her. Maybe it was the quality of the photography in those days. It showed a little brown-skinned boy in a party hat blowing out candles on a birthday cake. For a doting father, she wondered why he kept that of all pictures in his wallet. Why not a graduation picture or maybe a wedding snapshot? Given the man's apparent age, his son might be old enough for that. Then again, it was none of her business.

She handed the photo back. "What a cutie."

The man shrugged as he replaced the photo in his wallet. "I know I should probably replace that with another photo, but that's how he'll always be to me, my little boy."

In a way, that was sweet, but in another way it was sort of twisted. She wondered how the son felt about being kept forever young in his father's mind. But again, it was none of her business, so she kept silent.

The cashier handed the man his bag and change. But obviously the man wasn't through talking yet. He stepped to the side as Liza presented her purchases to the cashier. "You're not from around here, are you? What brings you to the Sunshine State?"

Liza didn't figure she had much of a New York accent, but what little there was this man must have picked up on. She gave him the most innocuous answer she could think of. "My father retired out here."

The man nodded. "Enjoy your time with him." He offered her one last smile and a wave as he headed out the door. Beyond him, she could see Jim had moved the car to park it right outside the door to wait for her. He wasn't looking her way, which was a good thing since it meant he didn't see the determined expression on his face. He might not know it, but as soon as they got home, he had plenty of explaining to do.

* * *

"Okay," Liza said, as they entered the house. "Who is that man and what has he got to do with my mother?"

He'd spent the time waiting for her to come out of the store rehearsing what and how much to tell her. The full, flat-out truth was out of the question. Nonetheless, the time of reckoning was at hand. "Can we sit and do this like civilized people, or do we have to stand in the hallway?"

She shot him a droll look and gestured for him to precede her. He did, but rather than sit, he stopped behind the couch. "Would you like something to drink?"

She sat on the sofa and crossed her legs. "No stalling, Fitzgerald."

"I'm not. I thought you might appreciate a glass of wine right now." He knew he would. No matter what he told her, she was likely to (a) not believe him, or (b) to pepper him with questions until he spilled everything he knew. Since he didn't know how she'd take any of what he planned to tell her, he'd rather do it with a mellower disposition than he now possessed.

"Whatever."

He went to the refrigerator and put the milk away. He opened a bottle of Chardonnay and poured them each a healthy glass, before rejoining her in the living room. She took her glass from him without really looking at him. "Thank you."

Jim sat in the teal leather seat across from her. He gulped down half his drink in one swallow. "What do you want to know? I thought for sure you were listening from the other side of the door."

She sipped from her glass, then set it on the glass coffee table. "I tried. I couldn't hear anything except mumbles. I came out when I sensed a lull in the conversation. So, what did he tell you? How does he know my parents?"

"How do you know he's not your father?"

She shot him another one of those looks. "I don't doubt that he knew me and my mother in some capacity. He knew too many things about my early life for a perfect stranger. But he said my mother wasn't into taking pictures, which couldn't be less true. You would have loved my mother. If I sneezed she took a picture of the tissue. If he'd been my father, he would have had other pictures of me. No matter how bitterly my parents might have parted, I doubt she would have denied my father a few mementos of his daughter. So, I ask again, how did he know my parents?"

It hadn't occurred to him that her questions were designed to test Paul rather than simply to get to know him. It appeared Liza was both more crafty and less gullible than he'd hoped. Two strikes not in his favor. His plan not to tell her the truth flew out the window.

"Honestly, I didn't ask him."

"You didn't ask him?" she echoed, an incredulous tone to her voice.

"No. It seems we have a bigger problem. You remember that little fire in your apartment building?"

"How could I not? What has that got to do with anything?"

"It's my belief that the fire was set so that one of Paul's former associates could search your apartment."

"For what? I don't have anything anyone would want."

"Diamonds. According to Paul, they lucked into them on some job he pulled with some friends. The friends think he has them, but he says he doesn't."

She sat forward. "Whoa, what kind of 'job' was this? You've got to backtrack for a moment." Despite her words, she held up a hand to halt him. She grasped her wineglass, took a large gulp from it, and then sat back. "Okay, now I'm ready."

He didn't know how to tell her except flat out. He told her how he met Paul and what little he knew of the thirty-year-old job. With a rueful smile, he finished with, "I'm sorry, sweetheart."

She shook her head. "Don't be. It's funny, but I can't imagine my mother knowing such a person. She was always so . . . so . . . proper, I guess the word is for it. She wore white gloves and carried a patent leather Jackie Kennedy pocketbook, for heaven's sake, and Jackie had been out of the White House for fifteen years."

She took another sip from her glass. "Why didn't you tell me any of this before we got here?"

"That the man you thought was your father was a crook and a con man? Paul's been straight for five years. I thought all that was part of his past, not his present. If it weren't for this diamond business—"

He stopped, seeing a horrified expression come over her face. She retrieved the gift Paul had given her from her lap and tore at the paper. Once she got the plain white box open, she sat back and sighed. She tipped the box toward him so that he could see its contents: a tiger's eye necklace. He'd never been a big fan of the stone, but the size and color of the gems were impressive.

"For a moment, I thought . . ."

Jim relaxed, too. He'd thought the same thing.

"So where does that leave us?"

"I don't know. Paul says he's going to meet with his partners tonight to settle things."

"Isn't that dangerous if they think he cheated them? Shouldn't he call the police?"

"Honey, the police are for law-abiding folks. What would he tell them anyway? Some guys I pulled a job with thirty years ago want to beat the crap out of me for cheating them?"

An Important Message From The ARABESQUE Publisher

Dear Arabesque Reader,

I invite you to join the club! The Arabesque book club delivers four novels each month right to your front door! It's easy, and you will never miss a romance by one of our award-winning authors!

With upcoming novels featuring strong, sexy women, and African-American heroes that are charming, loving and true… you won't want to miss a single release. Our authors fill each page with exceptional dialogue, exciting plot twists, and enough sizzling romance to keep you riveted until the satisfying end! To receive novels by bestselling authors such as Gwynne Forster, Janice Sims, Angela Winters and others, I encourage you to join now!

Read about the men we love… in the pages of Arabesque!

Linda Gill
PUBLISHER, ARABESQUE ROMANCE NOVELS

P.S. Watch out for the next Summer Series **"Ports Of Call"** *that will take you to the exotic locales of Venice, Fiji, the Caribbean and Ghana! You won't need a passport to travel, just collect all four novels to enjoy romance around the world! For more details, visit us at www.BET.com.*

A SPECIAL "THANK YOU" FROM ARABESQUE JUST FOR YOU!

Send this card back and you'll receive 4 FREE Arabesque Novels— a $25.96 value—absolutely FREE!

The introductory 4 Arabesque Romance books are yours FREE (plus $1.99 shipping & handling). If you wish to continue to receive 4 books every month, do nothing. Each month, we will send you 4 New Arabesque Romance Novels for your free examination. If you wish to keep them, pay just $18* (plus, $1.99 shipping & handling). If you decide not to continue, you owe nothing!

- Send no money now.
- Never an obligation.
- Books delivered to your door!

We hope that after receiving your FREE books you'll want to remain an Arabesque subscriber, but the choice is yours! So why not take advantage of this Arabesque offer, with no risk of any kind. You'll be glad you did!

In fact, we're so sure you will love your Arabesque novels, that we will send you an Arabesque Tote Bag FREE with your first paid shipment.

* PRICES SUBJECT TO CHANGE.

YOU'LL GET 4 SELECT ROMANCES PLUS THIS FABULOUS TOTE BAG!

ARABESQUE

Visit us at: www.BET.com

THE "THANK YOU" GIFT INCLUDES:

- 4 books absolutely FREE (plus $1.99 for shipping and handling).
- A FREE newsletter, *Arabesque Romance News*, filled with author interviews, book previews, special offers, and more!
- No risks or obligations. You're free to cancel whenever you wish with no questions asked.

FREE TOTE BAG CERTIFICATE

Yes! Please send me 4 FREE Arabesque novels (plus $1.99 for shipping & handling). I am under no obligation to purchase any books, as explained on the back of this card. Send my free tote bag after my first regular paid shipment.

NAME _____

ADDRESS _____ APT. _____

CITY _____ STATE _____ ZIP _____

TELEPHONE ( ) _____

E-MAIL _____

SIGNATURE _____

Offer limited to one per household and not valid to current subscribers. All orders subject to approval. Terms, offer, & price subject to change. Tote bags available while supplies last.

AN055A

Thank You!

Accepting the four introductory books for FREE (plus $1.99 to offset the cost of shipping & handling) places you under no obligation to buy anything. You may keep the books and return the shipping statement marked "cancelled". If you do not cancel, about a month later we will send 4 additional Arabesque novels, and you will be billed the preferred subscriber's price of just $4.50 per title. That's $18.00* for all 4 books for a savings of almost 30% off the cover price (Plus $1.99 for shipping and handling). You may cancel at any time, but if you choose to continue, every month we'll send you 4 more books, which you may either purchase at the preferred discount price. . . or return to us and cancel your subscription.

* PRICES SUBJECT TO CHANGE

THE ARABESQUE ROMANCE CLUB: HERE'S HOW IT WORKS

THE ARABESQUE ROMANCE BOOK CLUB
P.O. BOX 5214
CLIFTON NJ 07015-5214

"The statute of limitations must have run out on that crime by now."

"Maybe." If that's all there was to it. But Jim suspected more existed to the story than Paul had told him. For instance, he'd said four of them robbed the store, yet only two of the other men were after him. What happened to the other man? Then again, Paul had never said that the fourth was a man at all. What if it had been a woman who'd escaped prison and been content with the share she'd received? Could Liza's overly conservative mother have fit that bill? Not from the way Liza described her, but if she did she wouldn't be the first woman to leave a life of crime to err too much on the other side of the line.

Come to think of it, maybe Liza's father had gone away, but not in the usual sense most people used. As much as he hated to entertain the thought, could Liza's father be one of Paul's jailed accomplices? The more likely candidate was Grady, the more vicious one, which could explain why her father hadn't tried to see her over the years. He would have had to do so through the reinforced glass in the waiting room at the state penitentiary.

So many thoughts circled around in his brain, he wondered if he hadn't watched too many reruns of *Law and Order*. Maybe he was complicating things way too much. He only knew he needed to protect Liza as best he could.

He glanced over at her. Her gaze centered on the dregs in her wineglass, a pensive expression on her face. "Baby, say something."

Her lashes lifted and she focused on him. He saw pain, confusion, and a profound tiredness in her expression. "A month ago, I thought I had this amazingly normal life. Where did that go again?"

He snorted. "I don't know. Do you want to lie down for a while?"

She nodded. "I feel like I could sleep for a week. Excuse me."

She rose from the sofa and walked toward her bedroom. He followed a short distance behind, not wanting to crowd her. She paused at the doorway to her room and turned to face him. She leaned her back against the wall. "Thank you for being honest with me. I appreciate it, though a couple of times there I wouldn't have minded the proverbial little white lie."

He cradled the side of her face in his palm and her eyes drifted shut. He kissed both of her eyelids, her cheeks, and finally her mouth, a kiss not of passion, but of comfort. Pulling back, he said, "It will be all right, Liza. I promise you that."

She smiled and shook her head. "Thanks for the brave face, but you can't possibly know that." She slipped inside the room and shut the door.

Jim leaned his hands against the painted oak surface and rested his forehead against the wood. No, he couldn't know that, but he'd do his damnedest to make it true.

Hours later, Liza checked the clock next to her bedside and groaned. Three o'clock and, for the second night, sleep proved elusive. At least this time she had an excuse. She'd slept the entire afternoon away. She'd awakened in time for a dinner of broiled steaks, wild rice, and salad. Afterward, Jim had let her win a few hands of poker. Then they'd put on some movie she'd never seen before and couldn't remember now. Her thoughts had been too thoroughly consumed by the health and well-being of the man she'd once believed to be her father. Not only didn't she want to see any human being hurt over something as stupid as things that didn't belong to him in the first place, but she'd bet her last money that whoever Paul Mitchell really was, he knew the answers she sought. She wanted the answers more desperately now than ever.

Though Jim hadn't said so, she knew her involvement with Paul had put them in danger, too. And people who were willing to burn down an apartment building might be willing to do all sorts of other nasty things if they thought a great deal of money was involved. Fearing for all their lives wasn't completely out of the question.

Liza shifted onto her stomach and sighed. Once he'd noticed her flagging, Jim had sent her to bed again. She'd dozed off fairly easily, but she doubted she'd get back to sleep any time soon. She leaned up to look out the window above her headboard. What she really needed was to use her muscles rather than her mind. Something to tire her out. She needed a swim. Unfortunately, on her little shopping foray in the city, she hadn't possessed the foresight to pick up a swimsuit.

For a minute she contemplated the wisdom of a late night skinny-dip. Surely at this hour, Jim would sleep through it, saving her from any compromising situations. He'd promised not to push her before she was ready, and she didn't want to do the same to him, either. As far as she knew, the only way onto the back of the property was through the house, so she wouldn't be putting herself at any additional risk by being outside. The high fence and foliage prevented the prying eyes of any night-owl Peeping Toms.

Ten minutes. That's all she'd give herself. Ten minutes, and then she'd try to sleep again. She took off her nightgown and slipped into her robe. As quietly as she could, she made her way through the house and outside to the small blue and white cabana. As she expected, there were towels inside. She grabbed a white one and slung it and her robe on one of the deck chairs. Gingerly, she got into the water at the shallow end, not wanting to splash too much and risk awakening Jim. She lay on her back in the water and floated. She sighed out her pleasure at the feel of the warm water on her skin. In another moment, she'd start a few laps to tire herself out.

But suddenly, she had the sensation of someone watching her. Maybe it hadn't been such a bright idea to come out here after all. She opened her eyes and looked around. She spotted him almost immediately, but she still gasped when she saw him. Jim crouched next to the pool wearing nothing but a pair of black pajama bottoms and a smug expression.

He leaned down to splash her with a handful of water. "Liza, Liza, Liza. We've got to stop meeting like this."

Without thinking she obeyed her first impulse. She reached up and pulled him headfirst into the water.

Eleven

Jim came up sputtering a second later. He wiped the chlorinated water from his face and turned to find her. The grin on her face told him she'd pulled him in as a joke, but the sight of her nude body didn't arouse anything in him close to humor. He closed the distance between them in the water and stood. Still laughing, she backed away from him, until her back hit the side of the pool. He braced his hands on either side of her.

"If you wanted me to join you, all you had to do was ask."

"I was more interested in washing that self-satisfied look off your face."

He leaned closer to her until their bodies were almost touching. "If I were satisfied in any way, the only thought on my mind would not be, as you put it, ravishing your delectable body."

"I do remember mentioning something about ravishment, though I'm sure I didn't use the word *delectable*. But come to think of it . . ."

Her words trailed off as her fingers trailed down his chest and lower. He caught her wrist as she reached his waistband. He shook his head. "Didn't your mother ever tell you that playing with fire you're likely to get burned?"

She smiled at him, the smile of a woman who knows exactly what she is doing to her man. "Are you on fire, Jim?"

"You know I am. Now, do us both a favor and go back to bed."

She sighed, a gesture of capitulation. "All right. Kiss me good night and I'll go."

Every other time he'd sent her to bed, it had been with a kiss to her cheek or forehead. That wouldn't suffice this time. His brain screamed, *mistake, mistake,* but his body did what it wanted to do. His mouth lowered to hers. One little kiss, he told himself, a peck, really. He pulled away almost immediately, only to be drawn back by the sweetness of her kiss. Again he pulled away, far enough to see her face. Her eyes flickered open and she regarded him with such an expression of longing that whatever control he had eluded him.

Without thinking, his arms closed around her and he took her mouth again, in earnest this time. His tongue plunged into her mouth to find and mate with her own. His hands roved over her bare skin in ways calculated to excite. She responded by pressing her body to his and moaning in a way that left no doubt as to his effect on her.

One of his legs insinuated itself between her thighs. His fingers pressed into the soft flesh of her buttocks, bringing her in intimate contact with him. She whimpered and rubbed herself against him.

A ragged groan forced its way from his chest. God, he ached to be inside her. There was nothing stopping him except the damn pajamas stuck to him like a second skin and the fact that he had no means of protecting her.

That thought sobered him, like a splash of water in

the face. He broke the kiss and when she looked up at him with questions in her eyes, he pressed her cheek to his chest and kissed her temple. He was in no shape to answer any of her questions, if indeed he actually had any answers. He had enough trouble just trying to breathe and hoping his heartbeat would settle down to something resembling normalcy. It didn't help that her fingers continued to weave tantalizing patterns on his skin.

He unwound her arms from around his with his hands on her wrists. He stepped away from her, opening a gap between them. "Liza?"

Her head lifted and her eyes opened. Despite the warmth of the night, her body trembled, setting off tiny ripples in the water. "Jim."

That one breathless word, coupled with the entreaty in her eyes, let him know he'd really gone too far this time, or rather he'd taken her too far to leave her in the state he'd brought her to.

He brought both of her hands behind her and held them in one of his. "What do you want, baby? This—" He cupped and lifted one of her breasts and lowered his head to lave her nipple with his tongue. She jerked and a soft sound of pleasure escaped her lips. "Or this?" He drew her nipple into his mouth and suckled her.

She gasped and struggled against his hold on her, but he held fast, knowing he'd never be able to do what he wanted if she put her hands on him. His free hand skimmed lower, over her midriff, her navel, and beneath the line of the water to her belly. "Or this?" he murmured before taking her other nipple into his mouth while his fingers trailed lower to find the soft folds of sensitive flesh between her thighs.

She jerked and called his name, bringing a smile of satisfaction to his lips. He'd barely touched her, but already he could feel the tension building in her. He slid two fingers inside her, while his thumb strummed the sensitive core of her.

"Jim!"

"I'm here, baby."

He lifted his head to look down at her. Her throat arched and her mouth worked, but no sound came out.

He said nothing, not wanting to rush her, but the rapturous expression on her face told him it wouldn't be long. He buried his face against her throat as her body started to tremble, small shivers at first, then larger tremors that racked her body. He released his hold on her and her arms came around his neck. His free arm went around her, holding her to him as she cried out her pleasure against his ear.

As she quieted, he brought his other arm around her, to stroke her hair, her back, to soothe her. Her breathing came in gasps and sighs. He had to admit his wasn't much better. It was a heady thing to watch this woman come apart in his arms knowing he was the man responsible for making her feel that way.

He kissed the delicate juncture between her throat and shoulders. "Are you all right?"

"No," she whispered, but he heard the humor in her voice.

He chuckled and squeezed her more tightly to him. But he knew she'd recovered when she began to move again, rubbing herself against his erection.

He stroked his hand over her hair one last time, allowed himself one last kiss to her shoulder. Then he took a step away from her. "Go to bed, Liza."

She lifted her head and stared back at him in confusion. "What did you say?"

"I said, go to bed."

"Yours or mine?"

The teasing quality of her voice let him know he'd miscalculated again. She saw what he'd done as a prelude to more, not him simply giving her what she needed. "I'll see you in the morning."

She bit her lip, considering him. "You're kidding, right?"

He shook his head. "Sweetheart," he started, not really knowing what he intended to say.

"Why are you being like this?" She lowered her gaze to his chest. Her thumb brushed against his nipple. "It wouldn't have to mean anything."

With a finger under her chin, he tilted her face up to his. "For me it would."

She shook her head, either in denial or confusion about what he said. "Go to bed," he repeated. He didn't care what she thought at the moment as long as she got out of the pool. In another moment, he'd forget all about his promise to himself that the next time they came together for that ultimate act, she'd come to him for no other reason than that's where she wanted to be. He'd have her in his bed, her legs wrapped around him, and handle the repercussions later. His body hardened again with the prospect of it.

"Fine." She pushed away from him and started toward the steps at the shallow end of the pool.

He could tell by the stiffness of her gait as she rose from the pool, snatched up her robe, and fastened it around herself that he'd angered her, though he wasn't sure why. He'd make it up to her tomorrow, in the clear light of day when both of them had their clothes on.

After she'd gone into the house, he submerged himself completely under the water. Its warmth did nothing to dispel the heat raging in his body. While he'd given her the release she'd craved, their interlude had heightened, not quenched his thirst for her.

He considered swimming a few laps, just to burn off some of his frustration, but a noise coming from the back of the grounds stopped him. There was so much foliage back there an elephant could be hiding in the shrubbery. "Is anybody there?" he called. Not that he actually expected anyone up to no good to answer, but his neighbor's elderly grandmother wandered off often enough to make her presence a possibility.

Hearing nothing, not even the sound of leaves blowing in the breeze, he let out a pent-up sigh. Maybe he was just getting paranoid in his old age. Paranoid or not, the time for fun and games was over. He got out of the pool, stripped off his sodden pajama bottoms, and retrieved her towel from where she'd left it on the chair. Wrapping it around his waist, he let himself in the house, secured the door behind him. He checked the other door and the locks on the windows, before heading to his room for a brief yet frigid shower. He got into bed thinking about Liza at the other end of the house. For the first time and for completely unselfish reasons, he wished her bedroom were closer to his own.

Liza woke after a fitful night of sleep, still irritated at Jim, and still not sure why. She certainly couldn't fault his technique in arousing her or bringing her to a shattering sexual climax. She'd asked for that in more ways than one. But in her mind, pulling him into the pool had been an invitation for mutual pleasure, not a solo ride. She should have stopped him, but once he put his mouth on her, she was way too gone to register much of a protest.

Maybe that's what bothered her. What he'd done was a classic male stunt designed to prove he had the control and you didn't. If that was his intent, he'd proved his point in spades. Only moments before she'd promised herself she wouldn't do anything to stir the chemistry between them. All she had to do was see him to forget her own convictions.

But she doubted Jim acted on any macho impulse. No one would be giving him the Alan Alda True Friend of Feminism award any time soon, but he'd always treated her as nothing but an equal, not just sexually, but in every way. He hadn't lied to her, like another man might, when it came to Paul and the mess he'd gotten himself into. Perhaps he hadn't told her everything, but he'd told her enough that she appreciated the danger Paul may have put her in. She expected that as soon as they knew the outcome of Paul's meeting they would make a decision together about what they should do next.

She sat up, drawing her knees to her chest, and brushed the hair from her eyes. So how could she blame him for putting on the brakes when she hadn't been able to? Okay, she had been able, but she hadn't wanted to. She'd wanted his strength and his caring and, most of all, his heat. And while he'd shown her that, she'd wanted more. She'd wanted all of him.

Maybe her ego simply smarted after she offered herself to him, no strings attached, and he turned her down. In what version of reality did that make sense? Their sleeping together had to mean something to him. That had to be some sort of joke that had gone straight over her head. No man turned down free sex, especially not a man like him, unless he was holding out for something more. That would mean, at least in her mind, that he'd started to care for her much more than she'd believed.

Damn that man. Every time she thought she had some sort of handle on him he went and changed things on her. If that was the case, she wished he'd hurry up and tell her. Not because she knew what she'd do if it were true, but at least she'd feel she was a little bit closer to understanding him.

Sighing, Liza rose from the bed and stretched. The

smell of brewing coffee reached her nose, alerting her Jim must already be up. Damn. She could use a few more minutes of not seeing him to collect her emotions. She didn't know what she planned to say to him this morning, how to act. She only knew she couldn't afford a repeat performance of last night. Her sense of self-protection wouldn't allow that.

She showered and dressed in a sleeveless beige knit tank top and a flowing black and beige skirt that swirled around her ankles. After last night's swim she had to blow out her hair and take a curling iron to it to make it behave. After putting on a touch of makeup and donning a pair of low-heeled beige sandals, she declared herself ready to face the world. The world yes, Jim no.

Jim looked up from the task of pouring more batter into the frying pan as Liza entered the kitchen. As usual, she looked very feminine and soft on the outside, though he knew she possessed a core of strength underneath. Yet, this morning there was something else in her expression, something he didn't like. He remembered thinking he'd angered her last night. Apparently, he'd been right.

"I hope you like pancakes," he said as she moved past him toward the coffeepot.

"Nothing for me today. Just coffee." From the rack on the counter she got a mug and filled it.

He flipped the pancakes. "Cream and sugar are on the table."

She nodded and sat in the same chair she'd occupied last night. He watched her over his shoulder as she turned the morning paper toward her in order to read it, ignoring him.

Mentally he shrugged. In his experience, it didn't do a man any good to try to guess what was on a woman's mind. Invariably you were wrong and you just looked stupid for the attempt. Sooner or later, she'd get around to telling him. He only hoped it was sooner.

He retrieved the cakes from the pan, added butter and syrup, and brought his plate and coffee cup to the table. Though he sat in the seat across from her, she didn't look at him or acknowledge his presence in any way. He cut into the pancakes and forked some into his mouth. As he ate, she alternately flipped pages and sipped from her cup.

After a while, he said, "I'm feeling a bit of gender confusion here. Isn't it the guy who's supposed to have his head buried in the morning paper?"

She flipped the newspaper closed and looked up at him. "I'm sorry. I was thinking about Paul. Did you hear from him?"

If she really thought he believed Paul's whereabouts were her uppermost concern, she was mistaken, but for the time being, he'd let it slide. "Last night. His friend never showed up."

Her brow furrowed. "Is that a good thing or a bad thing?"

"Who knows?" It gave Paul a reprieve, but he'd have to face the other man sooner or later. One thing Jim did know was that he didn't intend to hang out here with Liza waiting to find out what he'd do. "I think you're going to have to put your reunion with Paul on hold."

She sighed. "I figured as much. Can we at least say good-bye before we go?"

He nodded. He didn't see the harm in that. As long as it was quick and no one who didn't need to noticed them. Then they'd come back and pack the few things they'd brought with them and go.

"All right. Let me get my purse."

After she left, Jim reached for the kitchen phone and

dialed Paul's number. After six rings he hadn't picked up. That wasn't unusual. First thing, Paul was generally in his pool and wouldn't bother with callers of any kind. Jim hung up the phone and cleared his space at the table. He spotted Liza waiting for him as he finished loading the dishwasher. Not only had she gotten her purse but she'd put on the necklace Paul had given her.

She fingered the largest stone. "It's a bit more ostentations than I'd pick . . ." She trailed off, shrugging.

"I'm sure Paul will appreciate seeing it on you."

"Thank you."

She turned to walk toward the front door. He caught up with her and spun her around with a hand on her arm. "Is there any chance you're planning to tell me what's bothering you before we go?"

She shook her head. "None whatsoever."

At least she hadn't lied to him and pretended nothing was the matter. "Why not?"

"Because right now it doesn't make a bit of difference anyway."

That was helpful. "Well, whatever it is, if you're willing to talk, I'm willing to listen."

"Whatever it is, it will keep. Can we go?"

"Sure." He gestured for her to precede him, but he didn't like this silence of hers one little bit. Hadn't they been through this before—her not trusting him enough to tell him what was on her mind? But he'd thought, after a few bumps and false starts, that they'd gotten past that. It felt as if they were moving backward a step, rather than moving forward—the direction he wanted to go. Maybe after they dealt with Paul, he'd drag her back here and make her tell him what he wanted to know.

But when they got to Paul's house, the door was ajar and someone had obviously trashed the place. Jim pushed the door open a bit more to reveal Paul's body lying facedown a little farther down the hall. A dark brownish stain covered the floor on one side of him. Blood.

"Call 911," Jim told Liza, pointing to the bedroom where Paul kept his one and only phone. Not only was the call necessary, but he wanted to give her something to do in case it turned out Paul was dead. If that were true, he didn't want her to be the one to figure that out. Once he got closer he heard Paul groan. Relief flooded through him, not just for his friend but for Liza's sake as well.

Kneeling, he turned Paul over to reveal a bullet wound at his shoulder and a nasty gash at his temple. The gash had stopped bleeding, but the shoulder wound was still active. He got a dish towel and pressed it to the wound.

Paul's eyes opened slowly and focused on him. At first Paul didn't seem to recognize him, then a look of alarm came into his eyes. "Liza."

"She's calling 911."

Paul gripped his arm in a surprisingly strong grasp. "Get her out of here."

"I will. As soon as the ambulance gets here."

Paul shook his head. "Get her off the island. Grady didn't want money. Didn't want diamonds. Revenge."

Paul didn't say anymore, but Jim figured out the rest. Grady planned to use Liza to avenge himself on Paul. Jim bit back a curse as Liza came into the room. He stood and tried to block her path to Paul. She didn't need to see him like that, but she wasn't having that. She brushed past him and knelt beside Paul.

Tears in her eyes, she took his hand. "Hold on. The ambulance is on its way."

Paul's other hand lifted to touch her cheek. "So much like your mother."

Jim checked his watch, though he didn't know what that was supposed to prove, since he didn't know what time they'd gotten there. But considering the island was no bigger than a postage stamp he figured the ambulance should be there already. Thankfully, it took only another few seconds for him to hear the sound of sirens and another minute before both the police and the paramedics were at the door. Jim was glad to see his friend Bill was one of them.

Jim pulled Liza into the living room as the EMTs began to work on Paul. He tried to get her to sit, but she refused, preferring to watch what was happening with Paul.

Bill came over to where they stood. He gave Liza a once-over, but as far as Jim could tell, he didn't recognize her. "The fun never stops with you, does it, Fitzgerald? What happened here?"

Before Jim had a chance to answer, one of the other officers called, "Hey, Sarge. You ought to see this."

The younger officer led Bill out the back door. Bill was back a few moments later with a younger officer in tow. "Would you mind going outside with Officer Freeman?" he said to Liza.

Liza looked at Jim, but he could only shrug. He had no more idea of what had happened than she did. But he appreciated Bill not giving any more details with Liza present.

After the two of them moved off, Bill turned to him and said in a hushed tone, "How much do you know about what went on here?"

"We walked in and found Paul that way."

"You didn't go out back?"

"No. What's going on?"

"Must have been some party your friend threw. We found another of his cronies out back."

"Why don't you ask him what happened?"

"I'd love to, but there's a problem. He's dead, Jim."

Twelve

"You're sure there's nothing you'd like to add?"

Liza offered the young officer taking her statement her best ditzy-girl smile and shook her head. In the five minutes the policeman had been trying to take her statement, she'd told him precisely nothing. True, she didn't know much of anything, not about what had gone on here before they arrived. Besides, she didn't want to give herself the chance to contradict whatever it was Jim was at this minute telling his friend Bill. The two of them were huddled together off to the side in the way that any woman would recognize as the international symbol for men who are up to something.

The officer gritted his teeth. "Thank you, Ms. Morrow."

He stalked off just as Jim began walking toward her. When he reached her, he led her over to the small living room. "Was I mistaken or were you giving that young pup a hard time?"

She shrugged. "He kept insisting on asking me questions and I insisted on not answering them. I didn't want to mess up whatever story it was you told Bill."

"I appreciate that."

"So what did you find out?"

"Nothing good. According to Paul, Grady wasn't entirely truthful about his reasons for wanting to meet with him. He's not interested in the diamonds or any money Paul might have given him. Grady is out to revenge himself on Paul—through you."

A tremor of pure fear raced up her spine. "Why me? Paul hardly knows me. How does he even know I'm here?"

"Maybe Grady doesn't know that. I don't know. Paul wasn't too clear on the reason behind all this. But all someone had to see was you and Paul at the front door to know some relationship existed between the two of you."

"You think we were being watched?"

He shrugged. "It's what I would do, if only to make sure Paul hadn't double-crossed me and called in the police. But that's beside the point. The point is you're in danger here."

Liza shut her eyes and her head swam. That was one hell of a point. It had been bad enough when she thought all Grady was after was a payoff from Paul to disappear. Now this man, a murderer who had tried to kill Paul, was after her. That was too much.

She felt Jim's hands at her elbows, steadying her, and she knew she had to get a grip on herself. She didn't want him to think she was on the verge of falling apart, though that might not be too far off. She straightened her shoulders, opened her eyes, and met his gaze. "When did Paul tell you this?"

"When you were calling the police."

"What's happens now?"

"We're getting out of here."

She'd figured out that much herself. "What about Paul?" The ambulance attendants had wheeled him out a few minutes ago, where to, she didn't know.

"Believe it or not, they have a pretty decent medical

center on the island. Given the population, they have to."

"We're just going to leave him here?"

"Sweetheart, the police are on the case. His room will be watched. The Dade County Sheriff's office has been notified. They'll be beating the bushes looking for Grady. If he's here, they *will* find him. For now I want to take you somewhere safe."

"All right."

Jim pulled her into his arms, and she melted against him, laying her cheek on his shoulder, making him grateful that she neither argued with his plan nor fought his embrace. Given her mood that morning, he considered the latter more of a a possibility. He didn't question her about it now. She had enough to worry about. Despite her calm demeanor, he knew she had to be worried, though he suspected her concern was more for Paul than for herself.

He could live with that. He was more than afraid enough for both of them. Although there was no identification on the body found at the back of Paul's house, the corpse was the right age and body type to suggest they'd found Slim.

Despite what he'd told Liza, he had serious doubts about the abilities of the San Pedro Police Department, which consisted in its entirety of six officers that worked in three two-man shifts. Although all of them were on duty now, he doubted any of them, with the possible exception of Bill, possessed the wherewithal to hunt down the kind of man who would kill one of his own friends and wound another.

The last homicide on the island had been in 1997, when old Mrs. Beasley got tired of her cantankerous husband criticizing her cooking and stabbed him with the knife he was supposed to use to carve the roast. She hadn't even intended to kill him. The knife wound hadn't been fatal; the ensuing heart attack had.

He'd never had any experience with the sheriff's office to know if their presence bettered or worsened their situation, but he didn't plan to stick around long enough to find out.

He stroked his hands up and down her back. "Are you ready to go?"

She lifted her head and met his gaze. "I want to see Paul first. I want to make sure he's all right."

Why was he not surprised? "All right. Let's go see Paul. Then we're out of here."

When they got to the hospital, Paul was still being seen by a doctor. Unable to sit still, Liza paced in the small waiting room with her arms crossed in front of her. How much time did it take to remove one bullet and sew up one gash? That's if that's all there was to it. An image of Paul lying prone on his kitchen floor flashed in her mind. There had been an awful lot of blood. Both her clothes and Jim's were stained with it. She sighed, wondering how she'd come to care so much for this man in so short a time. She'd felt connected to him from the moment she met him, even after she figured out he couldn't be her biological father. She didn't understand it, but she remained powerless to settle her emotions.

She'd left Jim in one of the waiting room seats while she paced, so feeling him come up behind her startled her.

He wrapped his arms around her waist from behind and pressed his lips to her shoulder. "Relax, baby. Paul will be all right. He's too much of a hard case for one little bullet to do much damage."

Liza inhaled, trying to calm herself. Jim was right. There was no point worrying herself to death when she didn't know anything. "I'm okay, really."

"Good. I was starting to think I was going to have to rescue you from the basement after you wore a hole in the floor."

She let him lead her to one of the banks of seats that lined the walls, but it was another twenty minutes before a doctor came out to say that Paul could have visitors one at a time. She insisted on going first and was glad that Jim didn't try to talk her out of it. She followed the doctor to a private room on the other side of the floor.

"Try to keep it brief," the doctor said before continuing down the hall.

She nodded, and taking a deep breath for courage, she pushed the door open and stepped inside. Paul lay in bed, his arm in a sling, his eyes closed. For a moment she stood rooted to the spot, watching the shallow, rapid rise and fall of his chest. Seeing him, she was flooded by a host of questions, the chief of which was, what was this business with Grady really all about. She didn't ask any of them though. He'd probably never answer any of them anyway. He struck her as the sort of old-school male who believed that keeping a woman ignorant was tantamount to protecting her.

She stepped farther into the room and around the bed. She touched her hand to his uninjured shoulder. "Paul?"

His eyes flickered open and he looked at her with a vague expression in his eyes. "Liza, what are you doing here?"

She pulled a chair over to the bed and sat. "I'm not going to stay long. I just wanted to make sure you were okay." She took his hand. "How are you feeling?"

"Don't look like that, sweetie. I'm fine, really. Only a

little worse for the wear." He squeezed her hand. "How's it going with Jim? How are you two getting along?"

"I haven't wanted to brain him with something in the past couple of days, so I guess we're getting along fine."

"That's not what I meant."

She gazed down at her hands. She didn't suppose he did, but despite the affinity she felt with him, she wasn't ready to confess the depths of her feelings to this almost complete stranger. But she still wanted to tell him something, if not for his edification, then for hers. This man knew Jim, much better than she did. Maybe he could give her some idea of what made the man tick. "He confuses me."

Paul chuckled. "I'm not surprised. Don't get me wrong. He's a good man, Liza. He's treated me better, been a better friend to me, a better son than my own flesh and blood would have been. He's so busy trying to convince the world he's got all the depth of a rain puddle, but once you get to know him you realize a river runs through that boy."

He'd just described her feelings exactly. And in her case she had her hands full trying not to get caught in the undertow.

"What he needs," Paul continued, "is a good long look in the mirror. So far, no woman's been able to get him to do that. Do you know what I mean?"

She nodded. He was telling her not to get her hopes up that she'd be the one to succeed where others had failed. That was fine. She had no intention of making a fool of herself over James Fitzgerald, at least no more than she already had.

"Good, because if he hurts you I will have to kill him."

She smiled. "We can't have that."

"No, we can't. Now come over here and give an old

man some sugar. Then I want you to send Jim in here. I
need to talk to him."

She rose from her chair and leaned down to kiss his
cheek. He enveloped her in a surprisingly strong embrace. "You take care of yourself, young lady. I want to
see you back here in one piece when this is over."

Stepping back, she said, "You do the same. You
promised me some answers and I intend to get them."

"I'll tell you anything you want to know. I promise."

"I'm going to hold you to that." She kissed his forehead. "I'll go get Jim now."

One of the policemen outside Paul's door walked
her back to the room where Jim waited. As she got
closer she saw him, sitting forward in one of the chairs
with his elbows on his knees and his fingers steepled,
his chin resting on his fingertips. She didn't know why
seeing him calmed her. Maybe because he seemed
more pensive than worried. Maybe because even if she
didn't understand him, she trusted him.

As if he sensed her approach, his head came up and
he stood. When she came to stand beside him, he
asked, "How's Paul?"

"Weak, but all right, I guess."

"Did he tell you anything?"

"About Grady? No, but he wants to see you, so I'll be
expecting a full report."

"Are you sure you'll be all right?"

She gestured in a way that encompassed the room
and the several police officers around her, including
the one that escorted her from Paul's room.

"Point taken," Jim said. He kissed her cheek. "I won't
be long."

As he walked away, she sighed. And once they left
here they'd be on their own. That thought scared her
most of all.

Thirteen

Jim pushed open the door to Paul's room. Paul lay on his back, his eyes closed, a pained expression on his face. Jim stepped farther into the room and let the door shut behind him. "Cut the crap, old man. Liza might fall for that poor me crap, but this is me you're dealing with."

Paul opened his eyes and glared at him. "What the hell are you two still doing here?" With his good hand he lifted himself into a sitting position. "Didn't I tell you to get her out of here?"

Jim ground his teeth together. Paul had the nerve to be angry with him? He wasn't the one who put Liza in danger. Paul had, both by his past actions and by his lies to her in the present. All Jim wanted to know was exactly what he was up against. Then as far as he was concerned, Paul could fend for himself. "I intend to. But she refused to leave without making sure you were okay."

"She's looking after her papa."

Jim crossed to the chair beside the bed and sat. "Oh, please. She already knows you're not her father. And no, I did not have to tell her anything. She figured it out for herself."

"How?"

"She caught you in a lie. Imagine that."

"Damn. If she knows I'm not her father, why is she so concerned?"

"Because that's the kind of woman she is. She . . ." He searched for the word he wanted. "Cares. She cares."

"How much does she care about you?"

More than she wanted to and certainly more than she thought was wise. But that was none of Paul's business anyway.

"I didn't come here to discuss my relationship with Liza. You've got two seconds to explain what this business is about so I can take Liza out of here. What does he want to take revenge on you for? Cheating him?"

Paul shook his head. "He only brought up the diamonds because he figured I'd agree to meet with him if I thought it was just about money. I should have known something was up when he wanted to meet at my house. I don't know why I didn't insist on meeting somewhere public, except I've gotten soft in my old age."

"If he didn't want the diamonds, what did he want?"

"I'm pretty sure his initial plan was to kill me."

Jim leaned back and crossed his arms in front of him. "Now why would the man want to do that?" Paul sighed and shifted position, which Jim recognized as an attempt to stall. "Don't get shy on me now."

Paul nodded, resigned. "Like I told you, Grady, me, and the others went to rob this store. Now, Grady was one of the meanest sons of bitches I've ever known, but he had a kid, a baby he was crazy about. He didn't care about the woman enough to make it legal, but he was an absolute fool over that kid. When he went away, he made the woman promise that she'd raise him to know who his father was.

"For a while, she brought the kid up to visit him, sent

him pictures. Then all of a sudden everything stopped. No visits, no letters. When he called her apartment the phone had been disconnected. But he was inside. What could he do? His buddies on the street couldn't find her and he had no money to pay someone to look for her. She was gone."

"What happened to her?"

"She married someone else and moved out of state. The kid grew up thinking his stepdaddy was his real daddy. When Grady got out, he finally tracked her down, only to find a son who didn't know him and didn't want to know. Grady had a smile on his face when he told me, 'I fixed that bitch.' "

Jim could imagine what kind of "fixing" Grady had done. "Why does he blame you? Because you were free all those years he was locked up?"

"Partly, I guess. He blamed me because I brought along the fourth guy at the last minute, someone I was trying to school in the ways of the world. He screwed up and everyone but me got caught."

"Then this had nothing to do with Liza's mother?"

"Of course not."

Jim snorted. That's what he got for letting his imagination run away with him.

"Grady had a lot of years for his rage against me to foment. Finding out his kid was lost to him must have been the final straw that sent him after me."

"How did Liza get into this?"

"You showed up at my door. He was watching my place, from where I don't know. I told you she looks just as she did as a baby, just like her mother. Anyone seeing her with me would figure out it was her. He said he wanted to take from me what was taken from him. He figured I'd suffer more if he hurt Liza than if he killed me outright. And he's right."

Jim shut his eyes and massaged his temples with his thumb and middle finger. It didn't cheer him any to know that he'd been right in thinking nothing good would come from this trip or about Grady watching Paul's place. He lowered his hand and looked at Paul. Paul's head was down, a doleful expression on his face. But Jim didn't feel sorry for him. His own choices led him to the point where he was now. Jim intended to make sure Liza didn't pay for this man's mistakes.

"If Grady changed his mind about killing you, why did he shoot you?"

"He didn't intend to. It seems he hadn't confided his change in plans to Slim either. Slim was all for helping Grady recover the diamonds from me if I had them. He was willing to burn down a building or two if he thought he'd get something out of it, though he claims he had nothing to do with the fire in Liza's building. But what else is he going to say? I don't think Slim would have minded if Grady went after me. But Slim said he wasn't about to, as he said, 'hurt no woman.' Grady killed him for what he considered his disloyalty."

Paul shrugged. "At least I think that's what happened. I got in the way of the first shot. I whacked my head on the counter when I fell. I don't know what happened after that."

Jim stood. He'd heard enough. "I'm going."

"Where are you taking her?"

"My brother has a place on Long Island. I don't think anyone will look for us there." Besides, once they were in New York, he'd call Jackson and see if his friend could send him some help. Jim held no macho delusions about his own ability to protect Liza, either. He'd do whatever he needed to keep her safe.

Paul nodded. "Promise me you won't let anything happen to that girl."

Jim huffed out a breath, annoyed at himself for letting his emotions soften toward Paul. Whatever he really was to her, his concern for her was obvious. "I promise."

* * *

When he got to the waiting room, Liza was waiting for him like a vulture waiting for her prey to die. She pulled him over to one side. "What did Paul say?"

He led her over to a corner of the room, away from the cluster of cops that appeared to be talking amongst themselves, but who he was sure would listen to every word they said. "According to Paul, Grady blames him for the loss of his son. He wants Paul to suffer the same loss."

He watched Liza's face and knew when his meaning became clear to her. "Lovely. A crazy person I've never met wants to kill me. At least that tops all the other nonsense that's happened to me this summer. No sense in going backward."

He drew her closer with his hands at her waist. She rested her temple against his shoulder and sighed. He knew she hadn't said what she did in an effort to sound self-pitying but as an attempt at humor. The problem was there wasn't much funny about the situation in which they found themselves.

He was about to suggest they get going when he noticed a blond man in an ill-fitting blue suit coming up to them. Jim recognized him as a cop by the badge he wore clipped to his belt and the particular brand of sour expression on his thin face. Jim disliked him immediately.

"We have company," he told Liza. She lifted her head and looked at him, then toward the cop.

"Ms. Morrow, I'm Detective David Wright of the sheriff's office. May I have a word with you?"

"Of course," Liza said.

But Jim wondered why, with the two of them standing there, Wright focused his comments and his gaze only on her. To test the waters, Jim said, "Yes, Detective, please go ahead."

The man cast him a quelling look before returning his attention to Liza. "First of all, I want to assure you that we and the San Pedro Police Department are doing everything to locate Mr. Grady and make sure he no longer poses a threat to Paul Mitchell."

"I appreciate that."

"I understand there have been some threats made against you as well."

Jim couldn't imagine that Paul had shared that information with the police, which left Bill as the culprit. He'd promised to leave Liza out of it if he could, but that must not have been possible. Then again, the officer stationed outside Paul's room could be an adept snoop.

"If that's true," Liza said, "I can't imagine why. I'd never even heard of Harold Grady until this morning."

"I don't know what kind of game the two of you are playing, but I warn you, it's a dangerous one. Grady was released from prison less than three weeks ago. The first stop he made was the home of the woman he was seeing thirty years ago. The least of what he did was to slit her throat. You both know what he did to Mr. Mitchell and George Watkins this morning."

Jim couldn't think of any reason for Wright to launch on this litany of doom other than to scare Liza. Unfortunately, he'd succeeded. Although she displayed an outer calm, he felt her tremble.

"George Watkins?" Liza asked.

"The man found dead at the back of the Mitchell property. I believe he went by the nickname Slim."

Damn. He'd known she had to find out about Slim sometime, but the glee with which Wright provided that tidbit of information made Jim want to deck him. "We get the picture."

"I'm not sure you do." He reached into the breast pocket of his jacket and pulled out a photograph.

Although he extended it toward Liza, Jim snagged it

before she could take it, fearing Wright intended to terrorize her with a graphic reminder of what Grady had done. He stuck it in his shirt pocket without looking at it.

Wright's expression grew more belligerent. "That photograph you choose to ignore is of a man with nothing left to lose. If we so much as pick him up, he's going back to jail for violating his parole. He's got to know that."

"Your point being?"

Wright cleared his throat. "We'd like to offer you our protection while you are on the island, Ms. Morrow. Even if our sources are wrong, and I don't think they are, you're in danger every moment you're here."

"What are you suggesting?" Jim asked.

Finally Wright focused his attention on him, but grudgingly and with little pleasure. "With your permission, Mr. Fitzgerald, we'd like to put a pair of police officers in the house with you. Your neighbor across the street has seen the wisdom of staying with friends until this affair blows over. She's given us permission to use her house in her absence."

In other words, they wanted to lie in wait using Liza as the bait to trap Grady. How stupid did this cop think they were that they wouldn't see through that plan? If they were really concerned with Liza's safety, they'd put her up somewhere else under police guard and, if necessary, set up a decoy policewoman in her place.

But Jim suspected Wright cared more about catching Grady than he cared about what it took to get him. It probably meant a feather in someone's cap for whoever captured Grady first, considering he was wanted now in three states. Someone would have to win that accolade without their help. He was more determined than ever to get Liza away from here.

"Thanks for the offer, Detective Wright, but we won't

be staying. We've already made plans to visit some friends for a while. In California. No one will think to look for us where we're going." Especially if they believed what he said was true. They'd be looking west, not north.

"Famous last words." Wright sighed. "With all due respect, Mr. Fitzgerald, what if you're wrong? If Grady finds you, any shots taken will not be the type that require film."

"Then why don't you and your men do your job and find him? If it makes you feel any better, you're welcome to plant as many people in my house as you want, as long as you understand we won't be there."

"If you leave this jurisdiction, we won't be able to help you."

That was supposed to be a bad thing? "We'll make do." Jim tightened his grip on Liza's waist. "Come on, sweetheart. Let's go."

"Well, that was fun," Liza said as they walked toward where he'd parked the car.

"What do you mean?"

"Being one of those law-abiding citizens for whom going to the police is an option, I don't particularly like lying to them."

"Why did you?"

"Because I didn't trust him, which is a good thing since all he wanted to do was dangle me in front of Grady to see if he'd bite."

He smiled, pleased she'd come to that conclusion without him having to point it out. "Is that why you let me do all the talking?"

"No, I enjoyed watching you drive someone else crazy for a change. Why didn't you tell me about the other man, Slim?"

He figured she'd question him on that considering his total lack of surprise to find out another man was dead. "*I* wasn't trying to scare the wits out of you to get you to cooperate."

"Good point."

They reached the car and got in. Liza fastened her seat belt and turned to him. "Just out of curiosity, let's see the picture Wright gave you."

Jim pulled it out and glanced at it. It must be Grady's mug shot from thirty years ago. The man in the picture had a tough-looking meaty face topped off with an Angela Davis 'fro and a unibrow. "Very attractive."

He handed the picture to Liza and started the engine. He was about to pull into traffic when something about Liza's continuing silence got to him. He turned back to find her staring transfixed at the photo and her hand was trembling.

He cut the engine and turned to face her. "Baby, what is it?"

She looked at him, a horrified expression on her face. "Th-this man. I've seen him. I spoke to him. He was in the gas station when I went in there."

Jim swallowed. This man had been that close to her and neither of them had known how dangerous he was at the time. "What did he want?"

"Nothing. Or he didn't seem to want anything. At the time, I thought he was just being friendly. He showed me a picture of his son. I remembered thinking it was odd that a man would carry around an old and faded baby picture of a son that had to be a grown man. Oh God, I practically told him I was out here visiting my father. That was a mistake, wasn't it?"

One she couldn't have possibly foreseen. "Don't sweat it. I'm sure Grady already knew who you were. He might have been looking for confirmation."

"He told me to enjoy my time with him. When he said it, I thought it was his way of saying good-bye. But now . . ."

Now, Jim agreed, it sounded like a threat.

Fourteen

Jim gritted his teeth as he pulled to a stop across the street from his house. If Grady had any doubts as to Liza's whereabouts, the combined forces of the sheriff's office and San Pedro police forces would have obliterated them. Not only had they been escorted from the hospital by Detective Wright in a black sedan with tinted windows—the ubiquitous "unmarked car" that didn't fool anybody—but two patrol cars bearing the imprimatur of the Miami Police Department were parked practically on his lawn, lights flashing. Wouldn't it have been easier to post a sign in his front window that said Liza Morrow Slept Here? They'd outed her, probably as another means of ensuring her cooperation, since it was no longer tenable to stay here. Damn.

Another blue-suited man opened the door to them. Just to be contentious, Jim stared pointedly at the man's suit, back at Wright, who'd followed them in and back again. "What, do you guys get some sort of volume discount on those things?"

The man gave him a sour look, but said nothing. Jim stepped aside to let Liza precede him through the door. Two uniformed officers milled around his living room.

Exactly how stupid did they think this guy was? He'd never show up with so many boys in blue present. Jim consoled himself with the knowledge that it wasn't really his problem. Now more than ever, he just wanted to get Liza out of there.

With a hand on her elbow, he led her off in the direction of the kitchen, middle ground between their two rooms and out of the earshot of the others. "How long will it take you to pack?"

"Two seconds. I packed this morning. I figured we'd be leaving."

"I knew there was a reason I liked you. Then you can help me round up some of my stuff."

"What stuff?"

"Some of my equipment. I don't mind if they raid my refrigerator, but I'll be damned to come back and find my cameras missing."

"How many do you have?"

"Five, plus assorted lenses and other gizmos. Plus the laptop."

"You're bringing all that?"

"I'm removing all that." He realized how cryptic that comment sounded, but he'd have plenty of time to explain it later.

Liza followed Jim to the door to his room that was painted a deep purple. Somehow the color suited him, as did the dark wood furniture, particularly the king-sized bed that dominated the room. For a moment, she tortured herself wondering precisely how many women he'd shared this room with.

"Come on in," he called to her. "I won't bite unless you ask me to."

Mentally, Liza shook herself. Wasn't she beyond questioning his sexual exploits? Besides, from the grin on his face, she knew he knew exactly what she'd been thinking.

"I'm not asking." She'd meant to sound flippant and cavalier. Instead she sounded petulant. Oh well. She did feel irritable and out of sorts, frightened for herself and for him and as sexually frustrated as she'd ever been in her life. It wasn't surprising that some of that edged itself to the surface.

Instead of focusing on that bed, she turned her attention to the bookshelf in the corner of the room. Though she could see him pulling things from his closet in the periphery of her vision, she tried to pretend that the titles on the books fascinated her.

"In answer to your question, not as many as you'd think."

Although she knew what he meant, she said, "I don't remember asking you a question."

He chuckled. "Have it your way, Liza. I'll be ready in a few seconds."

She said nothing to that, as one of the titles actually did snag her attention. She pulled the oversize hardcover from the shelf and examined the cover. *Winter in New York*. There had been some buzz about this book that had come out a few months before, but she hadn't equated the J.T. Fitzgerald who'd taken the pictures for the coffee table book with the Jim Fitzgerald she knew of.

She glanced over her shoulder at him. "I didn't know this was you."

"Yeah, well, that's how I spent my summer vacation two years ago."

She opened the book about a quarter of the way in. A smattering of text took up the left-hand page. On the right was a striking black-and-white picture of a homeless woman dressed in several layers of clothing wearing a crown made from what looked like a paper bag and holding a walking stick as if it were a scepter. Despite her lowly stature, there was something regal about this woman brought out through the photograph, something moving.

"How did you get involved with this?"

He shrugged. "I found out my uncle had Alzheimer's. It started me thinking about how other seniors coped with getting older, feeling their own mortality. I told this to a friend of mine, a writer for the *Times*. The collaboration was her idea. We talked our publisher into donating ten percent of the profits to the FAA."

"The Federal Aviation Administration?"

"The Federation on Aging in America."

"I'm impressed." She turned to the center of the book and a manila envelope slipped out and fell to the floor. Several papers, held together with a paper clip, slid halfway out the envelope. Actually, the topmost item was a photograph of a woman with almond-colored skin and laughing hazel eyes. "What's this?"

She bent to scoop up the papers, but Jim beat her to it. He shoved them into the bag he was packing. "Nothing."

"I see." So much nothing that he had to hide it from her. Too late. She'd already noticed the resemblance between him and the woman in the picture. And she knew he'd lied to her when he'd said he had no interest in the woman who'd given birth to him. For now, she'd let it slide, but that didn't stop her from wondering why he had.

After a moment, he zipped the bag and said, "Ready to go?" Although he smiled at her, his eyes were hard.

"As soon as I get my bag."

"I'll get it for you as soon as I take these out." He loaded himself down with two separate camera bags, a laptop case, and another bag, the one he'd shoved the papers into.

She followed him out into the living room. Ten minutes later, the car packed, Jim came back inside to get her. "We're all set."

His voice held a somber tone, or maybe it was her own sense of dread that lent a doleful note to his voice. Once they left, they were on their own. She'd known that from the beginning, but somehow that reality hadn't hit her fully until now. Now that she knew Grady really did mean to harm her, it hit her like the proverbial ton of bricks. And worse yet, she'd dragged Jim into this mess, since he refused to abandon her. She walked toward him until she stood by his side. "I'm ready."

Detective Wright, who stood in the hallway watching them, said, "Ms. Morrow, Mr. Fitzgerald, take care of yourselves and keep in touch. We'll let you know as soon as we find him."

Jim winked at the other man. "You boys just make sure to lock up when you leave."

"You don't like him very much, do you?" Liza teased as Jim seated her in the car.

Jim slid in beside her. "How'd you guess?"

He put his hand on the key to start the engine, but she forestalled him by placing her hand on his. "You don't have to do this, you know."

"Do what?"

She tilted her head to one side. "Go on the lam."

He put his hand in his lap and stared at her. "First, you've been watching too many episodes of *The Sopranos*. Second, what do you expect me to do? Leave you in the hands of those bozos in there? Walk out? Exactly how many people do you want ready to kick my ass? Eamon, Jake, Paul. Even Detective Wright would probably wait in line to have a go at me."

He stroked the backs of his fingers along her cheekbone. "It'll be all right, sweetheart. Have I been wrong before?"

"Yes. Quite a few times, in fact."

"Then I'm due to get one right, aren't I?"

She couldn't argue with that logic. She leaned closer and kissed his cheek. "Thank you."

He shook his head. "Pretty soon you're going to start insulting me." Before she could say anything else, he gunned the engine and pulled from the curb.

"By the way, where are we going, really? You told Wright we were going to California."

"I bought a couple of tickets to LAX, as well. As far as anyone knows, that's where we're headed. Bill's the only one who knows we're going back to New York."

"And you did this, why?"

Jim sighed. "I don't know this man, who he knows, or what he's capable of finding out. The fewer people who know what we're up to the better."

Liza sat back contemplating what he told her. Obviously he'd thought this out way more than she had. Or maybe that's the plan he'd cooked up with Bill that morning. Either way, she was grateful, since for the first time in her life she was too scared to tackle a situation rationally. To occupy her mind, she watched the traffic signs they passed as they exited the bridge that brought them onto the mainland.

"Isn't that the turnoff to the airport?" she asked as they whizzed past the exit.

"We're not going to the airport."

"We're not?"

"No, we're going to drive back."

Her eyebrows lifted. "That will take days, won't it?"

"Precisely. I called Eamon's neighbor who looks after his house when he isn't there. It'll take a couple of days to get the electricity and phone turned on. And who knows? Maybe by then, they'll have caught the son of a bitch and it will all be over."

She could only hope. She noticed Jim frequently checking the rearview mirror. "What's wrong?"

"Just making sure our tail is still with us."

"Someone's following us?" Despite the humor she heard in his voice, alarm skittered through her and she turned to look over her shoulder.

She felt his hand on her thigh. "Relax, baby, it's Bill."

Her hand went to her chest and she tried to breathe normally. She glanced over her shoulder again. "Which one is he?"

"The Harley about three cars back on the left."

Now that she knew what to look for, she spotted him easily. "Why is he following us?"

"To make sure we make it to his house in one piece."

"Oh."

He squeezed her thigh. "Understand this, Liza. I don't intend to let anything happen to either of us."

They had entered a residential neighborhood, a mix of ranch and two-story beige stucco houses, most of which sported iron balconies painted in bright colors. Jim pulled into the driveway of one home. One side of the two-car garage opened as he drove up. The door rolled down as Jim cut the engine, leaving them in semidarkness.

"Bill's house?" Liza asked.

"Come on." Jim got out of the car and opened the trunk. When she came up beside him, he said, "We're switching wheels."

Liza glanced at the only other vehicle in the garage. She knew nothing about cars except they required gas, but she took one look at the low-slung black convertible and put her hands on her hips. "You've got to be kidding."

The picture of innocence, Jim asked, "What do you mean?"

"Tell me all this subterfuge isn't an excuse to ride in your friend's muscle car."

"Not at all. If Grady comes after us, I want enough power to get away."

She tilted her head to one side. "I'm shocked you

could say that to me with a straight face. Whatever happened to being inconspicuous?"

"And here I thought this was the point when you'd be thanking me. Your only other choice is the Harley. Consider that I spared you that."

Liza rolled her eyes. Men and their expensive toys. Thank God women were more sensible.

"How's it going in here, kiddies?"

Liza turned at the sound of Bill's voice. He'd let himself in through the door that led to the house. "This person is trying to convince me that there is some practical reason we need to ride around in this shining example of testosterone on wheels."

"Don't look at me," Bill said. "I can't do anything with him either."

Liza shook her head. Like Bill was any better. There was no hope for it, not that she really minded. She stood aside as the men transferred most of the contents of one car to the other. The only item left, the second camera bag, Bill put inside the house.

When he came back a moment later, he was carrying a blue thermal tote. "I made you guys a little care package." He set it on the floor next to her and embraced her. "You take care of yourself. I have a barbecue every Labor Day. I expect to see you here."

Liza hugged him back. "I'll see what I can do."

Stepping back, Bill added, "And watch out for this bum. If he gets out of line, give me a call and I'll smack some sense into him."

She glanced at Jim, who looked heavenward in disgust. "I will."

Sensing the men wanted a moment alone, she slung the bag over her shoulder and got into the car. The windows were tinted dark enough that she knew they couldn't see her watching them. For a moment the two men embraced.

Liza smiled. She liked Bill and appreciated his loyalty to Jim and indirectly to Paul. Though he was a police-man, she doubted he'd shared all Jim had told him with his fellow officers. If he had, they wouldn't just be watching Paul's hospital room, they'd probably have him handcuffed to the bed, as well.

Always judge a man by the caliber of his friends. Liza straightened up in her seat hearing her mother's voice intone in her head. "Shut up, Ma," she said aloud. Not that she would have argued the point with her mother had she been here. But at the moment, she didn't need any schooling in Jim's fine points. Had it only been two days ago that she'd pondered the possibility of falling in love with him with dread? She didn't un-derstand him any more now than she did then, but she knew her feelings for him were deepening. She was falling all right, and there was no landing pad in sight.

Abruptly the car door opened and Jim slid in beside her. "We'll get going in a minute."

Liza schooled her features into the best benign ex-pression she could muster and met his gaze. "What are we waiting for?"

Jim nodded toward his own car, drawing her atten-tion to the fact that Bill sat behind the wheel. An instant later he backed out of the garage as the door opened for him.

"Why is Bill driving your car?"

"A little misdirection. If anyone followed us, they'll be watching for that car."

And following it now instead of them.

"What all is in Bill's supposed care package?"

Although she knew he'd only asked that question in order to distract her, she was willing to indulge him. She unzipped the bag at her feet. Several cold packs fit into slots on either side of the bag. She pulled out one of the two thermoses and removed the lid, surprised to find nothing but ice chips.

Jim leaned over to peer into the thermos and chuckled. "Bill told me he was packing us his stakeout special. I guess he wasn't lying."

She looked at him quizzically. "What does that mean?"

He sat back. "Most of the time cops are on stakeout in a car or van—some place lacking in facilities, shall we say? The ice chips keep you hydrated without sending you to the bathroom every two minutes."

Never would that have occurred to her. "See what you learn when you hang out with the right people?"

He winked at her. "And I haven't exhausted my repertoire yet."

The suggestiveness in his wink and the low timbre of his voice suggested schooling of an entirely different nature. One she didn't want to contemplate considering he'd been the one to send her to bed last night.

"Shouldn't we be going?"

"We should." He cast her a look as if there were something more he wanted to say. But instead of speaking he sighed and backed the car out of the garage into the deepening twilight.

Fifteen

The sky was rapidly growing darker as Jim merged onto I-95 North. His stomach rumbled, reminding him that neither of them had eaten since breakfast that morning. He glanced over at Liza, whose attention was taken up by the passing highway scenery.

He shifted into the far lane and gunned the engine. As he expected, Liza glanced at him, a startled expression on her face. He winked at her, then turned his attention back to the road. "Did Bill pack anything to eat in there?"

"Sure. There are some sandwiches on club rolls and, as if you might not have guessed, doughnuts."

"You can take the policeman out of the doughnut shop . . ."

She chuckled. "So what will it be? Ham and cheese or turkey and Swiss?"

"Surprise me."

In the periphery of his vision he watched her remove one of the sandwiches from the bag and begin to unfurl the plastic wrap covering it. The sandwich had been cut in half. She offered one end to him.

He glanced at her. "You've got to be kidding. You expect me to feed myself and drive at the same time?"

"Well, if you weren't going ninety miles an hour . . ."

"It's called keeping up with the flow of traffic." He eased off the gas pedal a little, but not enough to make much of a difference. "Have you no compassion for a starving man?"

She made a disgusted sound in her throat. "Oh, please." She lifted the sandwich to his mouth. "Here."

He turned his head slightly to bite into the sandwich she positioned next to his lips. He chewed, tasting neither ham nor turkey, but roast beef. When he could speak, he said, "You were holding out on me."

"You said to surprise you." She took a bite from her end of the sandwich. "Actually, I surprised myself, too. I didn't realize this was in there at first."

She raised the sandwich again. He took a second bite and grew pensive as he chewed. Now that they'd hopefully put some distance between themselves and Grady, other concerns came to the fore. While he enjoyed the easy banter they now shared, he also remembered her as she had been this morning—distant, and loath to explain the reason for her aloofness. He didn't intend to go to bed that night without knowing.

He took the third bite of sandwich she offered him, but refused another. "Are you ready to tell me what was bothering you this morning?"

She looked away from him and wiped her hands on a napkin. "That seems like a lifetime ago."

No kidding. Way back then they weren't running for their lives. "Was that a yes or a no?"

"Why did you do what you did last night?"

He didn't pretend not to know what she meant. "It was either that or carry you to my room and have my way with you in every way I wanted." He slid a glance in her direction to gauge her reaction to what he'd said, but it was impossible to tell in the darkened interior of the car. "I hadn't intended for things to go that far."

"Then that wasn't some line about wanting it to mean something?"

He snorted. She'd misunderstood him. He didn't mean that he *wanted* their lovemaking to mean something for him; he'd meant that it *would* mean something to him. Like crossing a threshold, a point of no return. He'd been half in love with her since the moment he met her. He'd never admitted that to himself before, but he knew it to be true. Why else would he have gone to such lengths to find her? Making love with her now would be like jumping off the big cliff while wearing a blindfold—an exhilarating ride, but no way to tell if he'd land safely in the water or splatter himself on the rocks.

"No, baby, it wasn't." He ran his hand down her arm until he found her fingers and laced them with his. He brought the back of her hand to his lips and kissed it. "Somehow I got the impression that we were both past the stage where all that mattered to us was satisfying mutual lust."

She pulled her hand from his. "So where does that leave us?"

Damned if he knew. He didn't know if he'd done himself good or ill by bringing up the events of the night before, but at least he knew she wasn't angry with him. That had to count for something.

Six hours later, after he'd yawned for the third time in fifteen minutes, Jim decided to call it a night. Save for a fifteen-minute pit stop a couple of hours ago, he'd been driving making good time up I-95 since he'd left

Bill's house. His goal had been to cross the North Carolina border, which he'd passed twenty minutes ago. At the next turnoff he'd hit one of the motels Bill told him about—some place out of the way where they'd accept cash and wouldn't ask too many questions.

He found the motel without problem, a seedy little place that in Manhattan would have charged by the hour. The building was a two-story brick number with a gallery running the length of the upper floor. Each second-floor room boasted its own small balcony that faced onto a large rectangular pool. While he would have preferred a more private arrangement, it would have to do.

After stopping at the rental office, he parked at the far end of the small lot reserved for renters. He turned to Liza. She'd been dozing for the past forty-five minutes. Despite the garish light of the neon sign that illuminated her, she, as usual, looked soft and peaceful in slumber.

Not wanting to wake her, he opened the glove compartment silently to extract the .22 revolver Bill had left there for him. Since he had no idea whether knowing he was armed would comfort Liza or freak her out, he figured the middle of the night was no time to find out. He stuck the gun in the front of his waistband and used his shirt as natural cover.

He snapped the glove compartment closed, then gently shook her shoulder. "Sweetheart, we're here."

It took her a few attempts to get her eyes opened and to focus on him. When she did, her eyes drifted shut and a lazy smile stretched across her face. "Jim."

He wished he knew what she'd been dreaming and how much clothing either of them had worn. "Yes, it's Jim. And you need to wake up long enough to go to bed."

Abruptly, she straightened up and looked around. "Where are we?"

"A little motel in the middle of nowhere."

"Please tell me Norman Bates doesn't own this place."

"I don't think so, but I'll stand guard while you take a shower."

She laughed. "My hero."

"That's me." At least he hoped so. "Now do me a favor and get your pretty little rear out of the car while I get the bags."

"Yes, sir."

Their room was on the second floor, third from the end. Not an ideal location, but it would have to do. He gave Liza the key to open the door while he carried up the suitcases. Once inside the room, he tapped the door closed with his foot and surveyed the furnishings. Industrial-grade faux wood headboard, nightstand, and dresser. The TV, which predated the use of a remote control, was bolted to the dresser, as if someone would actually steal it. The curtains reminded him of the ones Maria used to make play clothes for the Von Trapp children in *The Sound of Music*.

He set down the bags. "I love what they've done with the place—early tacky mixed with a hefty dose of drab."

Then his brain focused on the fact that there was only one bed in the room. Definitely not a king-sized, maybe not even a queen. Certainly not the double beds he'd been expecting.

He heard Liza's throaty laugh beside him. "I take it the sleeping arrangements weren't your idea."

"I can call down to the rental office to change our room, that is, if the receiver isn't bolted to the rest of the phone."

"Don't bother. We're both adults. I think you've

proven you have enough willpower not to ravish me in my sleep."

They'd have to see about that. Or maybe he'd do the honorable thing and bed down in the one uncomfortable-looking chair that sat in the corner.

She walked toward him, the same laughing expression on her face. Actually, he thought she was walking toward him, but she passed him by to pick up her suitcase. "I hope you don't mind me using the bathroom first. You can tell your friend Bill his ice chip trick doesn't work so well with women."

Jim shoved his hands in his pockets and rocked back on his heels as he watched her walk toward the bathroom. He wondered if she knew what effect the suggestive sway of her hips had on him. He supposed she did, considering that she glanced over her shoulder at him and winked.

Jim shook his head to clear it. If he didn't know better, he'd think she was feeding him back some of his own technique. Unlike him, she'd always been direct in what she wanted. He hadn't always obliged her, but he'd always known where he stood with her.

But that wink put him on the alert, not to mention revving his libido in a way that couldn't do either of them any good.

Jim sighed. He couldn't stand there contemplating the machinations of Liza Morrow's mind all night. Although he'd kept his eye on the road enough to be reasonably sure no one had followed them, he needed to secure their room, wash the grime and the weariness from his body, and grab enough rest not to fall asleep on the road in the morning.

He locked both the sliding glass door that led to the balcony and the room door, propping that lone chair under the knob. He rooted around in his own suitcase, located a T-shirt and a pair of lightweight sweats to change into. He pulled the gun from the front of his waistband and left it in the nightstand drawer. Then he sat on the bed to wait.

Liza patted a towel to her face, then smiled at her freshly scrubbed image in the cracked mirror above the sink. The expression on Jim's face when it dawned on him that there was only one bed had been priceless. She knew he was trying to do the right thing by her—what he thought was the right thing, which meant leaving her untouched as much as he was able. She realized he had something to work out within himself as far as being with her was concerned. She would probably consider his reluctance noble if some other woman was in this situation instead of her, but she'd had enough of this nonsense.

She wanted him and she was tired of waiting. With a killer on their trail, there was no guarantee that there would be a tomorrow to wait for. Tonight she needed him. She needed his heat and his strength and the release she knew she would find in his arms. She'd done her best to put on a brave face, to remain uncomplaining, though in truth she was scared out of her mind. She needed him, and tonight she would have her way, even if she had to resort to chicanery to get it. She'd worry about the consequences tomorrow.

After a brief shower, she toweled dry and slipped on the one nightgown she'd splurged on during her shopping trip in the city, a black silk number that dipped low between her breasts and was short enough to require matching panties. At the time, she'd had no ulterior motive in buying it, but at the present she was looking forward to seeing a different type of expression on Jim's face, both while she had it on and later.

She turned off the light and walked the small distance from the bathroom to stand by the side of the bed. Jim lay half on and half off the bed, as if he'd sat down, then decided to stretch out. Although his chest rose and fell in an even rhythm, she doubted he'd fallen asleep.

In a cheerful voice she announced, "Bathroom's free."

Jim's lashes fluttered and his head turned in her direction. A variety of expressions played out on his face—first surprise, then interest, then out-and-out lust. As if in slow motion, he sat up, never taking his eyes from her. He shook his head and muttered a single word. "Damn."

It took all her willpower not to laugh at his unguarded reaction to her. She'd never deluded herself about her physical charms. She'd always regarded herself as a pretty woman with the next best things to a boy's body. But her body heated knowing that despite her deficiencies she excited him.

He shook his head again. "What did you say?"

"The bathroom is free."

He stood and closed the gap between them. He stroked his index finger down the side of her face, drawing her gaze to his. "What are you doing, Liza?"

"I—I don't know what you mean."

He shook his head. "We haven't played games with each other so far. Let's not start now. And you damn sure don't have to resort to the use of lingerie to seduce me."

She tilted her head to one side. "Don't I? Tell me you weren't about to sleep in that chair or on the floor or maybe you'd hang from the ceiling. Anything but getting in that bed next to me."

He sighed and rested his forehead against hers. She could sense the indecision in him, whether to level with her or remain silent. She hoped to make up his mind for him. "Tell me."

He lifted his head and with a rueful smile cupped

her cheek in his palm. "Sweetheart, don't you realize you've been right about me from the beginning? I'm not exactly the go-to guy when it comes to forming permanent attachments. The only relationships I've had can be counted in days or weeks, not months or years. At least, I've never lied or made promises I didn't intend to keep. I've never been unfaithful to anyone who expected me to be true. I've never tried to force a woman into my bed or tried to hold on to one once she wanted to leave. I've never worked at being with anyone. It's always been easier just to walk away."

"Are you trying to warn me off?"

"You're a practical woman. You should appreciate a risk analysis."

"For my benefit or yours?" She sighed and took a step away from him. Maybe he was right. Maybe she'd been feeling sorry for herself and turned to him now simply to make herself feel better. Just hours ago they'd agreed that sex alone wouldn't solve anything between them. She knew he cared for her, but maybe this was his way of telling her that, despite his feelings, he found any sort of relationship between them untenable.

And despite her own feelings, she couldn't fault him for being honest with her. She looked away as, unbidden, the sting of tears burned her eyes. "Fine, Jim. You win. I'll see you in the morning."

Jim watched her as she slowly backed away from him. He had to be crazy for thinking what was in his mind. He felt himself teetering again on that precipice, caught between what was safe and what he truly wanted. Tonight didn't scare him, but what of tomorrow? What happened when the novelty wore off or she discovered she wanted something else? What if, as his brother claimed, he was simply a coward who had never risked anything in his life, the sort of man who would run away rather than fight for what he wanted?

With a hand on her arm he pulled her back to him. He sat on the bed, drawing her to stand between his parted legs. He took both of his hands in hers. "Is this how you want our first time to be, in a seedy hotel room in a bed that will probably give us both cooties?"

"It's not our first time."

Why did she have to be so damn literal? "All right, our first time when we know each other's real names."

She folded her arms and shifted her weight. "No, actually, I'd prefer the Plaza and a glass of champagne or at the very least a bathroom that didn't dispense condoms for two bucks a pop. But I don't have any of those things right now. Truthfully the only thing in this room that matters to me is you."

Sighing, he wrapped his arms around her legs and rested his cheek against her hip. "This is it, Liza. Understand that. There's no turning back."

"Don't you think I know that?"

He supposed he did. He supposed they'd been heading toward this moment as soon as she threw her drink in his face at Dani's party. He was tired of fighting it.

Her fingers went to the thin straps of her gown and pushed them from her shoulders. The flimsy material slithered to the ground, leaving her bare except for a tiny, nearly see-through triangle of the same gauzy material.

His gaze wandered over her, his resolve melting as his body hardened. "Oh, hell," he muttered. Leaning back, he pulled her down on top of him.

Sixteen

She shrieked and hit his shoulder as she landed on top of him. She leaned up, bracing one arm against his chest, and brushed the hair from her face. "Some warning would be nice the next time you're planning on doing that."

"Now what would be the fun in that?" His hands scrubbed up and down her bare back. "Come down here and kiss me."

She smiled down at him, the grin of a woman with devilment on her mind. "Sure." But instead of pressing her mouth to his, she unfastened the top button of his shirt and touched her lips to the skin she'd exposed. She leaned back, her grin broader this time. "How was that?"

"I've had better," he teased back.

Her fingers quickly unfastened his next two buttons to kiss the center of his chest. "And that?"

"You're getting warmer." So was he. His groin tightened and his heartbeat picked up. It didn't help that she straddled him now, as she undid the last few buttons on his shirt. He could feel the warm, moist heat of her even through the protection of his clothing. He wanted to feel it wrapped around him, and he doubted he could endure much of this sweet torture she seemed intent on inflicting on him.

His breath sucked in and his fingers at her hips flexed as her tongue darted into his navel. She leaned back and tossed her head, to shake her hair from her face. "Am I still getting warmer?"

"Liza." He'd meant that one word as a warning, but even to his own ears it sounded like an invitation. For an instant their gazes locked, her sherry-colored one to his hazel. Such an intense feeling of anticipation gripped him that it took all his willpower not to press her down on the bed and show her how that ravishment she liked to talk about was accomplished.

But before he had time to affect that plan or any plan, she scooted down on his body to sit on his thighs. Her teeth clamped down on her lower lip as her fingers tugged at his belt. In a few instants she had him free. A deep groan rumbled up through his chest as her fingers circled the head of his shaft and squeezed.

He called her name again, a rough growl of both pleasure and frustration.

The siren's smile was back on her face. "Having a little trouble coping with being at my mercy?"

No, not trouble, exactly, unless you counted the shallowness of his breathing and the layer of perspiration that now pebbled his skin. But more than anything, he ached to be inside her, to have those long legs of hers wrapped around him. Nothing else mattered.

But she slipped from the bed to kneel on the floor between his legs. She tugged at his pant legs. He obliged her by lifting himself up so that she could remove them. In a few seconds she'd divested him of the rest of his clothing.

He leaned up to pull her to him, shrugging out of his

shirt as he went. He reached for her, but she brushed his hands away. "Not yet."

Then her mouth was on him, like liquid heat moving over his skin. His eyes squeezed shut and his teeth clenched from the pure pleasure of it. He was too close to the brink already. With his hands under her arms he lifted her to straddle him again, his erection nestled at the junction of her thighs. Close enough to what he wanted to intensify the ache in him, but not close enough.

"Let's try this again."

She laughed as he turned them so that she lay on her back and he lay on his side next to her. Actually, it was more of a giggle. Never would he have imagined hearing such a sound from her. Propping his head on his hand, he looked down at her, while his free hand roamed over her waist, her rib cage, and higher to cover her breast. "How are you doing?"

She smiled up at him. "Come down here and kiss me."

He smiled, too, hearing her repeat his words from before. He behaved as obediently as she had. He lowered his head and took her nipple into his mouth. She gasped and her body arched toward him. Her knee lifted and she leaned her leg against his thigh. He could feel the restlessness in her body, the same turmoil that racked his own.

He ran his hand down her body to caress her buttocks, first over her panties and then beneath.

Moaning, she writhed against him. "Jim."

Hearing the urgency in that one breathless word, he pushed the silky material from her hips and down her body. He didn't doubt she was ready for him, more than ready, but he couldn't resist sampling the sweet juices that flowed between her thighs. He pushed her legs apart and brought his mouth down to her. Her hips rocked against him as his tongue flicked against her sensitive flesh.

He sheathed himself and knelt between her thighs. Her lips parted expectantly, and she looked up at him with eyes that had turned an incredible burgundy color. Her legs circled around his waist, drawing him down to her. "Jim!"

He sank against her, bracing most of his weight on his arms, but his entire body shivered as hers enveloped him. Her arms wound around him and her fingers gripped his back. He moved inside her slowly, reveling in the exquisite sensation of having her body wrapped so intimately around his own. He buried his face against her neck to rain soft, moist kisses against the length of her throat.

She called his name again, this time in agitation, and her hips rocked against his. Obviously, she wanted him to pick up the pace. He couldn't do that. He'd never felt like this before, not even the first time with her, wanting the journey even more than the destination. Holding her, loving her, letting her love him, that could go on forever—or as long as human endurance allowed. He lifted his head and stroked her damp hair from her face. "Not this time, baby."

But knowing she probably couldn't bear his weight comfortably much longer, he turned them so that they lay side by side facing each other, their legs tangled together. "Better?" he asked.

"No." She struck his shoulder with her fist. "You're . . . driving me . . . crazy."

A wicked smile spread across his face. "I know." From the restless way she moved against him, she wasn't too far from it. Truthfully, neither was he. Every moment inside her drew him inexorably closer to his own release.

She moved to hit him again, but he caught her hand and brought her palm to his lips. "Look at me, baby." He wanted to see her face, see the expression in her eyes as a deepening rapture claimed her.

She did as he asked, regarding him through half-closed lids.

His hand roved lower to cant her hips toward him. He thrust into her again. This time she trembled in his arms and her back arched. Her breath came in short gasps and sighs. Her eyes narrowed, but he could still see the look of entreaty in them. "Please."

He couldn't wait anymore, not that he really wanted to. He crushed her to him as he thrust into her again and again. Her eyes squeezed shut and her body contracted around his. Her nails dug into his shoulders.

Unable to hold back, he let his own orgasm overtake him, arching his back and tearing a ragged groan from his throat.

He lay back, dragging in air, and pulled her on top of him. For a long time, they lay together, silent, recovering. When he could move, he settled them the same way beneath the covers. She was so quiet that he might have worried about her were it not for the string of moist kisses she left along his collarbone.

His fingers tangled in her hair. "How are you doing?"

She sighed and shifted against him. "Fine."

He smiled. "I know you are, but how are you feeling?"

She lifted her head and cast him a droll look. "Don't start with the corny jokes and questions, okay? Can't you just let me savor the moment?"

He scrubbed his hand up and down her back. "Is that what you were doing?"

"Weren't you?"

"Kinda sorta."

"And since you asked, I'd give it a ninety-nine, but I can't dance to it."

"At the risk of sounding like a colossal egotist, why not one hundred?"

"This conversation." She laid her cheek on his chest. "I don't usually do this."

"Do what?"

"Cuddle."

He chuckled. She'd spoken as if she were discussing some dread disease. "I can turn over and snore if that would make you feel better."

Her fingers gripped his biceps. "No."

Her unguarded responses pleased him, though he wondered at it. "Why do I rate special treatment?"

"I haven't had the best luck in picking men in general, but they've all been pretty pathetic in the romance department. It's kind of hard to want to snuggle with a man who's just disappointed you. I know some women do it to feel like they've gotten *something* out of the encounter. Me, I'd rather the guy went home."

At the moment, he wouldn't mind rounding up all those men, whoever they were, and lining them up for his own personal firing squad. "So, you're telling me I'm the best of a very mediocre lot?"

"If it makes your ego feel any better, I think you'd be the best even if the lot weren't quite so mediocre."

She misunderstood him. He didn't need his ego stroked; he only wanted to make her happy. He squeezed her waist. "If it makes your ego feel any better, the same goes for you."

She lifted her head and cast him a skeptical look. "You don't have to say that."

He ran his thumb along her lower lip. "It's true. You make me feel things I haven't felt with any other woman." She made him want things he'd decided not to want. "I—"

He supposed he should be glad that her kiss cut off what he was about to say. Otherwise he would have blurted out the truth—that he was falling in love with her. He wasn't sure either of them was ready to deal with that right now, not when the most important item on their agenda was making sure they both stayed alive.

For the present, he concentrated on the warmth of her kiss and in a while the heat of her body as it enveloped him.

Jim woke up as the sun began to brighten the morning sky. It took a moment for him to recognize his surroundings, but he knew immediately whose head still rested against his shoulder. He brushed her hair from her face and kissed her temple. She stirred a little but settled down. After the last few nights when she didn't get much sleep, he didn't want to wake her.

Normally an early riser, he knew there was no way he'd get back to sleep himself, especially since last night's lovemaking still resonated in his body. Having her nestled so intimately with him was no way to reinforce his resolve not to wake her.

He extricated himself from her and rose from the bed. Nude, he padded to the bathroom to relieve himself, shower, and brush his teeth. Those important tasks accomplished, he figured he'd check on Paul. The older man might not be awake yet, but he'd answer. Jim found his pants, put them on, and went out on the balcony to call.

He leaned his elbows on the chest-high railing waiting for Paul to answer, giving him a clear view of the dry and discolored liner where the pool advertised in the rental office window used to be. Paul picked up on the fourth ring, just before the voice mail would have come on.

"Jim, I've been going out of my mind waiting for you to call. How's Liza?"

"Nice to hear from you, too. She's fine. Still sleeping."

"Good. She looked tired the last time I saw her."

Jim resisted the urge to remind him that the last time

he saw Liza she'd been half worried out of her mind about him. Tired hadn't entered the picture. "Where are you?"

"Still in the hospital. They're letting me out this morning."

"Any news?"

"What the hell do I know? I'm in the hospital."

Now he understood the reason for Paul's crankiness. No one including him had told Paul anything. "Let me see what I can find out, and I'll get back to you."

He disconnected the call and dialed Bill. "This better be good," said the sleepy voice that answered the phone.

"You tell me."

"Jim. How's it going? I was hoping I'd hear from you this morning. A little later this morning, though."

"How'd the sleepover at my house go last night?"

"Grady was a no-show and no one's located him yet. Word was passed to the local airports and the state police, but no luck so far. It's like the guy disappeared into thin air."

"Great." Although he hadn't held out much hope for the sting operation the police had going at his house, he'd hoped someone would have spotted him by now. Maybe he'd been pulled over for a faulty taillight. Anything. He was a convicted felon who'd already violated his parole just by leaving New York State. Any number of people had to be looking for him. "What does that mean?"

"Who knows? He could just be holed up somewhere till the heat dies down."

"How likely do you think that is?" He could tell by Bill's silence that the answer was "not very." And, to Jim's mind, if Grady hadn't been picked up at the airport, he'd probably hit the road before the word trickled down to the highway patrol to look for him.

"How's your lady holding up?"

Jim ignored his friend's question, as a sudden unease gripped him that had little to do with the contents of their telephone call. The fine hairs on the back of his neck bristled and he was certain someone or someones stood behind him. He didn't bother to tell Bill of his suspicion, considering he wasn't even sure what town he was in for Bill to send help. He only knew he'd been foolish enough to leave the one weapon he possessed in the nightstand beside the bed. How much damage could a three-ounce cell phone do unless it hit someone in the eye?

"Look, I gotta go." He heard Bill calling to him in the instant before he clicked off the phone, but he didn't care. Right now, he needed to worry about getting back inside to Liza and getting the two of them somewhere safe. That is, if he weren't already too late. Where could an intruder have gotten out here from, except through their own room?

He couldn't let himself dwell on that now. He had to stay focused on the present threat, not what might await him inside. Slowly, he lifted his arms from the railing. Maybe if he spun around quickly, he could at least have the benefit of surprise on his side.

But before he had the chance to move, an unfamiliar male voice said, "It's about time you noticed I was here."

Seventeen

Jim turned around slowly, his fists clenched. The voice sounded too young to be Grady's, and if anything was laced with humor, not hatred. He saw the man in the periphery of his vision: tall, dark skinned, closer to his age than Grady's, leaning against the wall to the left of the glass door leading to the room.

"Relax. If I'd wanted to kill you, you'd both be dead right now."

"That's a comforting thought. Now who the hell are you?"

The man extended a muscular arm toward him. "Tim Wyatt. Your friend Jackson sent me."

Jim shook the hand offered. "How did you know where we were?"

"I've been with you since New York. You asked Jackson to look into your girlfriend's former fiancé"

Yeah, and had told Jackson not to waste his time. "What did you find out?"

"Not much. Dad and sonny are squeaky clean. Mom ran off a year ago. I don't know what happened to her. I broke off the search when you guys decided to leave town. I can pick it up if you like."

Jim shook his head. There was no need. It was enough to know that no one Liza knew personally had been involved in wanting to hurt her.

But something the other man said bothered him. "Wait a minute. You've been with us since New York? Why didn't you let me know you were here?"

"I was under orders not to make myself known, unless something happened, and then only to you. This is the first time I've caught you alone since Grady made his motives known."

Jim could understand that. Aside from the brief time in the hospital when they were separated, he'd kept Liza with him at all times. Even before then, they'd been joined at the hip while awake. An unpleasant thought grabbed him, remembering the time two nights ago when he'd suspected he was not alone. "You watched us," he accused through clenched teeth.

Wyatt smiled in a way that neither confirmed nor denied anything. "I take it you people are headed back to New York?"

Jim sighed, willing the outrage he felt to dissipate. He should have learned his lesson way back with Mrs. Obermeyer that things done out of doors are likely to be observed. That didn't really make him feel any better. He supposed he'd live, but he never wanted Liza to find out that someone had been watching her at such an intimate moment.

In answer to Wyatt's question he said, "Yes. My brother has a place out on Montauk."

"You mean *in* Montauk. Folks up there say in Montauk."

Jim shoved his hands in his pockets and his gaze narrowed. What kind of pain in the ass had Jackson saddled him with? A Peeping Tom and a linguistics expert rolled into one? He was tempted to tell the guy to go to hell, but if there was a chance his presence would help keep Liza safe, he knew he couldn't do that now. But later. A feral grin spread across his face. "Whatever."

"How do you want to explain me?"

"I don't. Not unless I have to." He could imagine Liza's reaction, finding out he'd hired a bodyguard to look after her. Besides, he still hoped Grady would be apprehended before they reached the house *in* Montauk.

"Are you sure that's how you want to play it?"

Despite the voice in his head warning him that Liza would be furious if she learned of his deception, he said, "Yes. At least for the time being. I'll let you know if I change my mind."

Wyatt shot him a look that told him exactly what he thought of his plan, but Jim didn't care. "You didn't spend the whole night out here, did you?"

"Nah, I'm in the room next to yours." He nodded to the left. "I was out here debating whether to throw stones at the window when you came out."

Jim gritted his teeth. That's just what he needed—another wise guy. "There's a diner we passed on the way off the highway. I figured we'd grab some breakfast and get on the road."

"I'll be right behind you. Look for a tan Explorer."

Jim nodded. "Give us about twenty minutes." Then he went inside to wake Liza.

"Wake up, sleepyhead."

Slowly, Liza opened her eyes, but she didn't want to. She was enjoying the warmth of her bed and the lingering afterglow of the lovemaking she and Jim had shared the night before. Even without looking, she knew he was no longer beside her, not the way he had been last night. Her gaze focused on him sitting on the edge of the bed facing her.

She offered him a sleepy smile. "Hi."

"Hi yourself." He brushed his knuckles along her cheek. "You planning to get out of that bed any time soon?"

She sighed, letting her shoulders droop. If she could have her way, she'd pull him back into bed with her and keep him there all day. But that was not to be. The fact that he'd already dressed before he woke her spoke to the urgency with which he wanted to leave. "I suppose."

"Good. I want to be in New York by tonight."

She sat up and brushed the hair from her face. "Anything new since last night?" she asked, hoping to hear Grady had been caught and the whole episode was over.

"Not really."

Her eyes narrowed as she scrutinized his face. She didn't know what about his answer disturbed her. Maybe it was the fact that he hadn't really looked at her when he said that. Or maybe it was her suspicion that he kept something from her deliberately. If so, it wouldn't be the first time and she didn't like it.

She'd had enough of that from her childhood. To her mother, everything was a secret, especially the truth of what happened to her father. Whenever Liza brought up the subject, her mother would either dissemble or, as Liza got older, launch into one of her vaunted rules of selecting husbands, rules she'd obviously neglected in picking her own man. When she was little, she assumed her mother sought to protect her from unpleasantness. As an adult she realized that her mother sought to protect herself from having to answer for anything. That's why it took her so long to try to find Paul. She'd doubted her mother had in any way sought to tell her the truth.

Oddly enough with Jim, the closer they got, the more he seemed intent on keeping things from her. She didn't understand that, but she knew it was true. She'd had no idea where they were actually headed until she confronted him, nor had he informed her of the maneuvers he'd planned at Bill's house. And now, if her radar weren't completely off, he held back something more significant.

Well, if he did, she thought she knew what it might be. "Did you hear from Paul?"

"He's fine. They should be letting him out of the hospital this morning."

"No luck with Grady?"

"None. They're still looking for him."

That exhausted her two subjects of concern and she hadn't found out anything. Frustrated, she ran her hand through her hair. "It'll only take me a minute to get ready."

An hour later, after a breakfast of pancakes for him and a western omelet for her, Jim pulled onto the road that would lead them back to the highway. He glanced over at Liza. She'd been unusually quiet since he woke her that morning. Damn her ability to distance herself from him so easily. The only reason he could think of for her aloofness was the fact that she suspected he hadn't leveled with her.

Speaking of the reason for her aloofness, he checked the rearview mirror. Wyatt was behind him, far enough back not to look like an obvious tail, but at this hour of the morning there wasn't much traffic to provide cover. With any luck, Liza would remain as blissfully ignorant of his presence as they both had been until that morning.

Or so he hoped. But they hadn't been driving for more than an hour before he caught her looking over her shoulder at the traffic behind them. Fearing the worst, he asked, "What's wrong?"

"Do you see the beige SUV a few cars back?"

"Yes."

"I think it's following us. It was parked at the diner."

"How do you know?"

She shrugged. "The license plate. The numbers, 5309, like the song."

He hadn't noticed that himself. Who the hell looked at strangers' license plates? He could feel her eyes on him. "Why aren't you more surprised?"

There was no hope for it. He should have known better. "The man driving that car is named Tim Wyatt. He's a private investigator."

"A bodyguard?"

"More or less." He darted another glance at her and noted the grim set of her jaw and the flash of anger in her eyes.

"Why didn't you tell me about this more or less bodyguard? Was it some macho overprotective thing or was it a let's-not-scare-Liza-to-death thing?"

"It was a hope-she-doesn't-find out-what-a schmuck-I-am thing. Wyatt claims he's been with us since New York. I'm a photographer. I'm paid to be observant and I observed nothing."

"If it makes you feel any better, neither did I. Then again, *I* wasn't looking."

"Thanks a lot."

"You're welcome, but consider this, would you want some guy on the job who couldn't keep you from spotting him?"

"I suppose not."

Turning her attention to the scenery outside her window, she fell silent for a long minute, long enough for him to call her name and place a hand on her thigh in concern.

"Don't keep things from me, Jim. I don't need that kind of safeguarding. I don't want it. I can handle whatever is happening without falling apart. What I can't handle is dishonesty."

"So if you ask me if your butt looks fat in a particular pair of pants, I'm supposed to tell you the truth."

He saw her smile in the periphery of his vision. "No, then you can lie. I'm talking about the important stuff, and you know it."

He squeezed her thigh. He knew what she meant and he knew what she wanted from him, but that clarity didn't make it any easier to comply. The more he came to care for her, the stronger the urge to shield her from danger and unpleasantness became.

Unfortunately that macho overprotective thing as she called it had been drummed into him since childhood. Even knowing his brother Eamon had gotten himself into several different kinds of trouble with Jake over the same issue didn't make it any easier to let go. Maybe if he'd concentrated on developing actual relationships with women as opposed to cultivating bed partners, someone would have knocked that impulse out of him already. But now that someone had activated the programming, he found it difficult to shut it off.

"When do I get to meet this paragon of investigative virtue?"

If Jim had something to say about it, the answer would be never. "When we stop for food, I guess." They'd demolished Bill's stakeout feast the first night. "I don't want to stop too long, though."

"Why are you so hell-bent on getting to New York tonight?"

He grinned. "That's an I'll-show-you-when-we-get-there thing. You'll just have to trust me on this."

They didn't stop until it just past two o'clock. By then, her back ached, her stomach grumbled, and if she didn't find an unoccupied bathroom soon, there was going to be trouble.

The rest stop featured a McDonald's, a Roy Rogers's, and a Nathan's all in the same building. While Jim parked near the entrance, she looked around for the beige SUV. She spotted it pulling into a space a few cars down. Both she and Jim got out of the car and met at the trunk. They walked to the entrance of the building to await the other man's approach.

He looked more or less like she expected him to, tall, muscular, dressed in a pair of jeans and a cotton shirt that stretched across a broad chest. His walk said, as a former coworker of hers used to say, don't start none and there won't be none. With some humor she noted that the nearer the man got to them the tighter Jim's grip on her waist became.

The first thing Wyatt said after Jim made the introductions was directed solely at Jim. "Glad to see you changed your mind."

"*I* didn't."

Wyatt's eyebrow's lifted a fraction of an inch as he regarded her. "I see."

Liza wondered what that was about, but figured she'd have plenty of time to ask about it later. Right now she had more pressing concerns. As they entered the building, she spotted a sign for restrooms to the left. "I don't know about you two, but I see the first stop on my itinerary." She nodded in the appropriate direction.

Flanked by a man on each side, she made her way to the ladies' room. At the doorway she turned to face them both. She looked from one to the other, both of whom seemed more willing to follow her in than let her go alone. *Men!* She winked at Jim. "You boys try to behave while I'm gone."

A few minutes later, Liza stood in front of the crowded ladies' room mirror and surveyed her image. It would have been nice if someone had told her her hair was one step away from beehive status from the wind rushing past with the top down. She probably should have realized it herself, but for most of today, her appearance had been the last thing on her mind.

Ever since Jim revealed he'd hired some bodyguard to watch over her, her sense of dread had ratcheted up a notch. Oddly, she found Wyatt's presence more disconcerting than comforting. Up to today, she'd chosen to believe that Grady didn't really pose that much of a threat to her. She'd chosen to believe that they'd left their troubles back in Florida, like Jim said. She knew it wasn't logical, but every mile they passed, every hour they spent out of danger, she'd relaxed.

But if Jim felt he needed this man to help protect her, she couldn't afford to indulge in that self-delusion any longer.

She combed her hair, reapplied her lipstick, and left the bathroom. She found the two men exactly where she'd left them, though she suspected each had taken a turn in the men's room during her absence.

Jim slung his arm around her shoulders, leading her toward the area where food was sold. "What'll it be, fatty hot dogs, fatty burgers, or fatty chicken?"

"Fatty fries."

Fifteen minutes later, the three of them sat at one of the tables that lined the windows, a variety of fast food spread out before them.

Liza took a sip of her soda and set her cup on the table. "So, where do we stand?"

"As far as I can tell, we aren't being followed."

That came from Wyatt. At least that was something. But she noted the way he and Jim exchanged a meaningful look before Jim nodded.

Wyatt leaned closer to her across the table. "The San Pedro police found where Grady had been staying on the island. Unfortunately the owner of the house won't be needing it anymore either."

Eighteen

Jim watched as the color drained from Liza's face. She'd asked him not to keep her in the dark about anything, and in some ways he agreed with her desire. They needed to remain vigilant, even if the distance they gained gave them a sense of security—which was probably false. Yet he didn't relish seeing her afraid either. He wound his arm around her waist and gave it a squeeze.

"Then where is he?" she asked. Strangely, the color started to return to her face and she relaxed against his hold. "Not that I'm interested in seeing him, mind you, but if he's so hell-bent on retribution, you'd think he'd hurry up and get it over with."

Wyatt nodded in agreement. "The longer he's out there, the better chance he'll be caught."

"Let's hope so," Jim said. "With any luck, he'll be looking for us in the city, and the NYPD has already been alerted."

That's what Jim hoped, but he harbored an increasing sense of foreboding that Grady was neither as linear nor as lacking in cleverness as they assumed. Aside from that, if he was so intent on avenging the loss of his son on Liza, why didn't he do so in New York? Why didn't he snatch her instead of hunting around in her apartment? The only possibility that came to Jim's mind was that she'd gotten out too quickly for him to do anything except under the watchful eyes of both the police and the fire department. Even that thought didn't hold up to too much scrutiny, though he remembered thinking at the time that the devastation in her apartment looked like it could have been done in anger.

It was a puzzle for which he had no solutions. He consoled himself with the knowledge that, unless Grady followed them, there was no way he could know where they were.

He took a last sip from his drink. "Maybe we should get back on the road."

Sensing a lack of forward momentum, Liza opened her eyes and straightened up. She'd been dozing the last few hours since it turned dark, falling in and out of sleep as Jim drove. It took her a moment to recognize her surroundings—the driveway beside Eamon's house. She glanced over at Jim, who regarded her with a sleepy, yet satisfied expression. "What time is it?"

"A little after midnight." He brushed a lock of hair from her face. "How are you feeling?"

The man was insane. He'd driven all day and into the night while she'd slept and he wanted to know how she was feeling? Considering the speed at which he'd completed the trip, grateful to be alive was the first thought that sprang to mind. Her second thought was predicated on the rumbling in her stomach. They hadn't bothered to stop for dinner. Or if they had she'd slept through it. "Hungry."

"Glad to hear it," he said, but from the way he said it, she doubted he was talking about food.

"Why are we sitting here?"

"Wyatt wanted to check the house first. Make sure no one but the daddy longlegs were waiting for us."

"Oh." She tried to keep her expression as neutral as possible, but doubted she succeeded. Despite her nap, fatigue still pulled at her, making any sort of dissembling too much effort.

Besides, she'd asked for him not to spare her the unvarnished truth, whatever that might be. She didn't really want to change that, she'd simply prefer not to react to news the way she had that afternoon at lunch. Hearing Jim's neighbor's fate, she felt her head swimming and she was in serious danger of throwing up. To make it worse, her distress had escaped neither man's attention. She didn't want either of them, but Jim especially, to think that if worse came to worst she'd fall apart on them.

The front door to the house opened and Wyatt came out. He jogged over to the car and bent to look in the window. "All clear."

Jim winked at her. "Let's go."

The moment they got up to the guest bedroom on the second floor, Jim dropped their bags to the floor, shut the door by leaning his back against it, and pulled her to him. His mouth, warm, moist, demanding, claimed hers. She melted against him as his arms closed around her. She gave herself up to that kiss, reveling in his passion and sending him back the same.

When he finally pulled back, he kissed the tip of her nose. "I've been waiting all day to do that."

Looking up at his handsome face and devilish smile, she said, "Glad you didn't wait any longer. Is that why you were in such a hurry to get here?"

He shook his head. "Not exactly. I wanted the chance to make love to you in a decent bed, if that's okay with you."

"You won't get any objections from me."

"Good." He lifted her into his arms and spun them around. She laughed and clung to him as he carried her to the bed. He set her down and sat beside her. "How about some champagne?"

"I'd love some. Let's call up the nonexistent all-night liquor store in town and have them send over a bottle of their finest."

"O ye of little faith. It's already taken care of." He twisted around to face the nightstand beside the bed. He turned back with two glasses in his hands. A moment later he reached back for a bottle of Perrier Jouet—wet, she assumed, after having been chilled on ice—and began tearing the foil from the cage.

"How did you manage this?"

"I called the same neighbor who got the lights turned on and begged another favor."

She lifted one glass and then the other for him to fill. "Why?"

He set the bottle down in the ice bucket. When he turned around, he took one glass from her fingers and clinked it with the other. "It's not the Plaza, baby, but it's the best I could do at the moment."

For a moment she watched him as he brought his glass to his lips and drank. He'd remembered her cast-off comment about what she wanted and tried to make it real for her. Under the circumstances, the man had to be out of his mind. Nonetheless, it was the sweetest thing any man had ever done for her.

Laughing, she threw her arms around his neck, managing to spill some of her champagne on him. "You are a crazy person."

He grinned. "So they tell me. Drink up, then take your clothes off."

She brought her glass to her lips and sipped deeply.

Then she lifted it in salute to him. "Subtle, Fitzgerald. Real subtle."

He kissed her nose. "Real wet. I thought you might appreciate a hot bath before we hit the hay."

Now that she thought about it, a bath didn't sound half bad. Especially since she knew the tub in the bathroom adjoining this bedroom housed a Jacuzzi. "Lead on, MacDuff."

"How about I call you when the water's ready?"

"Sounds like a plan."

As he rose from the bed, she brought her glass to her lips and drained its contents. She put down her glass and began to strip. Without waiting for his call, she padded to the bathroom nude and barefoot. She stopped in the doorway, her hand braced on the door frame to watch the scenery: Jim fully nude, fully erect, and 100 percent gorgeous male.

For a moment, they simply stared at one another. "Come here, sweetheart," he said finally.

His voice was low and husky and his open arms inviting. She slipped into them and let him pull her to him. She lifted her face for his kiss—slow, erotic, made more so by the pressure of his erection against her belly. If this kept up, they'd be lucky to make it back to the bed, never mind the tub.

Perhaps sensing her thoughts, he pulled away from her. Taking both of her hands in his, he led her closer to the tub. They settled in the warm fragrant water, he on one end, and she on the other.

Jim sank back with a huge sigh and closed his eyes. "God, this feels like heaven."

She laughed and flicked the switch that turned on the Jacuzzi. The water pulsed with heat and bubbles surfaced. "How's that?"

"Mmm." His eyes opened and his intense gaze fastened on her. "All I need now is you." He curled a finger at her, beckoning her.

"I'll have to think about it," she teased. "Once a girl's got a good air jet going, men become extraneous."

He leaned up, grasped her wrist, and pulled her toward him. Once he had her arranged the way he wanted, with her sitting between his open legs, her back against his chest, he relaxed against the rim of the tub. "Much better."

She agreed, especially since his hands started a leisurely exploration of her body, roving over her breasts, her belly, between her thighs in ways intended to stimulate. She leaned her head back against his shoulder and closed her eyes.

His lips touched down on the side of her throat as his hands rose to cradle her breasts in his palms. He squeezed her nipples between his thumbs and index fingers. "How's that?"

Her breath sucked in and her body became restless. "M-much better."

He chuckled and his laughter reverberated through her, too. One hand strayed lower, over her rib cage, her belly, and lower, to slip between her thighs. Her neck arched and she cried out his name.

"I'm here, baby," he whispered against her shoulder.

It was too much. The heat and effervescence of the water, the warmth of his breath fanning her skin, and the skillful movements of his hands on her excited flesh pushed her over the edge. Her eyes squeezed shut and her body trembled, as pleasure washed over her like several powerful waves rushing up on the sand.

Still, he held her as she dragged in air and her tremors subsided. His lips rained kisses along her throat and collarbone. She turned her head to lean her cheek against his shoulder as best she could. Smiling, she said, "You did it again."

His hand cupped her shoulder. "Did what?"

She twisted around so that she faced him. "Indulging me without allowing me to indulge you. Unless you've got a scuba mask under there I don't know about."

He chuckled, but there was only heat, not humor, in his laughter. "Oh, I fully intend to let you make it up to me at a later date." His avid gaze roved from her face to her breast and lower before returning. "But right now I ache to be inside you. Indulge me in that."

His mouth closed over hers, and his arms pulled her flush with his body as he stood, drawing them both out of the water. She wrapped her arms around his neck and her legs around his waist, as the kiss grew more heated, more out of control. Her eyes closed, she felt a sense of motion and knew where he was headed. A few moments later, he lay down on his back on top of the covers and pulled her down on top of him.

She broke the kiss and sat up. His erection pressed against her belly. She stroked him with her hands, delighting in the groan that rumbled up from his chest and the way his eyes drifted closed in pleasure. She knew Jake kept a supply of condoms in the nightstand drawer in case any of her guests forgot. She found one now and rolled it onto him. She lifted herself up on her knees and guided him inside her.

With a more guttural groan, his eyes opened half-mast to watch her. But when he reached for her, she laced her fingers with his and pressed them back against the mattress. "Oh, no, you don't. For once we are going to do things my way."

"Whatever you say, baby."

"Mr. Agreeable," she teased, but there was a hitch in her voice as she started to move over him, slowly at first, but soon with greater urgency. Her mouth found his for a soul-stirring kiss that left them both out of breath and precariously near to climax. His fingers, still entwined with hers, rose to guide her hips to an abandoned rhythm. Her neck arched and her head lolled back on her shoulders as the tempest built inside her a maelstrom of heat, pleasure, and tension that threatened to explode.

She felt the tension in him also, as his hands left hers to grip her hips more tightly. His chest rose and fell with sharp, shallow breaths and perspiration pebbled his skin. She leaned down and circled her tongue around his nipple. His fingers flexed and his eyes squeezed shut. His body spasmed beneath hers, triggering her own orgasm. She clung to him as her body shivered in its rapture.

His arms closed around her, banding her to him. She laid her cheek against his chest, recovering.

After a few minutes she felt Jim shifting beneath her. "You're doing it again," he said in a voice remarkably reminiscent of her own.

She lifted her head and looked down into his smiling face. "Doing what?"

He tugged on a strand of her hair. "Cuddling with me."

"So I noticed. Do you mind if we continue under the covers?"

"Not at all."

Once they resettled themselves under the protection of a sheet and summer-weight blanket, Liza leaned up on one elbow. "Can I ask you something?"

The hands that had been conducting a leisurely stroll over her body stilled. "Here we go."

"What is that supposed to mean?"

"I find whenever a woman asks you if she can ask you a question she wants an answer you don't want to give her under any circumstances."

He appeared to be teasing her, but she noticed the smile on his lips was not reflected in his eyes. She wondered if he'd already guessed what her question might be and this was his way of warning her off. If so, she'd let him off easy. "You don't have to answer if you don't want to. In fact, forget it. It's none of my business, anyway." She laid her head on his shoulder.

Hearing the resignation in Liza's voice, Jim sighed. He knew what she wanted, and he supposed if anyone deserved an explanation from him, she did. That didn't mean he felt prepared to give her one, or that he even knew the answer fully himself.

His fingers tangled in her hair, drawing her head back so that he could see her face. "What did you want to ask me?"

She regarded him a long time, so long that he thought she'd changed her mind. Finally, she said, "Why did you tell me you had no interest in finding your mother when obviously you do?"

Nineteen

Jim sighed again, wishing he could avoid this line of conversation, but knowing he couldn't. "My mother has been dead for twenty years."

"You know what I mean. Your birth mother. The woman whose picture you keep in an envelope on your bookshelf. The same envelope that contains a private investigator's report telling you where she lives. Believe me, I know what one of those looks like. Why did you look for her, if, as you claim, you're not interested in finding her?"

He shrugged. "I was curious."

"And your curiosity was satisfied with a picture and a few words of personal history?"

"Yes." In a way it had been. Most of all he'd wondered what had led her to give him away the way she had. He'd figured her for a young, desperate girl, not a woman in her early twenties from a good family. He'd hoped that she might have felt some regret at his loss, but within a year she'd remarried and within four years she had three more children. So much for regret. "I wanted to know from whom I got my eye color and the cleft in my chin. I scored big on the first one, but struck out on the second."

She cast him a hard-eyed look of disapproval. He supposed he deserved that considering she didn't deserve the flippancy in his response. He stroked her back in a conciliatory way. "Look, Liza, I'm sorry. I'm not a bare-your-soul kind of guy."

"I'm not trying to get you to bare your soul. I just want to understand you."

He tugged on a strand of her hair. "That should be easy. I'm not that complicated."

"No, from what you've told me, you've lived your life letting women flit in and out of it, never caring for one of them enough to want her to stay."

She had no idea how close to his life, especially his twenties, she hit, not in the quantity but the quality of it. As a photographer, he'd been around the world. Women, even some of the most sought-after in the world, found him attractive. Some of them he had been with and some not. But it was also true that there were plenty of women who, like Jake, treated him as a jovial kid brother. And others who preferred to work with him since he was the only non-gay male photographer of any consequence who could take no for an answer without trying to ruin their careers.

But mostly he preferred his own company to that of anyone else's. Why did she think he lived on that godforsaken island in the first place? He was close enough to the heat and sensuality of Miami to partake when he chose, but more often than not, he didn't. Even his friendship with Paul was basically a meeting of two like minds—two hermits who periodically came up for air from their individual solitudes and sought each other out.

But he wondered how much of that self-assessment

would really matter to her if he told her. He thought he knew which question she'd really wanted answered when she started this conversation, though she was usually more blunt in asking for what she wanted. He didn't mind telling her what she wanted to hear.

"I'm in love with you, Liza. I'm not going anywhere unless you ask me to."

"Don't you mean *until* I ask you to? Isn't that how you see us ending up? One day I'll get tired or bored or whatever it is your other women do and that will be it?"

How foolish of him to think that telling a woman he loved her would actually appease her. Feeling testy, he fired back, "How the hell should I know?" That's not what he wanted, but, like her, he could be pragmatic when the situation called for it. At no point had she said anything about loving him back. She only took him to task for what she perceived to be his past sins. "That's the way it's always been," he said in a quiet voice.

She surprised him by cradling his face between her palms and bringing her mouth down to his. Until she pulled away, he lost himself in the sweetness of her kiss.

Then she laid her cheek against his shoulder, while her fingers wove an erotic pattern on his chest. "I'm sorry."

He grabbed her wrist to still its motion. She had nothing to be sorry for. They'd both known from the beginning that any relationship between them was doomed. All they had promised each other was the now, and since the now was pretty damn good, he didn't feel the need to jinx it with thoughts about the future.

He brought her palm to his lips and kissed its center. "Can't we just enjoy the time we have together without trying to analyze each other or our motives to death?"

She lifted her head and looked at him with an expression he couldn't begin to comprehend. Her eyes searched his face, and her mouth opened, as if to speak, but no sound came out. Instead, she pressed her lips to his, and in a moment, nothing else mattered.

Liza woke the next morning still in the haven of Jim's arms. His grip was slack enough for her to stretch her back without waking him, but tightened as she settled back against him. She kissed his chest and he mumbled something in his sleep but didn't wake.

God, she loved this enigma of a man. She'd wanted to tell him that last night, she'd started to, but the words wouldn't come. She didn't know why. Maybe it was because he'd uttered those words himself, words she hadn't expected to hear, especially not so soon. It had made her wonder how many other women he'd whispered those words to, hoping to gain what he most wanted, another turn in their beds.

She planted another soft kiss along his collarbone. Instinctively, she knew she was being unfair to him. He'd meant those words as best he was able. But what did you do with a man who vowed to protect your life, who'd all but told you he wouldn't fight to keep you in his? What would he do when all this was over—go back to his hidey-hole in Florida and leave her to her own devices back in New York? Part of her wished Grady would take himself a good long time to get caught. Maybe that would afford her enough time to change Jim's mind.

She doubted it, though. He might be the most gregarious recluse she'd ever met, but she recognized his withdrawal from the world for what it was. Maybe it was his profession that encouraged his detachment—always playing the observer, never the participant, or maybe it was his natural detachment that made such a career desirable. She could speculate about that all she liked, but she'd never come up with an answer. But she did know that what he needed, he sought out and what he didn't could go hang itself. Which category did she fit into? Unwilling to contemplate that much further, she figured it was time to get up.

But as she tried to extricate herself from him, his arms banded around her. "Where do you think you're going?" he asked in a sleepy voice.

"Bathroom." That was the only word she could manage with his hands perusing her body and his nose nuzzled against her neck.

She felt him smile against her skin. "I guess I can allow that." One of his hands strayed to her left buttock and gave it a gentle tap. "While you're in there, why don't you turn on the shower for us? Time to rise and shine."

"All right." Though as tired as he sounded, she'd bet he'd fall back asleep before she got the water started.

He gave her buttock another tap. "Then get going, woman."

Laughing, she left their bed. Halfway there, she glanced over her shoulder to see Jim watching her departure avidly. Maybe he wasn't as sleepy as she thought.

After relieving herself and brushing her teeth, she turned on the tap in the shower. Like the rest of the bathroom, the interior walls were tiled a royal blue, and like every other bathroom in this house, it came equipped with four separate shower heads, each adjusted to face center. Bathing solo under those conditions was a sensual feast. As she stepped into the circle of warm water, her body heated and moistened in anticipation of Jim joining her.

He didn't keep her waiting long. Nude, he slipped in behind her and pulled her back to him with his hands at her waist. Within seconds he was as drenched as she. And then his soapy hands were on her, skimming over her breasts, her belly, between her thighs, over her buttocks. The heat and intensity of the water and the ministrations of his hands tore a moan from her throat and made her unsteady on her feet.

She turned, hoping to stabilize herself by putting her arms around his neck. Seeing him brought an instant smile to her mouth, since he held a light blue condom packet between his teeth. She took it from his lips. "What are you doing with that?"

He leaned down to whisper a very stark and straightforward explanation of his intentions and her ensuing mental state. She'd meant why he hadn't put the thing down, not why he had it, but that didn't stop heat from stealing into her cheeks and a thunderbolt of desire from zinging through the rest of her.

He leaned back and grinned at her. "If that's all right with you."

"By all means."

"Then turn around."

She bit her lower lip, considering him. What exactly was he up to? "Why?"

"Because I asked you to."

No, to her mind, that had sounded more like a command. She indulged him anyway, anticipation mounting in her belly. A moment later, she felt him come up behind her. In one swift move, he was inside her, forcing her to her tiptoes to accommodate him. She braced her hands on the wall as a ragged cry tore from her throat.

His arms closed around her and his lips were at her shoulder. "That's it, baby," he said, but she didn't need any encouragement. He moved inside her again with an urgency she'd never felt in him before. Heaven help her, she wanted more of it. She tilted her hips to take him in more deeply and he obliged her, thrusting into her again and again as his hands fondled her breasts, her hips, and his fingers delved between her legs to pleasure her. All the while, the water sluiced down on them from all directions.

Liza gasped, trying to drag air into her lungs, trying to hold on to a little sanity. But it was no use. She was too far gone to try to hold back the inevitable. He thrust into her again, and she lost it. The strength of her orgasm arched her back and brought the sting of tears to her eyes.

Still he moved inside her, frantic and fevered until his body froze, only to convulse with its own set of tremors a moment later. He braced one arm on the wall, while holding on to her waist with the other hand. His lips explored the juncture of her neck and shoulder between short, ragged breaths. After a moment, he lifted his head enough to whisper in her ear, "Baby, are you all right?"

She turned in his arms to throw her arms around his neck and bury her nose against his neck. But she made the mistake of sniffling.

His arm around her waist tightened as his other hand tilted her chin up. His concerned gaze scanned her face. "Why are you crying?"

"I'm not." She swiped at her eyes with one hand. "I don't cry. I've lost my mind, I guess." She offered him a wicked grin. "Never let it be said you're not a man of your word."

He threw back his head and laughed. She pressed her lips to his chest, laughing, too. When they subsided he swatted her bottom.

"Maybe we ought to find out what Wyatt is up to this morning. We wouldn't want him coming up here to make sure we're still among the living."

She tilted her head to one side, studying him. Frankly, she'd forgotten the other man existed. Again, she sensed something adversarial between the two men, or at least antagonistic. Or maybe it was one of those Cro-Magnon, territorial things women would never understand in a million years. Either way, she decided to dismiss it from her mind.

They got out of the shower, toweled off, and dressed, he in a pair of jeans and a black, Black Dog T-shirt; she in a pair of black and white shorts and a white tee. But then there was the problem of her hair. With it still damp and starting to curl, she sent Jim downstairs while she attacked it with a blow-dryer and curling iron. It was probably a waste of time if she ended up outdoors on the beach. A little vanity was a dangerous thing. She fixed her hair, applied a bit of makeup, and headed down.

She found Wyatt right away, sitting on the living room sofa watching television. She took the chair perpendicular to him but facing the back of the house. "Where's Jim?"

"He went to the store."

Her eyebrows lifted. "You mean like the buying food kind of store?" Wyatt nodded, but somehow she couldn't imagine Jim food shopping, though she knew he had to do it sometime. "How did that happen?"

Wyatt shrugged. "We didn't have any food. I couldn't go and leave you unprotected and both of us agreed it would probably be best if you didn't make an appearance in town. He was the only choice left."

Liza frowned. Jim must have loved that particular bit of logic, and Wyatt seemed just a bit too happy to impart it. "What exactly is going on between you two?" Perhaps she was asking the wrong partner in the duo, but she couldn't take it anymore.

Wyatt smiled. "Nothing really. It's just that Jackson, our mutual friend, asked me to give Jim a bit of a hard time if the opportunity arose. It arose."

He said that as if it explained everything. It didn't. She'd heard Jim talk about Jackson with fondness, so why would the other man purposely want to bait him? On top of that, she wondered if this was the first time that the opportunity arose. She doubted it.

Liza leaned forward and fastened a glare on Wyatt. "This may be one of those things that only people with a penis appreciate, but I suggest you leave him alone."

A broad, satisfied grin spread across Wyatt's face. "Yes, ma'am." The sound of a car pulling into the drive-way drew their attention. Wyatt stood. "I guess that's my cue to help bring in the groceries."

As he left the room, Liza sank back in her chair. They were supposed to be here hiding out from a vicious lunatic and the two of them were playing games. *Men!*

That afternoon, Jim lay on one of the deck chairs facing the ocean under the shade of a huge umbrella. In a few minutes he'd get up and get the steaks he'd bought that morning going on the grill.

His thoughts wandered to Liza, who dozed under a light blanket in the chair beside him. They'd spent the first part of the day swimming in the ocean. She'd been forced to borrow a swimsuit from the much more buxom Jake and the suit had a charming way of reveal-ing much more than it concealed. After that, he'd pulled out one of his cameras and taken some pictures of her down by the water. When he pulled them up on his computer, she'd glanced at them and asked him in awe if that's what she really looked like. He'd had to laugh, since many of the "beautiful" women whose pic-ture he'd shot swore he must have some secret "ugly" lens that detracted from their appearance.

Now, looking at the glorious riot of oranges, yellows, and crimsons that made up the sunset, he wished he hadn't been so hasty in putting his camera away.

But otherwise he was content. Wyatt hadn't proved

to be as much of a pain in the ass as he'd expected. The other man had taken a position in a lounge chair on the other side of the wrought-iron table that housed the umbrella. He'd spent most of the day with his arms crossed and a baseball cap pulled low on his head. Jim doubted the man had been sleeping. He'd probably watched them every moment of the day, but not obtrusively, which made all the difference, Jim supposed. Or maybe the guy was growing on him. He hoped not.

Feeling Liza's hand on his arm, he turned to her. "Hey, sleepyhead."

She stretched, dislodging the blanket from around her to reveal the revealing swimsuit. "When's dinner?"

He chuckled. "Is that all you think about? The fulfillment of your bodily wants?"

"When I'm around you, yes."

He couldn't argue with that. "I'll get the steaks in a minute."

"Don't bother. I'll get them. I have to go inside and take care of another bodily want anyway. Why don't you get the grill started?"

"It's a deal."

It took him only a few minutes to get the fire going, yet Liza wasn't back yet. He didn't want to seem paranoid or to frighten her by running back into the house to check on her, but that was his first impulse. He looked to Wyatt, who was already sitting up with his feet on the ground. That settled it, if her absence made the Great Stone Face nervous, he was going in to find her.

He'd put Paul's gun in his camera bag. He got it now and stuck it in the back of his waistband and moved toward the door. Before he made it another step, he heard a crashing sound and one frantic word from Liza. *"Jim!"*

Twenty

Panic whooshed up through Jim like heat rising off a scorched sidewalk. In the second before he burst through the back door, he saw Wyatt trying to wave him off. Too bad. All Jim could think about was getting to Liza before it was too late. He didn't care what happened to him.

The minute he gained the entrance a bullet whizzed past his left ear. Jim dove behind the kitchen island for cover. But he'd already seen Grady, a tree trunk of a man, standing in the hallway that ran the length of the house. He had one arm around Liza's neck, his hand covering her mouth so she wouldn't scream. The other hand held a black revolver—one Jim suspected Grady had already used to administer the wound at Liza's left temple. Obviously he'd tried to knock her out, but she still struggled against him sluggishly, trying to pry his grip from her throat.

Fury replaced fear as Jim's primary emotional driver. If Grady had simply wanted to kill Liza, she'd be dead already. He had some other plan Jim didn't even want to contemplate. He called to Grady, "Let her go, and I won't have to kill you."

Grady's answer was another round that ripped along the edge of the island, but missed him. "Where's the other one?" Grady barked.

Good question. He looked toward the back door that still stood ajar. No sign of Wyatt, not even that damn hat. Then again, if he'd tried to follow Jim in, he might have been caught by Grady's first bullet. If that was true, then Jim was on his own and out of his depth.

"Don't worry about him. Worry about me."

Grady's answering snicker told him what the man thought of that challenge. Jim couldn't blame him. With every second, Grady got Liza closer to the door while he hid behind the furniture. Jim suspected the only reason Grady didn't cut and run was that he suspected Wyatt was somewhere waiting to ambush him.

What Jim needed to do was get closer. At this distance he had no hope of taking a shot at Grady or even leaping on the man and beating the shit out of him like he wanted to. Silently, he crept around the island. Much better. He stood and stepped out into the hallway. Aiming his gun at Grady's head, he said, "Let her go. You're not leaving here with her, I guarantee you that."

For the first time, he saw a hint of uncertainty in the man's dark eyes. And for a second he thought he saw a flash of something red behind Grady on the other side of the open door. He braced himself, knowing something was coming. The next voice he heard was Wyatt's.

Wyatt stood a couple of feet back, his gun pointed at the back of Grady's head. "Drop it and let her go, you sick son of a bitch."

Either Wyatt startled him, or he wasn't ready to go down that easily, but he turned toward Wyatt, loosening his hold on Liza. Jim grabbed her wrist and pulled her toward him as hard as he could. She stumbled forward into his arms. He half carried, half dragged her to the kitchen, content to let the two men in the hallway fight it out for a moment, as long as the right one won. He cradled her face in his palms and tilted it up to his. "Baby, are you all right?"

She nodded, but her legs gave out under her. He helped her down until she sat with her back against the refrigerator with her knees drawn up. "I'll be right ba—"

The last word was cut off by the punctuation of a single shot. Both he and Liza jumped. Her eyes searched his, but he had no answer for her yet. But the sound of footsteps reached them. Not knowing whom they belonged to brought Jim to his feet. He put himself between Liza and whoever stepped around the corner.

A second later he had his answer. He saw the bill of Wyatt's cap before he saw the man himself.

Wyatt took one look at Jim and the gun ready in his hand and a look of utter disgust came over his face. "You've got to be kidding."

Chuckling, Jim stuck the gun in the waistband of his pants. "One can't be too careful."

Wyatt cast him a sour look. "I'll do the honors of calling 911."

Jim nodded and went back to Liza. He sat on the floor and pulled her onto his lap. "Are you still with us?"

"Barely. My head feels like an elephant's sitz cushion and the elephant is sitting on it." Her hand lifted to explore her wound, but he pulled it away.

The gash had stopped bleeding, but it was probably large enough to require stitches. "Don't touch it. We've got an ambulance coming."

"I don't need an ambulance. I need a big bandage and a stiff drink."

"I'm sure they'll give you the former, but let's hold off on the latter for a little bit, okay?"

Wyatt squatted beside them. "The appropriate emergency personnel are on the way, as well as the cops. Maybe you want to give me that weapon to put in a safe place." He held out his hand. "You don't have a carry permit for it, do you?"

"Um, no." He retrieved the gun and handed it to Wyatt.

Wyatt shook his head. "Thanks for keeping him busy back there. If you actually want to learn how to shoot let me know. We'll go to the range."

As Wyatt straightened up, Jim fought down a strange urge to laugh. He couldn't care less whether he ever held another gun in his hand in his life. He was just glad that both he and Liza were safe and that the danger they found themselves in hadn't cost anyone else their life either. Grady had already claimed enough lives on his quest for revenge.

Feeling a twinge in his side, Jim shifted to rest his back against the refrigerator. He repositioned Liza on his lap, but the pain remained. He put his hand to his side to massage the muscle and his hand came back wet with blood. He lifted his shirt and found a patch of ragged, oozing flesh. Oh, damn. He'd been hit.

Twenty-one

Later that night, he and Liza lay in bed together spoon fashion to accommodate both their injuries. Both of them had been seen to by the EMT, leaving Wyatt to explain why there was a dead man in the doorway.

He pulled her more tightly against him, then groaned as pain shot through his side. "You know what really ticks me off about this whole thing?"

She leaned back to look at him over her shoulder. "What?"

"Those steaks. Those beautiful steaks." The crash he'd heard was her dropping the steaks when Grady hit her. "Ruined. You have no idea how much I was looking forward to eating them tonight."

She giggled, the reaction he'd been going for. "*That's* what ticked you off the most?"

"That and the fact that making love is probably out of the question tonight."

She cast him another look over her shoulder, this time a dubious one. "You can't even move without pain and you want to make love?"

"Baby, I could have been dragged a mile behind a

wild horse and it would still drive me crazy to have you in my bed."

"Tonight you're going to have to settle for holding me."

He rubbed his hand up and down her side. "I think you're getting addicted to this cuddling thing."

"Could be." She sighed. "What happens tomorrow?"

He knew his feeble attempts at humor wouldn't hold her attention very long. He also knew that as soon as the police and emergency people cleared out, she'd called Paul to tell him what happened. She was anxious to get back to Florida to make sure Paul was all right and to find out what secrets he'd kept from her. Jim couldn't blame her for that, but he also knew that every step she took toward finding her past led her away from him. Once she had the information she wanted, what reason would there be to stay with him?

"Not tomorrow, but in a couple of days, I'll drive you back. Until then we can act like locals: swim, surf, fish, leave our doors unlocked, and pray this place doesn't become the next Fire Island."

She laughed again. "Yeah, when neither of us is supposed to go in the water."

"I'll rent a boat and teach you how to fish."

"How badly do you think my head has been damaged?"

He chuckled and kissed her shoulder. "How about we play it by ear?" He nibbled on her left earlobe for emphasis.

"It's a deal." She covered a yawn with her hand. "I'm beat."

He imagined she was. She'd been a trouper while the action was going on. But once all of the fanfare was over and everyone had gone, they'd all been sitting in the living room when she started shaking uncontrollably. He'd pulled her onto his lap and held her until it subsided. She'd whispered one pained question against his neck. "Why didn't he kill me?"

"I don't know, baby," he'd answered. She'd have to hate him later, but that was one bit of honesty he wouldn't share with her. He thought back to Grady's original threat. He'd promised to hurt Liza, which everyone took to mean that he'd mete out the same punishment to her that he'd intended for Paul. What exactly had been in the man's mind, Jim neither knew nor cared any longer. He was simply grateful that he would never find out firsthand.

Now he stroked her hair in a manner he hoped she found soothing. "Go to sleep, sweetheart. I'll see you in the morning." He held her, fighting off his own drowsiness, until her breathing evened out and her warm, soft body relaxed against his. With a yawn of capitulation, he let sleep overtake him, too.

The next morning, Jim awoke to the scents of eggs and bacon cooking and coffee brewing. He sure hoped it wasn't Wyatt busy in the kitchen. The man would probably poison him.

He showered and dressed, leaving Liza sleeping. With Grady gone, there was no need to keep watch over her anymore. A surprise awaited him in the kitchen. Wyatt sat at the kitchen table with the morning paper spread in front of him. A diminutive woman in beige shirt and slacks stood at the stove taking the last few strips of bacon from the pan to drain on a plate lined with paper towels.

Both she and Wyatt looked up as he approached. "Good morning," Jim said to no one in particular.

The woman spoke first. "Good morning to you, too. Sit down. I'll have your breakfast for you in a moment."

Jim did as he was told. She might be small, but she

possessed the demeanor of a master sergeant ordering the troops.

True to her word, she plunked a plate in front of him two seconds later followed quickly but a cup of steaming, aromatic coffee. She wiped her hands on the chef's apron protecting her clothes. "Excuse me a moment."

Jim watched her leave, then turned to Wyatt. "Not that it's any of my business, but who is that woman?"

"My wife."

Just as he'd suspected. "Imagine that. Someone actually married you." He filled his mouth with a forkful of eggs. They melted against his tongue. "Good cook."

"Thanks." He shifted in his seat. "Look, if you guys are interested in heading back to Florida, we'll drive you, since neither of you is fit to get yourselves anywhere right now."

Jim's eyebrows lifted at the unexpectedly generous offer. "Thanks."

Wyatt shrugged. "We can visit her folks while we're there. They live in Deltona."

Jim hid a grin. "My condolences, man."

For the first time since their meeting, Wyatt laughed. "Thanks. I'll need them. By the way, Jackson wants you to call him."

Jim nodded. Jackson was probably the only person involved whom Jim hadn't spoken to last night. Once he finished his breakfast, he walked out back and pulled out his cell phone and made the call.

"Hey, buddy," Jackson answered. "Glad to hear you're still in one piece."

"Yeah, all except that chunk of me I left on the kitchen floor."

"How's Liza doing?"

"Still sleeping, but good."

"I don't suppose I need to ask you my question again."

Jim chuckled. What seemed like a lifetime ago, Jackson had asked him if he was ready to fight for her. No, Jackson didn't need to ask again, but he wondered what exactly had prompted that statement.

"Why do you say that?"

"Wyatt told me he thought you were about to leap on him and beat the crap out of him because you thought he caught you and the lady in question in a compromising position."

"Then he didn't see us?"

"I didn't say that. I'm just telling you what he thought."

Jim sighed. He couldn't even get annoyed hearing the humor in his friend's voice. He was simply grateful everything had turned out okay. "Thanks for looking out, man."

"Anytime. Where do I send the bill?"

Jim knew no bill would be arriving. It was Jackson's way of asking what they planned to do next. "Believe it or not, Mr. and Mrs. Wyatt are driving us poor souls back to Florida."

"You met Bea? Carly calls her Mussolini's illegitimate daughter. Have fun."

Jim ended the call and went back to the kitchen where Liza, fully dressed, was finishing the last of her breakfast.

Within two hours, Bea had them packed up, cleared out, and ready to hit the road. She'd even found people to fix the glass pane in the back door and to clean up the detritus from Grady's timely demise.

The trip back to Florida proceeded much more leisurely and took three days. Jim wasn't in any hurry. He enjoyed the countryside passing by his window and the nights spent with Liza in his arms. By silent mutual assent, they seemed to have put any burning questions on the back burner and simply enjoyed being together.

The only awkward moment came on the afternoon of the third day, when Bea had blurted out, "You know, the only thing I can't figure out is how he knew where to find you." She'd turned to her husband. "You're sure he wasn't behind you?"

"No one followed us," Wyatt said defensively.

Bea shrugged and let the subject drop, but she'd voiced the concern that had plagued Jim since Grady showed up at the door. Maybe the only answer was that Eamon's ownership of that house was less of a secret than Jim thought. After all, they'd held the company picnic for their family-owned magazine there a couple of summers ago. All Grady would have had to do was call up the magazine and say he was looking for Jim and someone might have told him to look there. That could have happened, but he doubted it.

Later that afternoon they crossed the bridge to San Pedro Island just as the sun was beginning to set. They stopped at his place first, but only to drop off their luggage. Liza insisted on going to Paul's house to make certain he was all right.

When they got there, both Paul and Bill were waiting for them. Paul grabbed Liza in a big bear hug that lifted her from her feet.

Bill offered Jim a more sedate handshake and demanded, "What did you folks do with my car?"

"Relax," Jim said. "We've got a kid driving it back next week."

Bill threw up his hands. "Great. My gears will probably be stripped and I'll be knee deep in potato chip bags and soda cans." Paul pointed a finger at him, but there was a smile on his face. "Next time you walk."

The four of them bade the Wyatts good-bye, then went into the house. Paul had fired up his grill with some steaks, supposedly to replace the ones Grady had cost them. After the meal, complete with corn on the cob and a pitcher of margaritas, Bill took his leave complaining of an early shift the next day.

When Bill left, Jim volunteered to do the dishes as a ruse to leave Liza and Paul alone. All afternoon, he'd felt certain anxiousness in Liza to get all the pleasantries over with so that she could talk to Paul, and he wanted to afford her that possibility. He gathered their dishes and headed to the kitchen.

Liza watched Jim leave the room, then sat back. She appreciated his discretion in leaving the room, but considering the size of Paul's place and the fact that all that was required of him was to stack the dishes in the washer, she knew he'd be listening to every word they said. She didn't mind, though. After all they'd been through, she figured he deserved answers as much as she did.

Her gaze slid to Paul. He sat forward, his hands clasped together, bobbing forward slightly. Finally, his eyes lifted and met hers, revealing a troubled expression. "I never wanted to have to tell you this, but there's no way around it, is there?"

Liza shook her head. "No. I need to know what happened."

He nodded. "I suppose you do. I suppose in your shoes I'd want to know." He sighed. "Thirty years ago, I'd just gotten out of prison. Two years on a B and E. A breaking and entering charge. My baby brother Frank said I could stay with him until I got on my feet, so being the s.o.b. I was at the time, I took him up on that offer. He was living with a woman, this proper, uptight witch he was planning to marry. She had no use for me whatsoever."

"My mother?"

"Yeah. In the time I'd been away, she'd gotten hold of Frankie and turned him into something. Made him give up the street and get a job at the post office. The two of them were planning their wedding as a baby was on the way."

"Me?"

He nodded. "I can't say why I did it. Maybe it was pure meanness or maybe I was jealous of him. Despite all my efforts, I'd never had anything worth a damn in my life: not a woman, not a home. All I had was this old red Camaro I'd fixed up to look like something.

"I convinced Frankie to come in with me on this one job. Just one job. He'd have enough money to pay for the wedding, maybe get a little house instead of living in that apartment. I told him what kind of man couldn't provide these things for his woman, but I knew by the type of woman your mother was that any kind of involvement with me would drive a wedge between them. I wanted to put one there."

Paul fell silent, giving her a moment to process what he'd said so far. He was her uncle, and not a very good one, by what he'd told her so far. He'd convinced her father to join him on the escapade that cost her father his life, her mother her husband. No wonder her mother hated him.

She supposed she should be content knowing that, but she suspected there was more to the story, and she wanted to hear it all. "What happened that night?"

"It was a disaster from start to finish. Slim didn't care that I brought Frankie along, but Grady was furious. This was his job and he didn't want anyone else along who might mess it up. Anyone looking at him knew Frank wasn't much for the life. He was the type you had to remind that fingers left prints. Grady told him to go stand by the back door, out of our way.

"We were almost ready to go, congratulating ourselves on our unexpected find. But then the old guy came back and Frank froze. He shot Frank where he stood. I guess anybody paranoid enough to keep their money in the floor is going to have some means to protect it. I'm sure he would have shot all of us if Grady hadn't taken him down first. I had the bag in my hands. I got out the window we'd come in and I just ran. I couldn't seem to stop running. The next thing I knew, I was by the river. I almost threw the whole damn thing in the water. I didn't know what else to do.

"I went to see your mother the next day. I'd read in the paper that the store owner died. Both Grady and Slim were picked up. Neither one of them had mentioned my name, and I knew why. Back then there was still a little honor among thieves, and besides, if I got caught, the money would probably have been recovered, as well.

"Anyway, I had planned to confess to her my role in getting your father killed. But something happened. In her grief she turned to me. She believed me when I lied to her and told her I had nothing to do with it. Your mother wasn't a woman a man could easily disappoint."

Or a daughter. There had always been something about Eloise Morrow that demanded obeisance. "If she believed you, what went wrong?"

"I did. My guilt finally caught up with me. You see, I was the one who sat in the waiting room while you were being born. I held you and fed you and it was me you called daddy. Somehow your mother managed to reform me, too. In the beginning, I doubted she saw me as a romantic interest. I was simply a man in need of a woman's hand. You were almost two years old when, for the first time, it appeared she might return the feelings that had been developing in me for some time.

"I had to tell her then. I couldn't build a life with her on lies. To say she was furious with me is an understatement. She threw me out and threatened to report me to the police. She didn't, but I believed she would. I wouldn't have blamed her."

Sighing, Paul stood. He rounded the sofa and went to stand by the picture window facing the street. "I have always regretted leaving that day. Running away. I should have tried to make things right with your mother. I should have stayed and taken my punishment like a man. A few years as opposed to a lifetime of punishing myself. If I'd done that, maybe she would have found it in herself to forgive me. I don't know, because I never tried. I never went back."

He had his back to her, but his head lowered and his shoulders shook. A lump of emotion formed in her throat and tears burned her eyes, but she went to him and wrapped her arms around him. Despite all he'd done, she couldn't bear to see him suffer alone.

He turned to face her and wrapped his arms around her. "I'm so sorry, sweetheart," he said against her ear.

Liza didn't try to stop her tears as they began to fall. She knew with absolute certainty that this man was the man her mother referred to as her father, the one who had hurt and abandoned her, not the man who'd sired her. This was the man who'd inspired her mother's invectives on not falling for the wrong man and who'd fueled her mother's late-night crying sessions that she wasn't supposed to know about. And worse, she suspected her mother regretted losing him and would have taken him back if he'd only asked.

God, what a bloody waste. She stepped back from him, swiping at her eyes. "Thank you for telling me."

He pulled a handkerchief from his back pocket and handed it to her. "Do you hate me now, too?"

She dabbed at her eyes. She'd get to his question later. She still had a few of her own. "How did Grady know about me?"

"A couple of years later, when Slim got out, he came to see me, looking for his share of the money. I gave him both his and Grady's share. I didn't want anything to do with either of them anymore. Slim joked that in about twenty years I should get you together with Grady's son. Slim wanted a picture of you to show Grady. I gave him one to get rid of him.

"I think Grady loved that kid more than he loved his own life, which is why it didn't surprise me that losing him would drive him crazy. He had plenty of years to let that rage fester into a desire for revenge. He had no way of knowing we'd been estranged all these years."

Yet, Paul had still sought to protect her, despite the long separation. He still considered her his daughter. That touched her more than anything he'd done repelled her. She supposed she was ready to answer his question.

"I don't hate you, Paul. I'm sorry you wasted your life the way you did. I really could have used a father."

"What about now? Got any use for a broken-down old coot?"

She tilted her head to one side considering him. She sensed the anxiousness in him, the need for any crumb of approval. Could she give him that? For her own part, she'd felt defensive of him from the start, without much provocation. She'd told herself she came to Florida seeking answers, but was that all she really wanted?

"I don't know. Are you going to be the kind of father who interrogates all my boyfriends and expects me to be home on time?"

She'd meant it as a joke, and as expected he laughed. He gestured in Jim's direction. "Only when it comes to that pain in the butt in the kitchen."

She glanced at Jim over her shoulder. He offered her a supportive smile, but said nothing. She turned back to Paul. "I tell you what, why don't we play this by ear and see what happens?"

"I can live with that. Come back and see me tomorrow?"

She nodded. "Good night." She felt Jim come up beside her. He laced his fingers with hers and led her outside into the sultry Florida night.

Twenty-two

When they got to his house, Jim unlocked the door and stepped back for Liza to enter. She'd been silent since they left Paul's house, not a pensive kind of quiet that wouldn't have worried him, but a melancholic sort of silence that did. Although she'd left Paul's house with a smile on her lips, enough time had passed for most of what he'd said to sink in.

Once they were both inside, he tapped the door closed with his foot, then took her hand. He led her to the sofa. He sat down and pulled her onto his lap. "How are you feeling?"

She leaned against him and wrapped her arms around his neck. "A little shell-shocked, I guess."

He didn't doubt it. Aside from the odd word here and there, he'd heard everything the two of them had said. He didn't know what he'd expected Paul's story to be, but it turned out to be much more than he'd anticipated. He only hoped, considering all she'd been through, that it wasn't too much for Liza to handle.

She buried her nose beside his neck and he rubbed her back in a soothing motion. "What am I going to do now?" she asked.

"What do you mean?"

"I came out here looking for my father. I put every-thing else on hold and now I've found him. What do I do now?"

You let me love you. Those were the first words that sprang to Jim's mind, but he didn't say them. Instead, he hugged her to him. "Stay with me, Liza. At least until you figure out what it is you want to do. You need time to regroup after all that's happened.

"Stay with me," he repeated as he cradled her face in his palms and brought her mouth down to his. Though he'd asked her for a temporary peace, he didn't have any intention of letting her go. Ever.

Liza spent the next two weeks at Jim's place, swim-ming, barbecuing, and in general recuperating from the experience at Eamon's house. She saw Paul almost every day, either with or without Jim accompanying her. Despite his past, Paul proved to be a kind and sensitive man. She supposed he must have been like many young men of every generation, drifting into places they didn't belong because there was no one to guide them else-where.

And Jim had been so sweet to her. Every day she spent with him she fell deeper in love with him and every night she found bliss in his arms. Yet, something was missing that kept her from being completely happy: the feeling that she was simply marking time, not get-ting on with her life. She still had no job, she hadn't done a thing with her apartment. At first, she'd been content to simply be with Jim, but in the last few days, restlessness had set in.

She shifted on the lounge chair she occupied, dis-lodging the magazine she'd been reading. Jim had gone out early that morning to do God only knew what, leaving her to fend for herself. Maybe all that was really wrong with her was that she was bored out of her mind without him.

The phone rang and Liza picked up the cordless receiver she'd brought outside with her for just such an emergency. "Jim's place," she said into the phone, trying to distract herself with a little humor.

"Liza?"

"Eamon? What are you doing calling here?"

"It's my brother's house?" he ventured.

She shook her head. "No, I mean, aren't you and Jake on your honeymoon?"

"We got back this morning and couldn't find anybody. What are you doing down there?"

"Long, long story."

"I bet. Is Jim there?"

"No, and I'm not sure when he'll be back."

Eamon muttered something under his breath she didn't catch. "I suppose you want to talk to Jake."

"Yes, please, if she's there."

"She's here. Hang on. Good talking to you."

"Thanks," she said, though Eamon seemed as pleased to be talking to her instead of his brother as he would if a rattler had answered the phone.

A second later Jake came on. "What are you doing in Florida and what happened in the house on Long Island? We came home to messages from four of our neighbors up there about some sort of homicide going on at the house."

"Oh God." It hadn't occurred to either her or Jim that such a thing might happen. She gave Jake a bare-bones rehash of what happened.

"So, you finally got to meet your father," Jake said when she was done.

Liza sighed. She should have known that murder and mayhem wouldn't interest Jake too much if more personal issues were involved. "Yes. He's not exactly what I pictured when I thought about the sort of father figure most girls have in mind, but I'm glad I met him."

"And what about Jim? Does this mean that the two of you are together?"

She didn't know how to answer that question. She knew her feelings for him, though she still remained uncertain about his. Neither one of them had mentioned that L-word again or any other issue of any consequence outside of her relationship to Paul. They'd been pretty much in a holding pattern since they got back to Florida, and now that she thought of it, that's what bothered her most of all.

"I don't know, Jake. I don't know. I do know that I love him."

Jake whooped, but Liza couldn't join in her friend's expression of happiness. Finally Jake asked, "Why is that not good news?"

"I don't know if that love is enough. There are things we need to work out."

"Will it help if I tell you I'm rooting for you?"

"Thanks."

Liza hung up the phone. Despite her friend's ebullience, tension formed a knot in Liza's belly. Jake's call reminded her that she had a life, an apartment in New York, even if being with Jim seduced her into neglecting them. He might be content to closet himself on this island, but she couldn't allow herself to. Finally, she understood her own restlessness. It was time to go home.

It was early evening when Jim finally came home. She was in the kitchen cooking a couple of salmon steaks under the broiler when she heard him call her name.

"I'm in here," she called.

A few moments later, he came up behind her and nuzzled her ear, making her giggle. "Looks like you've been busy in here." He planted a big smooching kiss on her neck. "Damn. I was going to take you out to dinner."

She turned in his arms to look up into his smiling face. He certainly was in a good mood, more so than usual. "Then you should get home before dinnertime," she teased back.

"So I should. I'm sorry I was gone so long."

She tilted her head to one side considering him. He offered her an apology for his absence, but no explanation of where he'd been. Did she really need one? He was a grown man and she wasn't his keeper. "Are you hungry?"

"Very." He lowered his head and took her mouth as his arms tightened around her. One of his hands dropped to delve beneath her skirt and cup her nearly bare buttocks. As he pulled away he swatted her bottom. "I guess that can hold me until after dinner."

She smiled, but she found his good humor disconcerting, she wasn't sure why. He walked away from her to look for something in the refrigerator, so she went back to tossing the salad. "Your brother called this afternoon."

Jim extracted a bottle of wine from the refrigerator and began to uncork it. "Eamon called?"

"He and Jake are back from France."

He pulled the cork from the bottle. "Looks like they lasted the whole month. We had a bet on that, didn't we?"

Liza pulled two glasses from the cabinet and set them on the counter. "Not a formal one."

"Too bad. I think I would have won." He filled each of the glasses. "I better go call him back. Let me know when the food is ready."

Taking his glass, he disappeared to the left in the direction of the bedroom.

Liza lifted her glass and gulped down half its contents, wondering if he'd notice she'd packed.

"Hey, big brother," Jim said when Eamon answered the phone on the third ring.

"Hey yourself," Eamon said. "Where were you this afternoon?"

"Let's get to that later, okay? How was the honeymoon?"

"Great, until I got home to find you gone, Liza missing, and several improbable messages referring to some sort of murder on Montauk."

"It would have to be murder *in* Montauk."

"Whatever. Both you and Liza are all right?"

"We're fine. Though I have to warn you we probably made the papers up there, too. Some reporters showed up snooping around."

"Wonderful. Anything else?"

A grin spread across Jim's face. "How do you feel about being a best man?"

"Whose?"

Jim had to shake his head. Had he been that much of a playboy that Eamon couldn't imagine him wanting to settle down? "Mine."

"You and Liza? What did you put in that poor girl's drink to make her agree to marry you?"

"Actually, I haven't asked her yet." Jim sighed. He'd intended to tonight but ruined his own plans by being late. But he'd wanted to wait until her ring was ready. He wanted some tangible proof to show her that he was serious. She didn't want him to treat his proposal the way she'd taken the one time that he'd told her he loved her as something to say to keep her interested but nothing more.

"Then aren't you being a little premature?"

"Maybe." But he knew she loved him, even if she hadn't admitted that fact to herself yet. She'd have been long gone if that weren't true. As it was, he sensed a certain disquiet in her, a desire for something more. He intended to give it to her. Like her mother, she was a woman a man found it hard to disappoint.

Eamon laughed. "I never thought I'd live to see the day."

"Don't rub it in."

"I'm not. Just know that I'm happy for you."

Jim hung up the phone. So far he had Paul and Eamon on his side. He could probably count on Jake as well. But truthfully, the only person whose opinion mattered to him was Liza. Did she love him enough to say yes? After dinner tonight, he intended to find out.

"What's the matter, baby?"

Liza shifted in her seat next to Jim on the sofa, turning so that she faced him with one foot tucked up underneath her. She scanned his handsome face, wondering how to explain to him her malaise. During dinner his buoyant mood had faded, probably in response to her own moroseness.

Still, she owed him an explanation. More than that, she wanted not only his understanding, but also his acquiescence. She wanted him to want what she wanted. If not, she feared she'd lose him, and that terrified her most of all.

She couldn't quite meet his eyes when she said, "I'm going home tomorrow."

"I see."

There was such coldness in his voice that she immediately started to explain. "Jake and Eamon are back. I have to see to my apartment. I have to find a job. I can't keep living off you like this."

He brushed a strand of hair from her face. "Why not?"

Finally, she met his gaze. "That isn't the way the world works."

"And you are a pragmatist, after all."

"When I need to be."

"What does that mean?"

She sighed. Nothing was coming out of her mouth as she intended. "You're content to hole yourself up here in this house."

"I have been. So what?"

"I can't be. I—"

His eyes flashed hazel fire as his derisive gaze raked over her. "For a woman who insists on honesty from others, you'd think you could manage a bit of straight-forwardness yourself. Why don't you say what you really mean?"

"I'm trying to."

"Let me help you out, then. How about, 'It's been fun, but see you around'? That wasn't so hard, was it?"

"That's not what I was trying to say."

"No? Then what?"

"I have enjoyed every moment we've spent here, but for me, life is back in New York. That's where my family is. Yes, I'm glad to have met Paul, but Jake, Dani, Eamon—they're my real family. Yours, too."

"So go back to them, Liza, if that's what you want. I wouldn't dream of trying to stop you."

Liza gritted her teeth as anger rose in her, too. Admittedly, she was doing a poor job of explaining what she wanted, but he wasn't listening, either. He'd already decided what she had to say. In frustration, she blurted out the first thing that came to her mind. "I am not your damn mother."

He reacted as if she'd slapped him. "Would you mind telling me what is the obsession you have with that woman?"

"It's not my obsession, it's yours. You're the one who can't get over the fact that your mother abandoned you."

He made a sound, half sigh, half exasperated growl. "My mother died when I was ten years old."

"That's right. She left you, too."

"Damn it, Liza. Enough. I do not need to have my head shrunk. It's cramped enough in there as it is."

She shook her head. He sought to dismiss her concerns with humor, but she refused to allow him to do that. "I have spent the last fifteen minutes trying to convince you to come back to New York with me. I was doing a lousy job of it, I admit. But it never occurred to you that I wanted you with me, did it? It was much easier to believe I was walking out on you."

"What do you want from me, Liza?"

"I want you to face the fact that you need to see her, if nothing else for a sense of closure. Believe me, I know what that feels like."

"I know what brought you out here to find Paul. I realize what courage it took to do that, and I admire you for it. But let's review what you're asking me to do here. You want me to give this woman the opportunity to tell me to my face that I was a mistake she'd rather forget. How is that to my benefit?"

"You don't know that she'll say that."

"And you don't know that she won't. And let's recognize something else. I don't give a damn."

She shook her head, knowing he lied to her. "Tell me something. How long ago did you get a copy of your book?"

He looked at her as if she'd lost her mind. "A few months ago, I guess."

"So that means that as recently as a few months ago you were thinking about her."

"All that proves is that I'm a glutton for punishment. I don't want to find her, Liza. I don't want to know. Why does it matter so much to you one way or the other?"

"Didn't you learn anything from Paul's story? He lived a life of regret because he was unwilling to take the chance that my mother would forgive him. Is that how you want to live the rest of your life?"

"The only thing I regret is this conversation."

"Fine," Liza said, tears stinging her eyes. "Have it your way. But know this, I just rid myself of all the old shadows in my past. I won't go back to that. I won't go back to having the weight of anyone's past pressing on me. I have a ticket on the eight o'clock flight to LaGuardia tomorrow. You do what you want to do."

She backed away from him and fled to the room she'd used the first few nights she'd spent in the house. She left the door open, hoping that maybe he'd follow her. Maybe he'd tell her something, anything to make things right. But he didn't. She waited, listening, praying he would come. A few minutes later she heard the front door slam, followed by the sound of Jim's car peeling out of the drive.

Twenty-three

For the third time in his life Jim found himself sitting in his car outside a comfortable home in an affluent neighborhood in a quiet Miami suburb. The first time he'd merely driven by, as if this house were a landmark. The second time, he'd parked, like now, across the street, but he'd never cut the engine. He'd simply sat there staring at the house as if by doing so, it would impart to him some secret information he'd been lacking. He'd sat there working up the nerve to get out when the front door had opened and a pair of women, one older and one younger, but both slender, had come out arm in arm. They'd seemed to look in his direction and he'd panicked and driven off. That was four years ago.

He sat there now, thinking not of the woman who lived here, but the one he'd left in his own home. He'd stalked out in anger after she'd run off to the guest bedroom. He could handle her accusations and predictions of doom. What he couldn't handle was seeing her withdraw from him so completely. He'd been a second away from storming after her and carrying her off to where she belonged—his bed.

Since he couldn't imagine what she would think of

him if he did what he wanted, he'd left. He drove to Paul's house and knocked until the older man got out of his bed to let him in.

"What happened?" Paul asked in a concerned voice. "Is Liza all right?"

"She's fine." Jim entered the house and headed for the living room, but rather than sit, he paced the carpet, his hands in his pockets.

Paul followed, taking a seat on the love seat and propping his feet on the coffee table. "You look like hell, boy."

Jim glared at Paul, willing the smug expression off the other man's face.

"I take it Liza wasn't impressed with your proposal."

"She never heard it."

Paul's eyebrows lifted. "Care to tell me why not?"

"No." Jim sighed. He supposed he did owe Paul some sort of explanation as to why he'd showed up on his doorstep in the middle of the night, but since that would entail telling how he'd screwed things up with Liza to the point she intended to leave with or without him, he decided to skip it.

Tightening his robe, Paul stood. "I don't know why you bothered to wake me up if you don't plan to tell me anything. It's not like the door's locked. You could have come in anyway." He walked out, off in the direction of his bedroom. It took Jim an hour to notice the other man had actually gone back to bed, leaving him alone.

He returned to his car and, for some unknown reason, he drove off the island into Miami. He stopped at a bar where he knew the owner, but rather than engage in conversation with the man and hopefully shake off his mood, he sat at one end of the bar nursing the same beer until that same friend kicked him out at closing time.

He should have gone home then, but he didn't. If

Liza was intent on leaving him, the least he could do was avoid being there to see her do it. The fact that he had nowhere to go didn't deter him from driving around aimlessly, trying to burn off steam. It didn't really surprise him that he ended up here. This was where she said he should come, although he doubted she meant at five-thirty in the morning.

He cut the engine and rested his hands in his lap. Liza was right. He did want answers. His presence here was proof of that. He wanted them almost as much as he feared walking up to that door only to have it slammed in his face. That much of a glutton for punishment he wasn't.

Liza was right about something else. Until she'd said that she wanted him to come with her, it never occurred to him that she did. It had been far easier to believe she simply wanted out. He realized that the ring in his pocket was less a tangible means of proving his earnestness to Liza than it was a physical means of binding her to him. How pathetic! It served him right that he hadn't been able to give it to her.

Jim sighed. As the saying went, it was time to shit or get off the pot. Considering that he'd been sitting there for over an hour, it was only a matter of time before some neighbor got suspicious and called the cops. He got out of the car and walked up to the front door. He still had no idea what he planned to say. The world being what it was today, he'd be lucky if anyone inside deigned to open the door for a stranger.

He rang the doorbell and waited, fighting the urge to get back in his car, drive away, and forget he'd ever done anything so stupid as to show up here in the first place. The only thing that kept him rooted where he stood was the knowledge that he could not win Liza back if he could not answer her honestly that he had tried to do what she asked.

The door swung open, revealing a tall, slender woman with hazel eyes and short, dark brown hair that had started to go gray at the temples. She wore a cream-colored robe, the collar of which she clutched together in one fist. He knew this woman from the picture Jackson sent him. Madeline Winters, his mother. He realized that picture didn't do her justice, as he recognized her now as the woman who'd come out of the house four years ago.

Seeing her, his thoughts scattered and his emotions churned a knot in his stomach. His mouth worked, but he couldn't think of a coherent thing to say.

A variety of emotions played out on her face: first, mild interest, then surprise, and finally an emotion he couldn't give a name to. For an instant, he would have sworn he saw tears in her eyes, but just as quickly they were gone. She said the last thing in the world he expected her to say. "Would you like to come in?"

He nodded, not trusting his voice. She stepped back and he crossed the threshold into a small foyer. She closed the door and came to stand beside him. "This way."

She gestured toward the living room on the left, a large, airy space tastefully decorated and immaculately clean. He sat in the chair she indicated while she took the matching chair across the coffee table from him.

For a long moment, neither of them said anything. For the life of him he couldn't fathom why she'd let him in unless she knew who he was. If that was true, why didn't she say something? He could see the edginess in her by the look in her eyes and the way she worried the sash to her robe. What did she expect from him?

It didn't really matter. He'd come here to have his questions answered, not the other way around. He'd start with the most obvious. "Do you know who I am?"

She nodded. "When I saw the car outside, I hoped it was you. I hoped you'd come in."

"Why?" It seemed like a reasonable question to him. Had she invited him inside to welcome her long-lost son or, more likely, to warn him away from her and her family from the comfort of her own living room? But her face crumpled and silent tears slipped down her cheeks. He pulled out his handkerchief and handed it to her.

"Thank you." She dabbed at her eyes. "I'm sorry. I promised myself if this day ever came I'd hold myself together better than this."

"You didn't answer my question," he said in a gentle voice.

"Last time you drove away. I didn't want to scare you off again. I've waited a long time for this."

She'd waited for this day? With anticipation or dread? He still didn't know? Did it really matter? Despite having made her cry, he wasn't looking for any teary-eyed reunion with this woman. He couldn't foresee any future for them as there was for Liza and Paul. He'd spent too many years resenting her for him to really want anything from her. It was time for him to get what he wanted and go.

"Just tell me one thing and I'll be on my way. Why didn't you keep me?" There, he'd said it, that question that had burned a hole in him for the past twenty-some-odd years, ever since he'd known he'd been adopted. He'd always be grateful for the family that raised him, but at a very early age he'd known he wasn't truly one of them.

Her eyes widened. "You don't know anything about me, do you?" She shook her head. "I should have known that, I guess. How did you find me?"

"A private investigator. I had a copy of my original birth certificate."

"I thought your uncle might have told you."

"*My* uncle? How would he have known?"

"Your parents did. Almost from the beginning they knew who I was." She twisted the sash in her hands. "Maybe I should explain."

He nodded. That would be nice, considering that, as he understood it, he'd been abandoned anonymously.

"At a young age, I took it into my head that I wanted to be a singer. I had no training, though I believed I had enough raw talent to make up for the lack. But I was raised in a small southern town by a father who was a fire-and-brimstone Baptist preacher. Saying I wanted to go to New York to pursue my career was like saying I wanted to pay Gomorrah a visit. He forbade me to go, but by the time I was twenty, I'd saved up enough money and enough gumption to go."

She shook her head in a self-deprecating way. "I thought I was something special. I was going to light up the world. I was so naive. I fell for the first guy that made a decent pass at me. He didn't stick around long enough to find out I was pregnant or even what I had for breakfast the next morning. That's how special I was. I fell into the same trap as every other country bumpkin with more stars in her eyes than brains in her head.

"One day, I found myself almost nine months pregnant, I'd been fired from my job as a waitress—you could do that in those days and no one would say anything to you. I was sharing an apartment with two other girls who did *not* want me there with a baby in tow. All I wanted to do was go home, but I knew I couldn't show up there with a baby. My father had already disowned me just for defying him and leaving.

"I used to go to St. Patrick's Cathedral to pray. I wasn't Catholic, but I figured God could translate Baptist. One day between masses, one of the priests found me crying in the pews. He tried to steer me toward an adoption agency, but I was afraid. I thought if they had my

name, somehow my father would find out. I figured if
he didn't know and I groveled enough he'd let me come
home. When you were born, I kept you with me for a
week, but I knew I was becoming too attached to you to
do what I needed to do. I brought you to Father Thomas
and asked him to make sure you went to a good home."

"How did my parents find out about you?"

"Well, I went back home. I married the man my father wanted me to marry, his protégé. I never regretted
that. He was a good man, but there was always a part of
me that wasn't happy. I think he knew that. The night
our first daughter was born, I couldn't keep my secret
anymore. I told him about you. He's the one who suggested I try to find you, not to take you back, but to make
sure you were all right, to give myself a little peace.

"With Father Thomas's help, it wasn't hard to find
you. Your parents were wonderful. The three of us
agreed that if you ever became curious, they would tell
you about me."

But he'd never asked them. As a child, he'd been
content to know he was loved and cared for. It wasn't
until after their deaths that he began to think about the
woman who'd given birth to him and feel contempt for
her. Which begged the question, if Peggy Fitzgerald
were alive today, would he have viewed the woman
across from him so harshly? He honestly didn't know.

"Unfortunately, that plan backfired when your parents died. We corresponded mostly by letters. Your
mother and I shared pictures of our families that way.
For a long while, all I knew was that they stopped coming and that your phone had been disconnected. My
letters started coming back unopened, but one of them
had the forwarding name and address on it. I wrote to
your uncle telling him who I was and to please contact
me to let me know how you were doing."

She gave a snort of mocking laughter. "He wrote me

back a curt note saying that you were fine and to please stop making a nuisance of myself. That's the last I heard from him."

An odd urge to laugh seized Jim. At this stage in his uncle's illness, he doubted the older man would even remember receiving such a letter. Even if there was a chance he did, Jim wouldn't ask him about it. Knowing his uncle, he'd done what he deemed necessary to protect the two young nephews that had just come into his care. There was no point in taking him to task for it now.

More than that, he felt lightened somehow. He understood what Liza meant now by not wanting to be burdened by the weight of the past now that it was lifted from him. He still didn't know what he wanted from this woman, if anything. But he appreciated her candor in opening up what was obviously a painful time for her. Come to think of it, he wasn't sure what she wanted from him, either.

But he did know that if he wanted to get on that plane with Liza, he had to leave now. He stood. "I have to go."

"So soon? You could meet your brother and sisters. They know about you."

That boggled the mind. There were three other human beings in the world who considered him their sibling. "Maybe next time. I'm going back to New York this morning."

She rose, nodding. "I understand. Will you do me a favor?"

"If I can."

"Please call me Maddy." She smiled. "All my friends do."

He'd tensed for a moment, thinking she was about to say "mother." Maddy he could handle. "All right."

She walked him to the door and opened it. "I hope the next time won't be too long."

For some reason he didn't understand himself, he hugged her. With a cry of surprise, she closed her arms around him. For a moment, he shut his eyes and basked in the warmth and tenderness of her embrace. A mother's hug. He hadn't had one of those in over twenty years. He pulled back, smiling, though his eyes burned and his emotions churned.

"See you," he said for want of something better, got in his car, and headed for the highway. With any luck, he'd make it to the airport in time.

Liza paced in front of Jim's front window. In another minute, she was going to have to give up hope that Jim intended to come back before she had to leave for the airport. He was going to let her leave. She admitted she'd pushed him too far last night. Everyone had to make their forays into self-discovery in their own time. If she were honest, she'd pressed him to meet his mother more because it was what she needed than what he wanted. She needed to start life over with the feeling of a clean slate. It wasn't his fault if he didn't.

She saw a car pull up to the curb and her spirits plunged even further. Earlier that morning she'd called Paul to ask him to take her to the airport. She'd hoped he'd only act as a backup in the event she really did need to get on that plane at all. She guessed she had her answer as to whether Jim intended to come back. She left the window and went to the front hall where she'd left her suitcase. She moved it aside so that she could open the door for Paul.

He came up the walk, a scowl on his face. "I don't know what it is about you women. Always have to get to the airport two years before the plane takes off." He picked up her suitcase despite the fact it had wheels and walked back to the car.

She supposed that was the best greeting she was going to get. She knew from her phone conversation with him that he wasn't pleased about her leaving. She took the keys that Jim had made for her from her pocket and locked the door. She deliberately didn't dwell on any last looks. Otherwise she might lose her nerve and stay. She slid into the passenger seat beside Paul and fastened her seat belt.

"Are you sure you want to do this?" Paul asked, hope evident in his voice that she'd change her mind before he had to drive too far.

"Yes," she lied. "It's time I got home."

Paul pulled away from the curb. "It's your funeral, but would you mind explaining to me this sudden urge to get back to New York? I thought you and Jim were happy here."

"We were."

"Then why are you walking out on him?"

"That wasn't my intention when this started. I wanted to go home. I wanted him to come with me, but he misunderstood."

"He thought you wanted to leave him. That should have been easy enough to straighten out."

"It might have been if I hadn't told him that he was obsessed with his mother leaving him and that he should go see her before he lives his whole life full of regret."

Paul's response was a long, low whistle. "All that?"

"I'm afraid so. I know I pushed him too hard."

"You figured that out by yourself?"

Liza turned her head to survey Paul's grim-set profile. He was angry with her, which she supposed she deserved. In self-defense she said, "Aren't you the one who said some woman needed to make him take a good long look in the mirror?"

"I said make him look, not whack him over the head with it."

"What can I tell you? I've always been an over-achiever."

Paul cast her a short, sharp glare. "Don't try to make jokes with me. Not when you've thrown him to the wolves in a way he never would have done to you. When you came out here to find me, he insisted you stay with him so that if it turned out I acted like a fool you'd have somewhere to go. And he knew me.

"What do you know about this woman you've sent him off to? And yes, if you want to know where I think he is, I'm sure he went to see her. When has he ever not done what it takes to please you? But if she disappoints him, or even if she doesn't, who does he turn to? You'll be in New York."

As Paul spoke, tears had formed in her eyes. Unable to blink them back, she let them spill down her cheeks. "I've really made a mess of things, haven't I?"

"It's not too late, you know," he said in a soft voice. "You don't have to get on that plane."

"I know." She sighed, letting her shoulders droop. "So much for my dramatic exit. Can you take me back to the house?"

"Are you sure?"

"Yes." That was the only thing she was sure of. She didn't care about being right or holding any moral high ground. Not if it meant she might lose him.

When Paul parked in front of Jim's house for the second time that day, she got out and waited on the sidewalk while he retrieved her suitcase. After he set it beside her, she hugged him. "Thanks for the ride and the dose of common sense."

"Anytime, kiddo. That's what I'm here for." He ruffled her hair. "Do you want me to walk you in?"

"No, I'll be fine." She waited until Paul pulled off before she took out her suitcase handle to wheel it up to the door. Just as she reached into her purse for her keys, the door opened and a familiar and totally unexpected man stood at the threshold.

"Ryan? What on earth are you doing here?"

"I got tired of waiting for you to get your skinny ass to New York." His arm lifted, revealing a vicious-looking gun. "Those diamonds belong to me and I want them back now."

Twenty-four

About halfway to the airport, Jim struck on a brilliant idea. In his absence Liza must have gotten Paul to take her to the airport. He'd call Paul's cell phone and get him to stall Liza at least until he could talk to her. He pulled off on the shoulder and took out his phone. He'd turned it off when he left the house, not wanting to hear from anyone. He switched it on, and it rang. He checked the display. What could Wyatt be calling him about?

"Hey, buddy, what can I do for you?" Jim said.

"Where have you been? I've been trying to reach you all night."

"What's up?"

"Is Liza with you?"

"Not at the moment, but she's here in Florida." He hoped she was still here. "What's the problem?"

"Bea and I got back to New York a couple of days ago. I picked up your case again. Something about it didn't sit right with me."

More than likely, little Bea had nagged him half to death about letting Grady follow them. "Did you find something out?"

"Remember I told you I didn't know what happened to Ryan Gilchrest's mother?"

"Yes," he said, but couldn't figure out where Wyatt was headed.

"She ran off with some hairdresser after cleaning out one of the family's bank accounts, but that's not the point."

Jim ground his teeth together. "Then what is?"

"Her father, Andrew Brooks, owned a store up in Harlem, Andy's Candy. Does that name sound familiar to you?"

"No. Should it?"

"It's the name of the store Grady and company robbed and from which the diamonds were never recovered."

Adrenaline rushed through Jim, putting every nerve ending in his body on alert. "What does this mean? Do you think Gilchrest had something to do with this? How would the two even have met?"

"The details of the robbery are public knowledge. The store owner's death was covered in the papers. Anyone with Internet access could find out where Grady was. His stabbing of a fellow inmate and subsequent transfer were cited in a recent *Times* article on prison violence. It's right there on the Web. I called a friend of mine up at Sing Sing where Grady served his time. About six months before his release he had a visit from a man fitting Gilchrest's description though the bastard probably used a fake ID to get in."

Jim's head swam. Thank God he'd decided to pull over since he'd probably have crashed by now. But one thought surfaced that would probably ease Wyatt's conscience somewhat. "Gilchrest's been out to my brother's house with Liza."

Wyatt didn't miss his implication. "Thanks, buddy. I'm sure Bea will be glad to hear that."

"But let me ask you this. I'm assuming Gilchrest is after the diamonds he thinks are still out there. Why would he send Grady after us if he intended to hurt Liza?"

"Who knows? Maybe Grady didn't tell him what his plans were. He didn't tell Slim either."

And Slim was dead now. So much violence over something that could never be recovered.

"There's one more thing," Wyatt continued. "You're not going to like this."

"Spit it out."

"It turns out Gilchrest did have a record, a sealed juvenile record that I used considerable charm to unseal. When he was sixteen he put some girl in the hospital. He claimed the sex was consensual, but she had the bruises to prove that it wasn't. I called his office yesterday, just to see if he was in town or out making trouble. His secretary said he wouldn't be into the office for the next few days."

A chill shot up Jim's spine. He'd left Liza alone and unprotected while this pervert was on the loose. Heaven help that man if he touched her. "I have to get to Liza."

"That was my next suggestion. Take care and tell us how it turns out."

"Will do." He disconnected the call and dialed Paul's cell phone and then his home number. He got answering machines at both places. He dialed Liza's cell phone and got more of the same. On an impulse, he called his own house. If by any strange chance Liza had changed her mind about leaving, she'd be there.

The phone was picked up on the third ring. A familiar but out-of-place voice said, "Is that you, Fitzgerald? Not very smart of you to leave your lady unprotected at a time like this."

Jim squeezed his eyes shut, wishing for the first time

she'd gotten on that plane. "If you hurt her, there isn't anywhere you'll be able to hide from me."

"Too late," Gilchrest said in an eerie high-pitched voice. "But if you hurry up and bring me my diamonds there might be some of her left for you when you get here."

The line went dead. Driven by fury and frustration, he wanted to hurl the damn cell phone through the windshield or smash something, anything, preferably Gilchrest's skull, and keep on smashing. Instead he put the car into gear and pulled back into traffic. He wasn't far from home, maybe fifteen minutes. But as he drove images of Liza hurt or worse plagued him. He wouldn't have believed Gilchrest for the type to resort to using his own hands for violence, not until Wyatt told him about that girl. But now he had to take his threat to Liza seriously. He only hoped he wasn't too late.

Liza glared at Ryan as he ripped off the piece of duct tape he'd hastily slapped over her mouth when the phone rang. Why he'd told Jim that nonsense she couldn't guess, unless it was to rile him up.

He pulled another of the kitchen chairs to hers and sat facing her. "Don't look at me like that, Liza. You're the one who just got herself tied to a chair. Remember that?"

She remembered it. She twisted her hands to test the bonds. Ryan must have flunked his Boy Scout training since they were neither tight nor secure. Given enough time she could get her hands free. Then what? He would surely notice her working her feet free. Maybe she'd just hop out the door.

Damn. It was her own fault. When Ryan met her at the door, gun in hand, she'd had enough. Without thinking, she'd thrown her keys in his face and leaped on him, trying to wrest the gun from his hand. She'd knocked him off balance, they'd crashed to the floor with her on top of him, and the gun had skittered off toward the living room. Before he recovered from the fall, she'd pummeled his face with her fists, not enough to knock him out but enough to daze him and bloody his nose. She'd gone for the gun then, but he'd grabbed the hem of her skirt, ripping it and tripping her. She hit the wall, knocking the wind out of her. By the time she got herself together, he'd recovered the gun and that was that.

"And you're the one who got beat up by a girl. Remember that?"

"Not quite, Liza. Though if you'd have shown half as much spirit in bed with me it might have actually made the experience worthwhile."

It hadn't occurred to her before then that it all must have been an act. He must have gotten closer to her thinking she could give him information about Paul and the diamonds or maybe he thought she had them herself. That stung and she wanted to sting him back. "If you'd been able to last more than a minute, I might have been able to say the same."

Rage flashed in his eyes. "Just because I haven't really hurt you doesn't mean I couldn't." His hand shot out to grasp her breast in a crushing grip.

It hurt enough to make her grit her teeth, but she was determined not to show it, not simply to spite him, but for the first time she sensed real danger in him. Seeing the man she thought of as a milquetoast papa's boy standing at the door pointing a gun at her had been too surreal for her to take seriously. But the pain, that was real, as was the jubilant look on his face knowing that he caused it. For the first time she feared what he might do to her, but more than that she feared letting him know she was afraid.

She tossed her head back and met his gaze. "I think I could manage to endure the full sixty seconds' worth of torture you might be able to inflict."

He released her and stood. "I'm not going to play this game with you, Liza. You're not going to goad me into doing things I hadn't intended to do, at least not yet. It'll be more fun once we have an audience."

A chill shivered up her spine, making the hair at the back of her neck stand up. Good God, who was this man she'd let into her life and into her bed? She'd been completely fooled by him. "The only thing that's going to happen when Jim gets here is that he's going to kick your sorry ass and I'm going to enjoy watching every moment of it. Too bad I don't have a video camera so I can watch it over and over and laugh."

He tapped the side of her face with the back of his hand, as if she were merely annoying him. "Why don't you shut your pretty mouth before I have to help you out in that regard? Unless of course you want to end this nonsense and tell me where the diamonds are."

"I told you, there aren't any diamonds. Paul dropped them. I don't know why they weren't recovered. For all I know a crooked policeman took them from the scene. Why do you want them so badly, anyway?"

"You have no idea what it's like to live under the dominion of a man like my father, to have to wait for every crumb that tight-fisted bastard decides to hand out. His own wife walked out on him because of it, not that I would have stood for that."

"You worked for him. You must have had a salary."

"Not what I wanted. Certainly less than I deserved. I know I told you differently, but he was never going to retire. I'd be saddled with him forever."

"You could have gotten another job."

He laughed, a chilling sound, especially since he stood behind her now and she couldn't see his face.

"Those diamonds are my chance to start over, to live the kind of life I've always wanted."

"You never intended to split them with Grady or Slim?"

"Of course not." A malevolent grin spread across his face. "I'll let you in on a little secret. Slim didn't set the fire in your building, I did. My mother's parting gift to me was to tell me about those diamonds. I didn't believe her at first, so I went to see Grady. When he finally agreed to see me, he told me what my mother said was true, that Paul Mitchell probably still had them or had given them to someone since Grady hadn't heard of anyone trying to sell them.

"Grady and I hatched a plan that day. He'd heard that Mitchell had left the city a long time ago, but he didn't know where he'd gone. But he knew about you. He figured if I found you, you might have the diamonds or at least lead us to Mitchell."

Liza scanned Ryan's face and found not a trace of the man she thought she knew. It had all been a lie—his hasty courtship of her, his claims of love, his proposal. Every time her interest in him began to flag he'd pull her along another step to keep her tied to him. She didn't know why that realization didn't bother her more, but it didn't. "I still don't see what any of that has to do with setting the fire."

"I had to get everyone out of the building in order to search your apartment. I tried once, during Jake's wedding, but that nosy old crone who lives across the hall from you saw me coming up the hallway. Though none of this would have been necessary if you didn't insist on kicking me out every night. Otherwise I could have looked all I wanted while you were asleep.

"But all I got for my efforts was a locked box full of papers. Grady was another matter. I thought he'd put enough of a scare into Mitchell to make him hand over the diamonds, but he wasn't even good for that. If I'd known he had no real interest in the diamonds I never would have told him where to find you in New York. I figured you'd taken the diamonds and run."

He was blaming her for setting the fire? Well, at least that explained why he'd begged off Jake's wedding only to show up on her doorstep the same night begging her to take him back. He hadn't gotten what he wanted, so he still needed her.

So this was all about greed. Oddly she preferred it when she thought Grady was the mastermind of the operation. At least she could understand his motive—wanting to avenge the loss of his son from his life. Ryan was upset because his father refused to let him squander the family money as he saw fit.

They both froze at the sound of a car pulling up outside. "Showtime," Ryan said. He slipped one hand around her throat while the other held the gun pointed at her head. "Keep your mouth shut and your boyfriend might stay alive—awhile anyway."

Liza swallowed, as fresh fear washed through her, not for herself but for Jim. There was no Wyatt to watch his back this time and she knew he'd returned Paul's gun to him. If he walked through that door, he'd do so unarmed and unprotected, just the way Ryan wanted him.

She wanted to scream at him not to come in, at least not alone. But perhaps sensing her desire, Ryan lifted his hand from her throat long enough to stick the tape back in place.

A second later, the front door burst open, and there was Jim. Ryan had positioned her in the hallway so that she was the first thing he saw. She noticed how Jim's gaze traveled from her bruised face to her disheveled top to her torn skirt and back again. As he did so, the set of his jaw hardened and his fists tightened. His eyes held such a look of fury that he frightened even her.

She knew what he thought, but at the moment she was powerless to tell him any different. That in itself scared her more. If he believed Ryan had hurt her, he might do something rash, like what he was doing, advancing on Ryan, even though Ryan had shifted his aim to train the gun on Jim.

"Stay where you are, Fitzgerald. I'd hate to have to shoot you. Yet."

Jim took another step toward them, his eyes on Ryan. "I've been shot before. It wasn't so bad."

"You heard me. Stay where you are."

It occurred to her that, gun or no gun, Ryan was afraid. She couldn't blame him. He'd actually taken a step back from her, releasing his hold on her neck and allowing her enough room to work on freeing her hands.

Jim took another step forward. "Why should I listen to you? You're nothing but a coward, Gilchrest, hiding behind women when you aren't beating them into submission. Why don't you put that gun down and let's settle this like men? If you can handle that."

Liza had no idea what Jim was talking about, but she knew how Ryan reacted to having his masculinity challenged. The knots that tied her hands proved more difficult to loosen than she thought. Her mind whirred, trying to find something to do to diffuse this situation before the inevitable happened and Ryan shot Jim.

"You bastard," Ryan said in a strangled angry voice.

In the periphery of her vision she saw Ryan adjust his aim, poised to shoot. Using her feet to push off, she threw all her weight backward. As she expected, she knocked into Ryan, throwing him off balance. The gun discharged and she screamed, though the sound never made it past the tape over her mouth. Ryan pushed her off him, sending the chair crashing sideways to the floor. Her shoulder and the side of her head took the brunt of the fall. Tears sprang to her eyes and for a moment the world went black with pain. Somewhere far off it seemed she heard the sounds of a struggle, mostly grunts of pain coming from which man she couldn't be sure. Her tears spilled as she remembered the last time she'd heard two men grappling over a gun only one man, the right man, emerged alive. Could their luck hold a second time?

She didn't have long to wait. The door burst open again, this time it was Bill and his partner with guns drawn. She'd never been happier to see any two men in her life. At first it didn't register with her why both men put their guns away as they entered the house. Especially since Bill rushed past her with a speed that surprised her.

"Damn it, Jim, enough," she heard Bill say in a quiet but commanding tone. "I'm only planning on taking one son of a bitch to jail today."

And then he was beside her. Little by little she was free. First the tape came off her mouth and then her feet were free. When the rope around her hands was removed she squeezed her eyes shut and groaned as fresh pain shot through her shoulder.

"It's probably dislocated," Harrison said.

Three pairs of eyes focused on the young cop.

"A master of the full freaking obvious," Bill said in an annoyed voice. "Go outside and call for an ambulance, would you?"

Liza tried to laugh but her body hurt too much in too many places for that.

Jim helped her sit up so that her back rested against the wall. He sat beside her. She closed her eyes as his fingers stroked her hair. "How badly are you hurt?"

She knew what he was asking. She opened her eyes and met his gaze. "Not at all in the way you think."

"No?"

"When I got here he was waiting for me. He thought I wouldn't put up a fight. He was wrong. That's how my skirt got torn." Surprisingly, emotion welled in her and she felt compelled to add, "He was saving that for later. Once you got here."

Jim's jaw clenched. "I knew I should have killed that bastard."

"From the sound of it, you almost did."

"Nah, but I bet the back of his head is going to be flat from now on."

She had to stifle the humor that rose in her. "Please don't make me laugh."

"I'm sorry, baby." He leaned down and touched his lips to hers.

With her good hand she pulled him back down to her and kissed him the way she'd wanted to ever since he walked in that door, with all the love, passion, and promise inside her.

"Get a room, would ya?"

That came from Bill. For a moment, she'd forgotten he was there. This time she did laugh. "The only room I'll be getting is a hospital room, which is not particularly helpful."

She glanced up at Jim, expecting him to share in her humor. Instead she found a troubled look that worried her. "I'm sorry, baby," he said. "I'm sorry I wasn't here for you when you needed me. But it's over, sweetheart. It's finally over."

She smiled up at him, this sweet, sweet man who loved her and whom she loved. Nothing else mattered to her except that. They'd work out the rest. She touched her fingertips to his cheek. "No, Jim," she said. "It's just beginning."

Twenty-five

After they touched down at LaGuardia Airport a week later, Liza and Jim took a taxi straight to Jake and Eamon's apartment. Liza's bruises had healed for the most part, though her arm was still in a sling. When Dani opened the door a broad smile broke out on her face. She launched herself at Jim, who scooped her up in his arms. "I'm so glad you're home."

"It's good to see you, too, munchkin."

He set Dani on her feet. Rather than offer Liza a hug, she stared at her with interest. "How did that happen?"

Obviously neither Jake nor Eamon had told Dani about her injury, and Liza certainly couldn't explain to her what really happened. "You know how Jake is always telling you to quit wiggling in your chair? Well, I didn't take her advice either and foink, I fell over and hurt myself."

Dani's reaction to that morality tale was a disgusted look and a disgruntled sigh. "Okay, don't tell me." She stalked off, calling Jake's name, leaving the adults at the door.

Laughing, Jim said, "You tried, sweetheart, you tried."

Yeah, but there would be no points scored for the grown-ups today.

They left their bags in the foyer and moved into the apartment proper. Jake came running out of the kitchen and hugged each of them. "Why didn't you guys tell us you were coming home? I would have made you a big dinner." Jake led them toward the living room.

Neither Liza nor Jim bothered to point out she'd answered her own question. She and Jim sat on the sofa while Jake sat in the adjacent chair. "It was a last-minute decision. The doctor finally gave me a clean bill of heath."

"And you, Jim. Don't you have better sense than to let someone shoot you?"

"It was only a flesh wound, ma'am," Jim said as if he were downplaying some horrific wound, but Liza thanked God that's all it had really been. His side had healed before her stitches came out.

Jake sighed dramatically. "I'm just glad both of you are all right. Eamon and I are both ticked that you didn't call us to let us know what was going on."

Liza snorted. "On your honeymoon? What were you going to do about if from France?"

Jake shrugged. "Worry, I guess."

For the second time that day, Jake had given herself her own answer.

Jim said, "Speaking of Eamon, where is he?"

"At work. He should be home any minute."

"In that case, I'm going to go see what my niece is doing, if you ladies don't mind."

Well, here was proof positive that she hadn't fallen in love with an imperceptive man. He'd picked up on the fact that, despite their polite conversation, Jake really wanted to be alone with her. Liza waited until he'd disappeared into Dani's room to turn to Jake. "Speaking of the honeymoon, how was it?"

"Oh God, Liza, like a slice of heaven here on earth. It took us five days to even make it out of the hotel room.

One of these days you'll appreciate the thrill of making love without having to worry that there's an impressionable child in the next room.

"After that, we toured Paris. We went to the house my grandfather left me. It's beautiful, but I'd rather sell it to pay for a couple of college tuitions."

That was the most practical idea Liza had ever heard Jake utter. "I must be rubbing off on you." Then she thought about what Jake said. "What do you mean a *couple* of college tuitions?"

"I'm pregnant, Liza. We found out while we were away."

Liza whooped and hugged her friend as best she could with only one good arm. She knew Jake and Eamon had been trying for a while. She was glad they'd finally succeeded. "Does Dani know?"

Jake nodded. "But I made her promise not to blurt it out before I got a chance to tell you. That's probably why she stalked off to her room. She didn't trust herself not to say anything."

"But I suspect Jim's already had an earful by now."

"Mmm," Jake mused. "Speaking of Jim, how are things going with you two? I was hoping I'd see a ring on your finger."

Liza glanced down at her bare hand, then up at Jake. "That will come, I guess. I don't want to rush this, Jake. I don't want to mess things up. I'm content to know he loves me and I love him."

"For now."

Sometimes she forgot how well Jake knew her. "Yeah, for now."

"Did you tell her yet?" Dani called from the other room.

"Yes, I did," Jake called back. "You can come out now."

Dani scooted into the room and knelt on the sofa next to Liza. "Isn't it cool? I'm going to be a big sister."

"It's very cool."

She noticed Dani staring at her neck. Her fingers automatically went to the necklace fingering the stones. "They're called tiger's eyes," she said to Dani's unspoken question.

Dani's eyes widened. "Real tiger's eyes?"

"No, that's what they call the stones."

"It looks fake. Did Uncle Jim give you that necklace?"

"No. Someone else did." She wasn't any more ready yet to call Paul her father than Jim was ready to call Maddy his mother. After their ordeal hit the papers in Miami, Maddy and her two daughters had come to the hospital, supposedly to visit her, but had spent all their time with Jim. Each of them had made a start, though.

"Can I wear it?"

"Sure. As long as you're careful with it." She had Jim, who had come to sit next to her, put the necklace on Dani.

After the transfer was complete, Dani twisted her upper body back and forth, sending the necklace swinging. "How do I look?"

Jake suggested, "Why don't you go look in the mirror?" As Dani scampered off, Jake speared Liza with a look that chastised her for entrusting an expensive piece of jewelry to an eight-year-old.

Eamon came home shortly after that, thankfully bearing a shopping bag full of Chinese food. After dinner, Eamon and Jim disappeared into Eamon's study for twenty minutes. When they returned, Jim rushed her out of the apartment so fast she forgot to collect her necklace from Dani.

Out on the curb, Liza asked, "Do you mind telling me where we are off to in such a hurry?"

"You'll see in a few minutes."

True to his word, after a short taxi ride they pulled up in front of a building on Fifty-seventh Street. Liza looked up at the tall structure with flags flying—the

Plaza Hotel. She turned to Jim and threw her good arm around his neck. "Do I get champagne, too?"

"And even a fruit basket."

"Now, that's living."

"Not unless you get out of the car."

She laughed and let the doorman help her out. By the time they got to their room, her giddy mood must have infected Jim, too. At the door to their room, he swept her into his arms and carried her into the room. He laid her on the cream-colored Queen Anne sofa, tipped the bellman, and returned to her. By then she'd peeled open the foil encasing the cork on the champagne bottle that had rested in an ice bucket on the coffee table. He took the bottle from her and finished the job. He filled a glass and handed it to her.

He filled a glass for himself, sat back, and winked at her. "So what do you want to do now?"

Watching him over the rim of her glass as she sipped, she let her gaze travel over him. Despite his relaxed posture, she sensed an undercurrent of intensity in him. She'd seen his laughter, the heat of his passion, his rage strong enough to make him want to kill another man, but she'd never seen him like this. He actually seemed nervous. "You're kidding me, right?"

"No, actually, I'm stalling." He gulped down half his champagne and set his glass on the table. He took her hand and laced his fingers with hers. "What would you say to marrying me?"

Those were the last words she expected him to say. She'd figured that eventually she'd have to hogtie him and drag him to the altar. Just to be sure, she asked, "Are you asking me to marry you or are you asking me what I'd say if you asked me to marry you?"

He reached into his pocket and pulled out a blue velvet ring box. He opened it and extended it toward her. "Does that clarify things for you?"

She looked from the ring, a two-carat emerald-cut stone in a platinum setting, to his face. "When did you get this?" For the couple of days she was in the hospital, he'd camped out there and refused to leave. They'd been in each other's company ever since.

"That day I disappeared without telling you where I was going."

"Oh." She remembered that day and the way he'd come home so happy and she'd accused him of not being able to see a future for them. Had he planned to give it to her that night? Talk about sabotaging her own desires.

She touched her fingertips to his cheek. "Will you put it on me?"

He grinned. "Are you saying yes, or are you asking me if I will put it on you if you say yes?"

"Yes, yes, yes." She grasped his chin in her hand and pulled his mouth down to hers.

His arms closed around her and the ring was forgotten until after they lay in bed together, both of them sated after lovemaking. Liza lifted her hand to admire the ring once again. "It's beautiful, Jim."

She rested her palm on his chest and looked into his smiling face. Happiness washed over her, both for herself and Jim, and for Jake and Eamon. "Did Dani spill the beans about Jake's going to have a baby?"

"Yup. I don't think I did a good job of acting surprised when Eamon told me the same thing."

She laughed and rested her cheek on his shoulder. "I'm going to want one of those sometime soon myself." She waited, unsure of what his reaction would be to that statement.

"We can make one tonight if you want."

She lifted her head to look down at him, certain he was teasing her. Unable to read the expression in his eyes, she decided her first impression was correct.

Unsure how she felt about that, she decided to tease him back. "You think that's all there is to it? You do it once and that's it?"

"Apparently, or I wouldn't be here. But you know what I mean. Let's start tonight. If it doesn't take, I'll give it another shot."

She laughed and hugged him. "Are you sure?"

"Hey, I'm not the one who's going to swell up like a balloon and puke my guts out every morning, so it's fine by me."

She sighed. "Be serious, would you? I need to know if you really want this."

He brushed her hair from her face. "I love you, Liza. I just asked you to marry me. What would make you think I don't want to make a life with you, have children with you?"

She tilted her head to one side considering him. "For a former commitment-phobe you are taking all this marriage, babies, domesticity thing in stride."

He laughed at her assessment. "I've never been afraid of commitment, or at least I've never doubted my ability to commit if the need arose."

"You just made sure it never arose."

"In some ways, I guess. It's easy not to find something if you're looking in the wrong places." He squeezed her waist. "You know when Jake and Eamon got together I was so envious of my brother. He'd been married, but he'd never been in love. I saw what Jake did for him and I wished there was someone in my life that would do the same. I should have known then that my days of tom-catting around were over. I think that's why I couldn't let go of you. You rocked my world from the moment you entered it."

She smiled. He'd done the same thing to her.

"So how about that baby?"

Her answer was to press her open mouth to his.

* * *

The next morning, Jim awoke first. Liza was still pressed against him, lying on her stomach with her arms tucked under her. He scrubbed his hand up and down her back, not trying to rouse her but enjoying the feel of her soft skin beneath his fingertips. He'd gone a little crazy last night, or rather she'd driven him there. It had been the first time he'd made love without the benefit of a condom. He hadn't expected there to be much of a difference, but the orgasm she had brought him to had been the most shattering of his life. Or maybe that little bit of latex had nothing to do with it. Maybe he finally felt freer because he had his life exactly the way he wanted it. Either way, he eagerly awaited the next opportunity to find out.

She stirred and shifted onto her back. Her eyes opened half-mast and she smiled sleepily. "How long have you been lying there watching me?"

His hand strayed over her belly. "Not long enough. Go back to sleep so I can watch you some more."

She giggled. "What time is it?"

"Almost ten."

Her eyes popped open. "What time is checkout?"

"Tomorrow morning at the earliest. We can stay here as long as you like, within reason."

Her eyes widened in indignation. "At upwards of three hundred bucks a night? I don't think so. You are definitely going to have to start being more frugal if you're going to marry me."

He thought to tell her that he made a comfortable living, even if he had spent a great deal of time in his hidey-hole, as she called it. But he knew that wouldn't make a difference to her. Wasting so much money on frivolities offended her sensibilities. All in all, he was just glad she had no idea how much he was paying for this room.

He circled his hand upward to cover her left breast. She'd never told him how she'd gotten the facing bruises here. He'd never asked her, but he knew. He bent his head and kissed each of the healing spots, five in all, then drew back.

"Who said you could stop?" she teased.

"Forgive me, mistress," he teased back. He lowered his head and pulled her nipple into his mouth to lave it with his tongue.

"Liza the Dominatrix. It has a nice sound to it."

He drew her nipple deeper into his mouth and sucked hard. She gave a gasp of pleasure. He liked the sound of that more. He liked the feel of her hand stroking over his back and shoulders and the way she'd drawn up her knees, pressed together, as the tension built in her. His hand skimmed over her belly and lower. Just as he would have parted her thighs, the room phone rang.

Damn, damn, damn. The only person he'd told where they would be was his brother. If Eamon was calling at this hour, it had to be something important. Or it better be.

He leaned over to press the button to put the call on speakerphone. "Yes?"

"Jim?" Jake's distorted voice asked. "Is Liza there?"

"I'm here," Liza called. "What's up?"

"I didn't call at a bad time, did I?"

Before he could get the word "yes" out of his mouth, Liza placed a silencing finger over his lips. The look in her eyes warned him to behave, but he wasn't inclined to do that. Jake sounded excited, not worried. If he had to guess the reason for her call, he'd bet that Eamon told her he intended to propose and she'd called to get the rundown. That could wait, he couldn't. He stroked his hand low on Liza's belly to remind her of that.

"Did I?" Jake prompted.

"N-n-n-no," came Liza's response.

He smiled against her skin as he pressed his lips to her abdomen, just above her navel.

"I wasn't sure I should call, except you both are early risers and I thought I should tell you right away.'

His tongue delved into her navel. She jerked and hit his shoulder. "Spit it out already, Jake," she said in a strained voice.

"Well . . . it's about the necklace you sort of let Dani borrow . . ."

He did stop then, knowing Liza might take news of her necklace seriously.

"What about it?" There was anxiety in Liza's voice.

"Well, Dani was convinced it was fake. You know that. I had to take it away from her. I caught her trying to bite open one of the stones."

Jim lowered his head to keep Liza from seeing him laughing. He knew that hadn't worked when she smacked his shoulder again.

"Did she damage the stone?"

"Not then. When I wasn't looking she took the necklace back and, well, she went at it with this nutcracker Jim bought her. Two of the stones broke and you'll never believe this, a couple of diamonds fell out."

For a moment he and Liza shared a look that was at once shocked and knowing. He should have known that Paul wasn't a poor enough thief to leave behind the most valuable part of his treasure. He also knew that Paul considered his gain that night Liza's birthright since that robbery cost Liza her father. Despite all they'd been through, Jim was relieved that neither Ryan Gilchrest nor any member of his family had gotten hold of them.

"Son of a bitch," was all the practical, pragmatic, sensible Liza managed to say.

Jim threw back his head and laughed.

Dear Readers,

I hope you enjoyed reading Liza and Jim's story. I knew I had to let them have their own story before I'd finished writing *Could It Be Magic?* What exactly that story was going to be, I had no idea. I just knew I had to start at the beginning, with their time in Florida. They started talking to me and the result was *Looking for Love in All the Wrong Places*.

I was asked recently what I thought was the main theme that ran through all my books. I have come to the conclusion that it is the risk factor in life: the fact that in order to open yourself to success, to love, to happiness you must be willing to risk the security of what you have now for what you really want. Life, whether fictional or real, takes courage.

As always, I would love to hear from you. You can contact me at aboutdeesbooks@aol.com or at P.O. Box 233, Bronx, NY 10469. Or stop by my website at www.dsavoy.com.

All the best,
Dee Savoy

ABOUT THE AUTHOR

Native New Yorker Deirdre Savoy spent her summers on the shores of Martha's Vineyard, soaking up the sun and scribbling in one of her many notebooks. It was there that she first started writing romance as a teenager. The island proved to be the perfect setting for her first novel, *Spellbound*, published by BET/Arabesque Books in 1999.

Spellbound received rave reviews and earned her the distinction of the first Rising Star author of Romance in Color, and she was voted their Best New Author of 1999. Deirdre also won the first annual Emma award for Favorite New Author, presented at the 2001 Romance Slam Jam in Orlando, Florida.

Since then, Deirdre has published seven other novels and one novella in the 2004 BET hardcover Mother's Day anthology. Her work has been featured in *Black Expressions* and has garnered many award nominations as well as rave reviews.

In her other life, Deirdre is a kindergarten teacher for the New York City Board of Education. She started her career as a secretary in the school art department of Macmillan Publishing Company in New York, rising to advertising promotion supervisor of the international division in three years. She has also worked as a freelance copywriter, legal proofreader, and news editor for *CLASS* magazine.

Deirdre graduated from Bernard M. Baruch College of the City University of New York with a bachelor's of business administration in marketing/advertising.

Deirdre is president of Authors Supporting Authors

Positively (ASAP) and the founder of the Writer's Co-op group. She lectures on such topics as Marketing Your Masterpiece, Getting Your Writing Career Started, and other subjects related to the craft of writing. She is listed in the American and international authors and writers editions of *Who's Who*, as well as the *Dictionary of International Biography*.

Deirdre lives in the Bronx with her husband of over ten years and their two children. In her spare time she enjoys reading, dancing, calligraphy and "wicked" crossword puzzles.